SOME PLEASURE THERE
TO FIND

Books by Elizabeth Rossiter

A MARRIAGE OF CONVENIENCE
SOME PLEASURE THERE TO FIND

SOME PLEASURE THERE TO FIND

by Elizabeth Rossiter

G. P. Putnam's Sons
New York

Portions of this book have been published
previously in *Woman* magazine.

SBN: 399-11728-8

Library of Congress Cataloging in Publication Data

Rossiter, Elizabeth.
  Some pleasure there to find.

  I. Title.
PZ4.R8293S03   [PR6068.O833]   823'.9'14   75-34383

I courted lovely Flora
Some pleasure there to find . . .

—Ballad

SOME PLEASURE THERE
TO FIND

One

ABOUT FIVE O'CLOCK on Friday evening, I knew that I wasn't going to get away early after all. The day had been like an obstacle race, I was leaving for the Continent first thing on Monday morning, and I had to finish clearing up my desk. I spoke to Sara on the intercom and suggested that she go on home and I would pick her up there: "Say quarter to seven, all right?"

"Certainly," said Sarah. She had her office manner on.

"I told Maddy not to expect us for dinner anyway. We'll eat on the way. Sorry about this, love."

"That's all right," she said. "I'll be glad of the chance to go home and have a shower. I'll have a long cold drink ready for you when you come."

"I won't be late," I said.

She laughed, adding, "I've heard that one before." But she said it without rancor. That was typical of Sarah, sweet Sarah, also efficient capable Sarah, a girl not for making difficulties, but smoothing them away. Of course, she did work for me; that made a difference. I thought of her with pleasure for a minute, and then forgot her, while I put a pile of memoranda and correspondence on tape for Mrs. Ferguson to deal with on Monday. Another calm, sensible woman; she came in with a folder of letters for me to sign, looking at me with a rather wary eye, I thought, so I shook my head at her. "Don't look at me like that."

"Like what, Mr. Hunter?"

"Suspiciously," I said, and she smiled her reserved, secretary-type smile. "I'm not going to keep you—this is all for Monday, when I've gone. Oh, I meant to ask you. How did Chris get on?"

9

Mrs. Ferguson was a widow, forty-odd, with two teen-age children, a boy and a girl, both exceptionally bright. Now and then I liked to ask her about them, not only from genuine interest, but because the change in her was so remarkable when I did. It was like throwing a power switch; without her knowing it, her face, normally so neat and neutral, became illuminated. Now, as I asked her about Christopher, the eldest, it happened as it always did and I watched her, thinking briefly so that's what it's like—to have a son and love him. But she only said in her usual even tone, "He was quite pleased with the papers. We think it will be all right."

"So it's Cambridge for him?"

"We hope so."

"Oh, come on," I said. "They've accepted him. He doesn't even need such good grades in A-level now. And you know he'll get them."

"Oh, well," she said, "I suppose I've got into the habit of never counting any chickens until they're hatched." She put an envelope on my desk. "Those are your tickets and reservations for Monday. Don't forget to take them with you tonight, will you? Check-in time at the airport is seven-thirty."

"Thanks. I'll remember," I said with a grin, knowing that she knew as well as I did that my habit was to board the aircraft at the last possible moment before the gangway's pulled away. "You get off home now. Have a nice weekend."

"And you too. Good night, Mr. Hunter."

"Good night."

I hate paperwork but it has to be done sometimes and I always get on better with the office to myself, with no phone calls, imminent conferences, or just Hugo chuntering on as he does all too often. With Mrs. Ferguson gone the place was silent except for the faint whir of a vacuum cleaner on the floor below, indication that the cleaners were already in occupation. I belted through the rest of the work, shoved all the papers into my "out" tray, switched off the machine and sauntered out to get my car. It was half-past six, a lovely, warm summer evening. Sliding behind the wheel of the car, I shut off the business problems from my mind and let the easy pleasant leisure-time thoughts take over: Sarah, the drive down to my sister's place through roads lined with summer green; the weekend, peaceful and relaxed.

Sometimes since I've asked myself how my life would have shaped if I hadn't been held up that evening, and Sarah and I had left London at the time we'd planned at first. I wasn't to know, at half-past six that night, that my mind wouldn't be at rest again for a long time.

Sarah had a nice flat on the north side of the Park, the upper half of a pretty little old house in a quiet street, one of the small backwaters you can still find around there, if you look hard enough. There were trees in front, and even tiny front gardens. It was like Sarah to have found such a place, and, of course, she had it to herself. That, in London, means money. Sarah didn't depend on her salary from Hunter's, she had money of her own. She also had, in abundance, what people call "background"—which gave her that special sort of confidence and sureness of touch which was so much a part of her cool personality. The flat was like that, too. There was nothing of the make-do, slapdash untidiness of the average career-girl's London pad, shared with two or three others, clothes and cosmetics all over the place, posters and postcard reproductions, lamps in bottles, paperbacks ranged on a ramshackle shelf. Sarah's flat was furnished with skilled and loving care, with odd and beautiful things her expert eye had culled from junk shops, and with nice old pieces brought from home.

I had first met Sarah when she had come, photographer in tow, to interview me for a magazine she was working on then, rather absurdly called *Gracious Living.* Come to think of it, they went in rather for absurd titles; the feature, when it appeared, was headed "Gregory Hunter—Chippendale of the Seventies"—which turned me cold with embarrassment. Sarah assured me later that the title had not been her idea, and it's true that the write-up she did on Hunter's was an honest enough affair. She had reported faithfully what my ideas were, to produce furniture which was beautiful, lasting, and a natural development from the traditions of the great craftsmen: no bare austerity in the Scandinavian manner, no blowup or paper chairs, no gimmicks of any kind: furniture

11

for the discriminating, for whom there are simply not enough antiques to go round.

Sarah liked all this, in fact she was enthusiastic about it. In the course of the interview we discovered another link—she knew my sister, Madeleine. They had been at school together, at that posh boarding school that Mother and her third husband, Russell, had packed Maddy off to, when she became too much of a problem at home. It seemed that Sarah and Maddy had been quite close at one time, though in more recent years they had lost touch.

"I admired her madly," Sarah said, smiling reminiscently. "I was a very good, obedient child, you see, and Madeleine was always so rebellious. It was the sensation of all time when she ran away."

I laughed. "That I can believe."

"Wasn't it you she ran to?"

"Who else? Our mother was abroad at the time, and Maddy wouldn't have gone there anyway. We sat up all night arguing it out and in the end I took her back next day and talked *them* into taking her back again. I was awfully dignified, doing the in loco parentis bit; it must have seemed rather funny, as I was only nineteen at the time myself. It worked, anyhow. Poor old Maddy, she really was hell at fifteen—not that she didn't have plenty to make her. You should see her now, the perfect wife and mother, extraordinary metamorphosis. Would you like to, by the way?"

"See her again? Very much."

"They live in the country. She's not often in London these days. I could run you down there one Sunday," I offered, "if you'd like that."

So we did that, and the friendship between the two girls was renewed. As for Sarah and I, soon we were going everywhere together. Later I cajoled her out of her job with *Gracious Living* and persuaded her to work for us as publicity manager. Hugo, I think, did not really approve of this, not believing in mixing business with pleasure. But he had to approve of Sarah, who had the art of keeping personal relationships out of the office, and did a superb job for us in it.

So far as I was concerned, it did seem as if the arid period in my life after the death of my wife, Tessa, had come to an end. I didn't need to be especially vain to know that Sarah was in love with me, and would marry me if I asked her. But I hadn't asked her, not yet.

I arrived at her door punctual to the minute, and punctual to the minute Sarah was ready for me, ready to leave the moment I was; her weekend case standing in the hall, the promised drink immediately forthcoming. I relaxed in a comfortable chair, and looked at Sarah with appreciation. She had changed into a cool, crisp summer dress, and looked just right, as always. A lovely, desirable girl, to be proud of when you took her out. But above all, it was her tranquillity that I valued. I said gratefully, "You know, Sarah, you are the most soothing person I know."

She smiled, and said, a bit dryly, "Well, thanks."

"Did I say something wrong? It was meant as a compliment."

"Of course," she added, laughing. "But it does sound a bit dull, doesn't it?"

"Dull? You know perfectly well I don't think you're dull. Come here and I'll prove it."

She came across the room to me rather slowly. In a vague way I thought she looked a bit sad; I don't know. I pulled her down on my knees and kissed her, and of course we got a bit involved in that, and after a bit I said, "Don't let's go. Let's just stay here."

She began at once to pull away from me and admonished, "We can't do that. Madeleine's expecting us."

"We can telephone. She'll understand."

"Hardly," Sarah explained. "She's probably made all sorts of preparations. Besides . . ." She slipped away from me and stood up. "I want to go, Greg. I feel like a weekend in the country." She smoothed her dress down, refusing to meet my eye. I hadn't really been serious and I didn't argue. Sarah had been like this more and more lately, and I knew why. What was that I had said, about her not making difficulties? If she did, I had only myself to blame.

So we set off to the country after all. It was a little late for the worst of the weekend exodus, and we made good time out of London. Once clear of the suburbs we stopped off for a meal at a pub. The heat of the day was gone when we started out again, heading into the west where the sky was a pale pearly green, dappled with clouds flushed with the sun's reflection. The hedgerows were clotted with dog roses and the waxy white bells of convolvulus. It did something to our mood, our swift passage through the lovely summer evening, the countryside garlanded for our coming. We were both happy, I believe. I remember thinking about Sarah, about marrying her and settling down in a house in the country, just near enough to London for me to go up and down each day. I could see it all in my mind's eye, the return in the evening to a house ordered and cared for by Sarah, who did all such things well. Later there would be children, rosy and sleepy and already in bed, perhaps, or shouting and scrambling to be the first to greet me; and I would be proud and content, the provider and pivot of their lives. A pretty picture. I thought, this weekend I shall ask Sarah to marry me. She wants it, and I can't possibly do better. I don't know why I haven't done it before.

Then, a few miles from my sister's house, it happened. We had turned off the main route on to a secondary road, which ran directly past the Institute of Environmental Science, where Paul, my brother-in-law, worked. The road was straight, rather narrow, with unfenced woods on either side; empty at that moment except for ourselves and another small car, a Mini, traveling towards us. It was still some distance away when a rabbit leaped out of the undergrowth and crossed the road with its bounding gait, followed a second later by a large mongrel dog intent on pursuit; it dashed straight into the path of the other car and we heard the screech of tires as the driver braked and swerved violently. We saw the car scramble and totter at the top of the bank; then it was over, almost on its side, with its nose in the ditch beyond.

I slammed on the brakes and Sarah and I jumped out of the car and ran. I got there first. The driver of the Mini had been thrown across the passenger seat in a heap. All I could see at first was the huddle of her body and a tangle of dark

14

hair and for a moment I feared she was unconscious, badly hurt perhaps. But almost immediately she began to try to struggle up into a sitting position. She turned her head, and our eyes met. Hers were very large, of that luminous clear gray one can only call the color of water, fringed with thick dark lashes, all her own. Not unexpectedly, she was as white as a sheet.

The most momentous things can happen in a few seconds, and that's how it was and I can't explain it. That single moment, looking at her, before we had exchanged a word, hit me where I live. That's all.

I found my voice and asked, "Are you all right?"

"I think so. I think I must have blacked out for a minute. Can you get me out of this?"

I got the door open somehow and half helped, half lifted her out. There seemed very little of her, it was rather like handling a kitten, there was the same lithe boneless feeling—light, yielding and sensuously sweet. I put her on her feet gingerly, holding her to steady her. Upright, she was much taller than I expected. She was wearing jeans and sandals and a bright shirt. She trembled lightly under my hand, and said in a small voice, like a child, "Was the dog all right?"

Sarah said, "Don't you think you ought to sit down a minute?"

I had forgotten Sarah. While I had been getting the girl out of the car she had run back to ours for a rug and a coat. She spread the rug on the ground and put the coat around the girl's shoulders; kind, efficient Sarah, she thought of everything. "There," she said. "I daresay you feel a bit cold."

"Yes," the girl replied in surprise. "Sort of shivery. Thank you. You're being awfully kind."

"You know," I said, "I think we should take you to hospital. It isn't far. Just to check up that you're all right."

"But there's nothing wrong with me," the girl protested. "I just feel cold, that's all."

"That's shock," Sarah said. "He's right, you know. And you could just have cracked a rib, or something. You should have some medical attention."

"But they might want to keep me in, and I *can't* stay, I must

15

get back to London tonight . . ." She stared at the car. "Will it go?"

"I doubt it. I'll see if I can get it back on the road."

In normal circumstances it's quite easy to manhandle a Mini, but it was firmly wedged on the bank and I couldn't shift it. I battled with it for a few minutes, and gave up. "Don't worry. It won't be a write-off, but we can't get it out of there without assistance. In any case," I added gently "I don't think you're fit to drive, you know."

"But I must get there," she pleaded. "I must, I've got a show at eleven and I must be there." Tears gathered in her eyes and ran down her white cheeks; shock, of course, she didn't strike me as a crying sort of girl. She stared helplessly at us through her tears. "I don't know what to do," she said. I heard her say it with a painful tightening of the heart. I didn't know her at all. I didn't even know her name. But there it was.

I said lightly, "Here, that won't do. We'll get you to hospital, that's the first thing, just to make sure. Then if you're all right, we'll have to find a way of getting you back to town. That makes sense, doesn't it?"

She nodded. "I suppose it does. You're very kind," she repeated.

I think, in a way, she was glad that we took command of her. I ran my car alongside and Sarah collected the girl's belongings and we tucked her into the rear seat, wrapped in the rug. On the way to the hospital, she became nervously voluble.

"I hate to bother you like this. I could kick myself, it was all so silly, but I couldn't bear to hit the dog . . . and I haven't been driving very long. If this hadn't happened, I would have had plenty of time in hand."

"Where's your engagement?" I asked.

"The Silver Rhino, it's a club."

"Oh, yes, I know the one."

"I'm singing there. I only started this week."

"What's your name?" I asked.

"Cass Clayton. Just Cass, for professional purposes."

"Short for Cassandra?"

"No such luck. My name's Kathleen really, but I mean I couldn't use that, could I? Too ordinary and anyway people would expect me to burst into 'When Irish Eyes Are Smiling.' Then I picked up this nickname and it stuck."

I introduced Sarah and myself and the breathless little voice behind me babbled on: "Well, how do you do? I simply don't know what to say about all this, I must be taking you miles out of your way, I hope I'm not making you late for a meal somewhere . . ."

"That's all right. We've eaten already."

Sarah murmured, "Greg, you shouldn't encourage her to talk so much," and this vaguely irritated me. However, at that moment we turned into the hospital drive.

When we had checked Cass into the casualty department Sarah and I sat down in the waiting room and looked at each other. Or rather, Sarah looked at me, and I had a strong disinclination to look back. I got up and lit a cigarette and wandered about the room.

"It says No Smoking," said Sarah.

"To hell with what it says. There's nobody else here."

I didn't mean to snap at Sarah. However, she ignored it, saying only, "I suppose we must wait and see what happens. We can hardly just dump her here and disappear."

"Hardly."

"But she must have friends in the district, or relatives. The hospital could get in touch with them."

"We don't know yet how far she's come already."

"That's true," said Sarah reasonably.

Silence again. I suddenly felt like a heel and said, "I'm sorry, Sarah."

"Sorry? Whatever for?"

I wasn't quite sure what for.

"Well, your evening's been spoiled."

She smiled. "That's all right. Your evening's been spoiled too. We couldn't help getting involved in this." Then she added, "I suppose if she hadn't been going so fast, she wouldn't have landed in the ditch."

"She wasn't going fast. She probably wouldn't be here at all if she had been."

Sarah didn't answer. I continued to fidget up and down the room, looked out into the empty corridor, came back in again. Sarah said suddenly with an edge to her voice, "Greg, do stop pacing about like an expectant father."

This was unlike Sarah. I said "Sorry" and sat down, and after not too long a time, I suppose, a nurse stood in the doorway. "You're Miss Clayton's friends?" she asked briskly, not giving us a chance to deny it. "She's quite all right, just a bit shaken up. She's talking to the police at the moment, perhaps you'd like to come along, they'd like a word with you too."

Cass was sitting in the reception office, talking to a young policeman; I suppose the hospital had put in a report. The policeman was treating Cass very gently, as if she might break if he talked too loud. Then he turned his attention to us, but as nobody else had been hurt and there was no dispute about what happened, he shut up his notebook and prepared to leave. "But you'll be wanting someone to get your car up, miss. Cossors in the village will do it. They're open now but they won't be able to move your car until morning. Forest Dale 23."

"Oh, thank you. Is there a telephone here I could use, nurse?"

The nurse indicated a pay phone in the hall outside, and we all moved out there. Sarah paused, but as if only on her way to the door, conveying, not too pointedly, that we had done what we could and now intended to get on with our own affairs. She said pleasantly to Cass, "You're sure you're all right now?"

A brief, level look passed between them. Cass, certainly, seemed all right. The panic had passed, she was in command of herself. She said coolly, "Yes, thanks, I'm fine now. Thank you so much for everything."

It was release to Sarah, dismissal to me. Sarah made some other civil farewell remark and went towards the door. Cass was looking for change in her handbag. I stood my ground, while she went over to the pay phone and dialed. As she waited, I said, "How are you going to get back to London?"

"Hire a car. I'll ask these people."

"They don't hire cars."

18

She peered out at me from under the hood surrounding the phone, looking at me in dismay. "Are you sure?"

"Quite sure."

The garage answered and she began to talk to them. After a bit she glanced back at me, shaking her head and spreading her right hand, palm downwards. She said to the garage man, "Just a minute." She put her hand over the mouthpiece and said to me: "Please go. I'm very grateful for all you've done. But please go. Your friend will be . . ."

I said, "Never mind that." I took out my diary, scribbled a telephone number on a blank page and tore the sheet out. "Try this. If it isn't any good, we'll think of something else. I'll be back."

Sarah was standing at the end of the hall by the door; her back, turned towards me, had a rigid look. But I was not afraid she would make a fuss. That was something Sarah never did.

Finding me beside her, she looked up and said brightly, "Well, that seems to be that, doesn't it?"

I explained slowly, "I don't think it is, Sarah. Look, this kid's got to get back to London. There's no local car hire firm. I've told her to phone one in Ringwood but it's a long shot at this time in the evening. I feel if she can't get anything, we ought to offer to take her."

"*Take* her? All the way back to London? But why? The accident wasn't your fault."

"Or hers, really. She's shaken up, and she's got an engagement to keep. A job to do. You know how you'd feel in the same circumstances."

This was a shrewd, indeed a cunning stroke. I must say I felt both triumphant and a bit ashamed, seeing its effect on Sarah, who was such a reasonable woman; too reasonable, perhaps, for her own good.

"Yes, I see what you mean," she said. "Well, I suppose . . ." She sighed, put a hand on my shoulder and gave me a friendly little push. "Go on, then. Go and see what she's up to. If she can't get a car . . ."

"She may have got one by now," I said, eager to meet Sarah halfway. "I'll go and see."

As I approached I could hear Cass saying, "You haven't

anything? Till what time? After ten? I'm afraid that's no use. Thank you." She put the receiver down and stood there for a moment with her head bent. I touched her shoulder and said, "Come on."

"Come—where?"

"We'll take you back to town," I said.

"But . . ." Relief, doubt, embarrassment warred in her face.

"I've just had a chat with Sarah. She doesn't mind. In fact she suggested it," I added, lying shamelessly.

"It would be wonderful, but I don't really think I ought to accept."

I looked at my watch. "If you stay here arguing, there won't be any point in accepting. We ought to get going."

"Well, if you're sure," she said. We went to join Sarah. Cass said in a small nervous voice, "This is very good of you."

"Don't thank me," Sarah said dryly. "Greg's got to drive." After that, there didn't seem much more for them to say to each other and Cass retired into the back seat as quiet as a mouse. We had hardly got going when Sarah said quietly, "Greg, I was thinking . . . we'll have to go close to the house this way, and anyway we'll have to let Madeleine and Paul know what's happened. I think if you don't mind, I'd rather you dropped me off there. I'm rather tired."

I felt an onrush of joy, immediately suppressed, and because I was rather ashamed of this I was especially tender to Sarah. "Well, if you'd rather, darling . . . are you sure?"

"Quite sure."

She didn't look at me. I was afraid that Cass might have overheard this exchange and would rush in with more protestations, but either she hadn't heard, or Sarah scared her. None of us said anything further until we reached the house. I got Sarah's bag out of the trunk and put it in the hall; the front door, as always in the summer, was open. I could hear the dog barking faintly from the other end of the garden. Maddy and Paul must have been in the garden too, as no one came out to greet us and I wasn't sorry. Sarah and I stood in the drive for a moment. "Don't wait, Greg. I'll explain. I suppose you'll be a bit late back, won't you?"

20

"I'll make it as soon as I can," I promised.

"Well, I expect we shall have gone to bed, anyway." Her face was turned away from me.

"All right, then. Give everyone my love. And, Sarah . . ."

"What?"

"You're being very sweet about this."

"Am I?" She put her hand briefly on my sleeve, adding, "Mind how you go," and went into the house. I got back into the car and drove away.

A mile or so down the road I pulled up and said, "Wouldn't you like to sit in front?"

"M'mm . . . yes." Cass scrambled out of the car and in again beside me. She didn't sit in the car as Sarah would, letting the back of the seat support her spine all the way down. She slid down in the seat and curled up in it, hugging her knees. There was something about her movements both gawky and graceful, like a young animal. Her hair had fallen forward like a curtain and she pushed it back with a thin small hand, bare of rings. She looked tired and disheveled, she had no makeup on at all and nobody could have called her beautiful, but she exuded magnetism like perfume. I was intensely, violently aware of her, which is no way to be when you're concentrating on getting from A to B in the shortest possible time without taking too many risks; I was a more careful driver these days, having learned to be the hard way.

"Feeling better now?" I asked.

"Oh, I'm fine. Just feeling angry with myself, busting up the car and being such a nuisance . . ."

"You've said all that once already," I told her with a grin. "It's getting monotonous. I wouldn't have driven you back to London if I hadn't wanted to. Pipe down, girl. Save your energy for your performance. Have a sleep, why don't you? I don't suppose you get to bed until the small hours."

"Well, no . . ."

"And you've driven down from London . . . today? And you were going to drive back and do a show tonight. I call that overdoing it a bit. Especially if you haven't been driving long."

She murmured defensively, "I'm not always doing it. I just

21

had to come this time . . . just one of those things," she added, without explaining any further. She sighed. "We will make it in time, won't we?"

"With a bit to spare," I promised. "Leave it to me."

"Oh, smashing. You've no idea how relieved I am." She yawned deeply, mumbled, "Oh dear, I do feel rather tired."

"Put your head down," I advised. "I'll wake you when we get there."

She did as she was told and was asleep almost instantly. As we went round a stiff bend she slid sideways until her head was resting against my shoulder. Now and then I was able to steal a glance at her. She went right on sleeping. Like that, with the long lashes resting on her cheeks, pink unpainted lips slightly parted, she had that touching, vulnerable look which children have when asleep.

She didn't wake up until we got to Knightsbridge. She said sleepily, "Where are we?"

"Just passing Harrods. We're doing fine."

"Really! I must have been asleep for ages . . . you've saved my life, you know, you really have."

On the one-way stretch down Piccadilly I asked, "Are you going to let me come and hear you?"

"If you want to, but don't you have to be a member?"

"I'm a member of every club in London, I should think."

"Heavens, you must lead a hectic life—"

"I don't, at all. It's just a blanket membership, a sort of credit card. Useful now and then, for entertaining visiting buyers."

"Oh, I see. What do you do?"

"We make furniture."

"Oh, yes. I thought I'd heard the name somewhere . . . it's just round this next corner—I don't know about parking—look, isn't that a space over there?"

The Silver Rhino was one of those tarted-up cellars, lit almost exclusively by the candles on the tables, where it's too dark to see what you're eating and you pay through the nose for the privilege. There was a jungle decor, very somber, what one could see of it. A small group of piano, drums and a chap clanking away on a double bass provided music for people to dance to, on the pocket-handkerchief floor.

22

As we came into the foyer a man emerged from the shadows: the owner or manager, I supposed, a pale, fattish character, the type that manages to look both old and young at the same time. He said to Cass in a flat, not especially unpleasant voice, "Oh, there you are then. Just beginning to wonder where you'd got to. I suppose you know you're on in ten minutes?"

Cass said breathlessly, "Yes, I know, I'm sorry, there's been an accident, to my car. Mr. Hunter just happened to be on the spot and gave me a lift." She looked from one to the other of us, as if uncertain what to do, and murmured the man's name which was Dominic something, I forget the other bit. We nodded at each other. Cass excused herself and fled.

I said, "Perhaps you can find me a table."

He said doubtfully, "Well, I'm afraid . . . we're very full tonight, sir."

I looked him over and said pleasantly, "I've been at considerable trouble to get your singer here on time. I'm sure you can find me a table if you try."

As I expected, his attitude changed into a servile affability; I signed the book, orders were given, waiters scurried, they squeezed me into a corner. I ordered a drink and looked about me. When I'd got used to the general gloom I recognized several people there who are called personalities. The Silver Rhono was having its day, so Cass had got in there at the right time, when it mattered; if it did matter. I felt faintly depressed. I had taken a dislike to Dominic Thing and hated the thought of Cass being dependent on types like him for her bread.

After a bit the band left the platform and she came on.

She was all in black: a long black dress, long sleeves, no jewelery, nothing to relieve it at all. Everything was black, the piano, her dress, her heavy straight hair looking black in the spotlight. It ought to have been effective but it wasn't; she simply melted into the background. For all the notice the audience took of her, she might not have been there. They went right on eating and talking.

She sat down at the piano, played a few bars and began to sing. The first thing I realized was that she had a real voice that didn't need the mike, a warm, full, golden voice; and the

23

material was good, too. One song, especially, had a good lyric—sad, ironic and witty—and a haunting tune. But she wasn't getting over, I knew that, and what was worse, she knew it too. She wasn't projecting her personality at all. I knew without being told that she was tired, shaky after the accident, and frightened to death.

She sang three songs and after each there was a faint, polite rattle of applause. The third time I clapped vigorously; I could not have announced my interest in her more blatantly if the message had been printed on my chest. An arrogant-looking blonde at the next table turned her head and stared at me as if she thought I was quite mad. I didn't give a damn about that, being only concerned about Cass, looking so small and defenseless at the piano with the spotlight on her, while the indifferent customers plied their knives and forks and drank their wine.

She took a bow, unsmilingly, and went away, her back very straight.

I said to the waiter, "Keep my table. I'll be back." Then I walked over to the pass door and pushed my way through it.

The pass door was a frontier between two territories: the nightclub on one side, and on the other, chipped brown paint, linoleum, fire buckets, the sound of kitchen clatter, a voice behind a closed door, telephoning. I almost collided with a man I recognized as the drummer. I asked him where I could find Cass.

He gestured behind him. "Second door on the left."

I went to it and knocked. There was no answer, so I turned the handle and opened it a little way. It was a tiny box of a room and just inside was the dressing table. Cass sat on a stool in front of it, her arms were spread on the tabletop among her makeup clutter, and her head was buried in her arms.

"Cass," I said.

Her head came up quickly and she sprang up. I don't quite know how it happened, perhaps she stumbled, but the next instant she was in my arms. I kicked the door to behind me and stood there holding her, not making anything of it. She put her head down on my shoulder and I said, "Never mind, love. Never mind."

24

She looked up and said in wonder, "You knew how I was feeling. You *knew.*"

"Yes. I knew."

"I was terrible, wasn't I?"

"No," I said. "Not terrible. You've got a lovely voice and the songs are all right too. Who writes them?"

"I do, mostly."

"Do you now," I said with respect.

"But I'm not getting over, am I?"

"Not yet, no."

"I'm only here to fill in," she said, "while someone they really wanted is ill. It's a chance, a sort of now-or-never chance . . ."

"Does it mean so much to you?"

"I'm afraid it does."

"Well then," I said. "Listen."

I couldn't go on holding her like that. I gave her a little affectionate shake and lowered her onto her dressing stool again, and pulled up the only other chair in the room. We sat facing each other, knee to knee. She folded her hands in her lap and looked at me and waited. She looked like a meek little girl, waiting to hear the words of wisdom from teacher. It occurred to me that the words had better be good.

"Now," I said. "You've got everything it takes. You've got the right sort of looks, a lovely voice, good material and a style of your own. The only important thing wrong is that you're overanxious and frightened of the audience. That's it, isn't it?"

She nodded mutely.

"So you've only got to go on there happy and confident, and it's all yours. Now I know this sounds corny, and it's been in every show-business film since the thirties I daresay, but I've got a feeling it works. It's just this: forget all about those people out there. Remember there's one person there who does think you're good, and that's me. Don't sing to them, sing to me. That makes it all personal, intimate, which is what is wanted in a place this size. Oh yes, and there's one other thing. Have you anything else to wear?"

"I've got a red caftan here . . ."

"Put it on. That black thing's horrible. Throw it away."

25

"Heavens," she giggled. "You certainly know your own mind, don't you?"

"That's what's needed around here just now. Let's see you in the red thing. I'll turn my back if you're modest."

"Oh, you needn't bother," she laughed. She unzipped the black dress and stepped unconcernedly out of it. In black briefs and bra she was no more naked than any one of a thousand girls in bikinis one can see, without disturbance, on any beach. But she was not any one of a thousand girls. Her flesh had a rosy sheen like a pearl. I had to turn away; I don't think she noticed.

"There," she said. "What do you think?"

I surveyed her, now wearing the red caftan.

"That's better. Now, you remember what I said."

"Yes. All right."

"And afterwards, I'll wait for you and take you home."

For the first time, her mouth trembled, and she pressed her lips together to stop it.

After a moment, she said, "I don't know why you should do all this for me."

I grinned. "Don't you?" I said.

I told myself that it was absurd to be so anxious. When she appeared again I was sweating lightly, my mouth was dry and my collar felt unusually tight. I could no more stand up and sing before an audience—always supposing I had a voice to sing with—than I could jump over the moon. Perhaps I was even more afraid for her than she was for herself; and I began to think that maybe all that stuff I had been saying to her was a lot of nonsense, and wouldn't work.

But it did.

I concentrated on her absolutely, and across the room I could see her eyes seeking and meeting mine, and immediately she began to sing I could feel the confidence in her and knew it would be all right, even before the chattering died down, before the significant, momentary pause at the end of the song before the applause broke out.

Cabaret audiences don't often go overboard and they didn't do that, exactly. But when, finally, she abandoned the piano, explained the story of the Eastern European folk song she was about to sing, and began to sing it unaccompanied in some strange language, clapping her hands, ranging up and down the little stage and leaving the mike to take care of itself—then I knew she had them. Their faces were turned toward her, they clapped with her, some of them even sang the refrain with her, they were smiling, enjoying her. Rapport with an audience is a mysterious business, all in the mind, you might say.

Satisfied, I settled my bill and went out to the car to wait. She didn't keep me waiting long. She came out of the doorway, looked about her, saw me and came bounding toward me like an excited child, her hair swinging, her hands outstretched.

"It worked," she cried. "It worked, how can I ever thank you?"

"Don't try. You did it yourself. You've really started something now. Fame and fortune, here they come."

"You really think so?"

"Why not?" But it's not what I want for her, I thought. I want her for myself.

It had been raining a little, earlier. The streets were blue-black, sleek, shining. It was very late, or rather very early, and London was asleep, but muttering in her sleep, the way great cities always do. We drove back along Knightsbridge, past the barracks and Kensington Gardens, the night air damp and sweet after the shower of rain, past the big department stores, windows gleaming goldenly even at this hour with the lights left on all night. All of it was touched with the kind of magic I thought I was past experiencing: because she was there.

She said suddenly, "You know, I'm not sure that I care."

"About what?"

"What you said, about starting something. I mean, about making money, that sort of thing. I want to prove myself. The rest doesn't really matter so much."

"But you're happy?"

"About having brought it off, yes. And being understood. You turn left at the next light, I think." She spoke naturally, absently, without looking at me. The lights turned red. I put out my hand, and she put hers into it, and we sat like that, without speaking, until the lights changed.

She lived in the hinterland west of Chelsea, where the dear little houses and the squares and the window boxes and the rich gloss of gracious living give way to a maze of gray streets, blocks of council flats, and tall houses rented out floor by floor or more often room by room. She directed me to a corner house, a door in a wall. She had what is called a garden flat, a semibasement really, only in her case, she told me, there really was a garden of sorts, a walled, paved space in which she tried to grow plants in pots; only it didn't get much sun, except in the middle of the day. I didn't get to see it and didn't expect to, not this time. As we drew up beside the door she sighed, smiled, and turned to reach for her bag.

"Cass," I said.

Her eyes were enormous, deep pools. One could take a dive into them and drown and I almost did. After a moment, she shut them. I held her with a passion that was more than desire.

After a bit we drew apart and she said shakily, "Don't rush me."

"No," I said. "All right, love."

"I'm not playing hard to get. It's just . . ."

"I know. I wouldn't want to rush you anyway. So far as I'm concerned, this is for real."

She shook her head. "You can't say that, not yet, it's too soon . . ."

"Is it? Don't you think one can come a long way, like that, in a few hours?"

"Yes. Oh yes, I do. Only it isn't always as simple as that. I feel rather bad about all this. Guilty."

"What about?"

"That nice girl friend of yours—Sarah."

The mention of Sarah's name was like a cold douche on my excitement and joy. "What about Sarah?"

"She was kind to me," Cass said slowly.

"What an extraordinary girl you are. That's the last thing most women would think of."

28

"I wonder," she said. "I don't know if that's true. If we really are as mean and petty as most men seem to think."

"I don't think you're mean and petty. Given the time and opportunity, I'll tell you what I really think. But seriously, that's my business, isn't it? I'm not committed. I'm not married to Sarah, I'm not engaged to her. I'm not in love with her and I've never told her I was."

"But she's in love with you," Cass said.

"I wouldn't know about that."

She was silent, and I said, alarmed, "You wouldn't really let all that make any difference?"

She sighed. "No. I ought to, but I shan't, I know that."

"Well, then, look. I can't get out of going back to the country for the weekend. But I'll be back on Sunday night."

She bent her head and said, "I don't go to the club on Sundays."

"Then can I come and see you? We could go out somewhere and eat, perhaps."

"If you still want to—"

"Of course I shall still want to."

She said gravely, using my name for the first time, "Greg, it's been rather an unusual evening. When you get back to the country you may feel differently. Sometimes these things seem real when they aren't. I'll be here on Sunday, but if you don't come, I shall understand."

"Do you want me to come?"

Her lips trembled, and she pressed them together in the same way as she had done in the dressing room. She said quietly, "Yes, I do. But that hasn't really got anything to do with it." She touched my hand and added gently, "Good night, Greg. And thank you for everything."

She got out of the car and the door in the wall opened and closed behind her. I started the engine and drove away.

Even though I made good time on the empty roads going back, the first streaks of daylight were showing in the east by the time I reached my sister's house. To avoid making a noise, I stopped the car before I got there, and left it parked in the road. I approached the house as stealthily as a burglar,

29

skirting the gravel drive and making my way across the lawn. I didn't really imagine that Sarah would be awake, checking up what time I had come in, still less that she would rush downstairs to confront me and demand to know what I had been doing. But you never know. I went round to the kitchen, where I knew Maddy would have left the door unlocked for me.

The house was silent and still, the night peaceful; the soft country air was like balm after the tasteless stuff one breathes in London. A bed of tobacco flowers glimmered palely, pouring out into the darkness their strong evocative scent, and in the stillness I could hear the scuttle of some nocturnal creature, and the first sleepy chirrups as the birds began to tune up. In common, I suppose, with everyone who has ever experienced the onset of romantic love, I had a heightened awareness of all such things.

I let myself into the kitchen. Honey, the labrador, who slept there, uttered a single grumbling growl, recognized me, and threw herself, silent and ecstatic, against my chest. On the kitchen table was a note in Maddy's sprawling hand: "I've taken Jane in with us and Helga . . ." (Who was Helga?) ". . . has got Jeremy so you're in the children's room If hungry raid fridge Don't make noise Jane teething and hell to get to sleep see you in the morning love M." She wrote without any stops, as usual.

I crept up to the children's room, which had washable rugs with bunnies on, a Disneyish wallpaper, and, apart from Jeremy's bed (he'd recently been promoted to a grown-up one), furniture scaled down to the appropriate size; I felt a bit like Gulliver in Lilliput.

This was the moment when often, even if dead beat and longing for bed, sleep eluded me. I was only too familiar with the pattern: going to bed in a good humor, contented, optimistic, believing all wounds healed, or rather not even remembering there were any. Then it would happen: in the darkness, the uneasiness beginning, the sudden sinking of the spirit. And there she would be, Tessa, creeping inexorably into my consciousness, a sad, inimical little ghost.

Thank God, I didn't dream about her anymore. Though I

suppose you could say that I never had, exactly. She didn't appear in the dreams, though in some weird way they were about her, I knew that. Any headshrinker would have a ball with those dreams, but none of them will ever get the chance. I had never told a living soul about the dreams and didn't mean to start; and they'd gone now, anyway, gone for good, and the haunting depression with them. Cass had done that, plunging into my life that sunny evening in June. Crashing her car and knocking herself out. Cass.

Thinking about her, I fell asleep.

Two

I SLEPT LATE, and like a log. I came up slowly through layers of sleep to a mild feeling of discomfort: there was a weight on my chest. The weight squirmed and wriggled. Somebody was saying shrilly right in my ear, wake up, Gegg, wake up. I opened my eyes and looked directly into another pair of eyes, close to my own, belonging to my nephew, Jeremy. The irises were a deep fresh blue and the whites very pure white—the exquisitely clear and healthy eyes of a small child after a good night's sleep. Looking at them made me feel about a hundred. I groaned and shut my eyes again and then opened them once more, just in time to forestall Jeremy from prizing them open with his fingers. "Stop that!" I yelled.

Jeremy giggled. "Gegg woke up," he said with satisfaction. "Get up, Gegg. You're *lazy*."

"Very lazy," I agreed, "And if you don't get off my chest, I shall be cross as well as lazy, and then I shall spank." I heaved myself up suddenly and he rolled off backwards onto my legs, squealing and giggling. He was up again in a flash, back on the attack, and we had a tussle. A foreign voice outside cried, "Jeremy! Where are you, Jeremy?" Jeremy didn't answer. A handsome strapping blonde, whom I had never seen before in my life, opened the door and walked in, stared at my naked torso, said "Excuse" and withdrew hurriedly.

"That's Helga," said Jeremy. "She's a pair."

"A what? Oh, I see."

Jeremy seemed to have worked off his aggressiveness for the time being. He hugged me round the neck. "You're in my bed. Why are you in my bed?"

33

"Because Mummy said." I was beginning to talk like him.

Jeremy looked at me with love. Golden with summer tan, flushed with health, his upper lip adorned with a milk moustache, he looked extremely beguiling.

"I like it when you come," he said. "I like *you.* I like you always."

"Good. I like you always, too."

"But you always go away again. You shouldn't go away again."

"I have to. I have work to do."

"What's work?"

"You'll know soon enough, poor infant."

"Daddy's going away," he announced importantly. "To Affiker. In a plane. Or a hellingcopter."

"Helicopter. But I should think it would be a plane. Is he really going, or are you making it up?"

Paul appeared round the door, winked at me over Jeremy's head and said rapidly, "Mr. Thing's prognostications are quite correct but we don't make too much of it in case of ructions . . . coffee?"

He proffered the steaming mug he was carrying and I seized on it gratefully.

"Who's Mr. Thing?" Jeremy asked.

"Nobody you know. Get down off there, and let your long-suffering uncle drink his coffee in peace."

Jeremy's face clouded. I began to say, "He's all right," but Paul shook his head at me. "Leave him to you, he'd be thoroughly spoiled. Helga wants you, Jeremy. Off you go, now."

Jeremy looked at his father reproachfully, but he climbed down from the bed and trotted away. Paul and I looked at each other and laughed.

"I'm sorry about last night," I said.

"Last night?" Paul looked vague. "Oh, yes, you had to go back to town. I wasn't home till late myself actually; everything's in a flat spin. I should be doing the apologizing, anyway. There's been some administrative slipup and this trip's been put forward a week; we're leaving tonight."

"What are you going to do out there?" I asked.

"They're setting up a research institute, something like

34

ours. We've been seconded to the scheme—myself, a colleague from our place, and another chap from Cambridge—to get it off the ground. Survey the problems, lay down guidelines, produce a preliminary report in six months—"

"Sounds a lot to expect in that time," I said. It was my turn to be vague.

"You can say that again. But it's a challenge. The Africans haven't had time to wreck their environment the way we have ours over hundreds of years. Now things are beginning to change. One can get in on the ground floor, monitor it, the effects of industrialization, tourism, movement of population—all that—on everything from soil and water to bird and insect life."

"Yes." I knew nothing about ecology and couldn't share his enthusiasm.

"What does Maddy think about it?"

"Well, not keen. But she wouldn't stand in my way. If it were for longer they'd let us take our families, not that I'm sure she'd want that either. It's a bit lonely for her here though. She'd be very tied on her own with the kids. Hence Helga."

"Oh, yes. The Brunnhilde character."

"A nice enough wench. Her English is a bit fractured and she's a dead loss domestically, but nice with the kids. Anyway, Madeleine will be able to get out a bit more. She doesn't do enough of that."

Something in his tone puzzled me. "She's all right, is she?" I asked, meaning Maddy.

"All right? Of course she's all right." He looked at his watch. "I must go down to the Institute; my chief's tearing his hair and wanting all sorts of last minute conferences. Why don't you come too? I shan't be long, I hope, and we can have a pint at the George afterwards."

I shook my head. "I'd hold you up, not dressed, not shaved—anyway, I must make my peace with the girls. I might come down later."

"Okay. Look, Greg, I'd like to ask a favor—"

"Ask away."

"The plane leaves at ten. Maddy wants to come and see me

35

off and I don't fancy her driving back on her own in the
dark, you know how night-blind she is—"

"You want me to drive you? We'll all come," I promised.

"I'm afraid it's messed up the weekend," Paul said.

The weekend, I thought, was messed up already.

Paul went off and presently I heard his car pulling away.
The house was quiet now except for the faint sounds of Maddy's activity in the kitchen. Helga had probably taken the
children out somewhere, perhaps to the local stables where
Lucy, the eldest, would trot proudly round on a fat docile
pony at the end of a leading rein. Sarah, I guessed, was having breakfast in bed.

I shaved and dressed and went downstairs.

It was another beautiful day. The sun was streaming
through the window at the end of the landing, and I stopped
there to look out on the open view, the land patchworked
with field crops; the chugging sound of a tractor, a red toy
seen faraway, came faintly on the warm morning air. All of
this seemed today invested with a special grace, the house
too, though that was at all times a pleasant place to be—
warm, sunny, a bit untidy with the vigor of family living, full
of comfortable chairs, books, music, a scatter of children's
toys, and in summer everywhere the smell of garden flowers.
Mother was fond of saying, on her infrequent visits, that
Maddy had turned into "such a homebody, darling." That
was something Mother had never been, for very long at a
time anyway; I felt Maddy had the right idea.

I found her now, in the kitchen, already busy on one of
her tremendous cook-ups.

"Hi," I said.

Maddy put down the knife with which she was cutting up
vegetables. She said dryly, "Oh. So there you are." Funny little thing: she wore shorts and a sleeveless top, had her fair,
fine straight hair scraped up into a rubber band on top of her
head. In this get-up she looked about twelve years old still.
She came over and stood on tiptoe to kiss me, and then stood
away from me a little, giving me a quizzical look. As she did
this I realized that she didn't look twelve years old at all. She

was pale, and there were lines round her eyes I had never noticed before. I thought, with a bit of a shock: Maddy will soon be thirty.

"Well?" I said, smiling.

"Well, yourself," said Maddy. "What have you been up to?"

"You know that already—"

"Oh, don't stall," Maddy said. She laid a place for me on the kitchen table, produced milk and cereal, and slapped bread in the toaster. She waved the frying pan at me. "You want eggs and bacon?"

"Please. Look, I'll cook it myself if you're busy."

"Oh, sit down and eat your cereal. I'll do it." Over her shoulder she added, "Sarah came in with some story about you going back to London with some young woman who sings in a nightclub. She was awfully calm and dignified about it all, a good deal more so than I'd have been in her shoes, I must say. What's it all about?"

"Nothing," I said. "She told you, didn't she, about the accident?"

"Oh, yes. That."

"Well, then. I'm sorry about it, love—I mean, not being here last night—but I don't see what else I could have done."

"What, indeed," said Maddy, "except take the girl to the nearest railway station and let her sweat it out." She added suddenly, "I bet you stayed to hear her sing. Is she any good?"

"Yes, I did. And she is."

"And, of course, you took her home, and you're going to see her again, and you fancy her madly. Poor Sarah."

"Now, look, Maddy—"

"I know. You're not married, or engaged, nor nuffin'." Maddy nodded. "Poor Sarah just the same. Say what you like, Greg—it's no good your claiming you haven't led her up the garden, because you have. Men!" she exclaimed suddenly. "They make me sick. You all make me sick. One egg or two?"

"Two, please," I said meekly.

Maddy put one egg in the pan, broke the other and missed

37

the pan somehow, dropping the egg, shell and all, on the floor. She stared at it and said loudly, "Oh, damn damn *damn!*"

"Hey," I said, "what's going on? This isn't like you, Maddy—"

"How would you know what's like me?" Maddy snatched a paper towel and began to mop up the egg. Crouched on the floor, she muttered, "Didn't mean to shout. Sorry."

I said curiously, "Are you getting yourself into a state about Paul going away? He's not going into outer space, is he? And it isn't for so long, after all."

"Oh, no. It won't even make all that much difference. He's never here when he *is* here. If you see what I mean."

"Well, I know he works hard. It's his career—"

"Of course. But I wonder if you've ever thought what it's like for *me,* stuck right out here in the country."

"I thought you liked it," I said. "Come off it, Maddy. You've got a lovely house, garden, everything you can possibly want. You've always seemed contented, and you're so good at the domestic bit—"

"Ever so. One's got to be good at something. One's got to do *something.* What makes you think it's enough?"

I said uneasily, "I've never heard you talk like this before."

"No. But then you're not usually listening to what I say, are you? I mean, when you come for the weekend, you bring your girl friend, or you and Paul go sailing, or you and Paul play golf, or you disappear down to the George. I'm just here to do the cooking and see there are clean sheets on the bed."

"*Maddy,*" I said, perplexed, "I didn't know you felt like this. If I've been imposing on you—"

"Of course you haven't."

"What have I done, then?"

"Nothing," said Maddy, "You haven't done anything. Eat your breakfast." She hesitated and added, "I've done your eggs both sides. The way you like."

I looked up, caught her eye, and we both started laughing.

"It's a long time since we had a fight," Maddy said.

"Yes. Must be years. You've turned into such a placid girl."

"I'm not. I'm just the same as I always was, underneath. Oh . . . hallo, Sarah."

38

Sarah looked as lovely and elegant as ever, and perfectly self-possessed; she smiled pleasantly at us both, and said nicely to me, "You got back all right then."

"As you see," I said. I busied myself with my breakfast; the girls began to talk of other things. You would have thought neither of them had a care in the world, so rapid and effective are the defenses women put up when they have to. I drank my coffee, and began, showing willing because of Maddy's mood, to clear up the breakfast things.

"Don't bother with that, Greg. It's such a lovely day, why don't you and Sarah go and sit in the garden or something?"

Sarah said with a smile, "She wants to get rid of us, I think." I suppose Maddy thought that whatever it was I had to get over with Sarah, it was best done as soon as possible. She had a point there. I followed Sarah, rather reluctantly, into the garden.

Sarah said pleasantly, "I'm going for a walk."

"I'll come with you," I said.

"You needn't, you know. I daresay you don't feel up to it. You can't have had much sleep."

"I wasn't as late as all that."

"I heard the car," Sarah said without emphasis. "It woke me."

"I'm sorry."

"It doesn't matter. I went to sleep again."

There was nothing to say to that. She moved off and I went with her as there didn't seem much else I could do. We made our way through the kitchen garden, out through the wicket gate at the end and into the woods. The path was a faint ribbon of beaten earth winding through a tangle of couch grass, bracken and brambles, wide enough only for one. Sarah walked in front of me, moving quickly and lightly; her hair, cut quite short at that time, grew down into little wisps and tendrils at the nape of her neck, and it moved me in a way that the bright smiling mask of her face could not. It was unfair, the whole thing. Here was I, for whom this lovely weather seemed made to measure, and Sarah, who must have looked forward to this weekend, for whom nothing was left of it but the ashes of a dead love affair. All considered, she was doing very well.

39

We stopped at the edge of the copse because there was no walking further that way, unless one picked one's way round the edge of the big field of young corn beyond it. We stood there, side by side, and looked at it, that silky, faintly moving mass of greenish-gold, the eye carried away beyond it into a purple-blue distance. A perfect spot. If it hadn't been for that chance meeting yesterday, I might, at this very moment, be asking Sarah to marry me. We would have embraced and made promises, and gone back hand-in-hand to the house to tell the others.

She was there beside me. It could still be like that. Just forget last night. Forget it. Say the right words in the right tone of voice and it will all be over and she'll be in your arms and the other thing with its ecstatic promise, so uncertain, so unknown and troubling, would be no more than a whisper on the wind. Well, after a few weeks anyway.

Sarah said, "Lovely view."

"Lovely."

"Maddy seems rather depressed, don't you think?"

"Not quite herself, perhaps," I agreed; thankful that for some reason Sarah had decided to talk about Maddy rather than us.

"I think she's upset about Paul going away. Anyway, I don't want to upset her, or complicate things. So I shall stay on until tomorrow, as we arranged. You can give me a lift back to town tomorrow afternoon, can't you?"

"Of course. But I was going to do that anyway. Were you thinking of leaving earlier?"

She turned her head away. "Don't pretend to be obtuse, Greg, it doesn't suit you."

"Darling, if it's about last night" I said, "I'm sorry—"

"Don't apologize," she said loudly. "And don't call me darling. You're moving on, aren't you, Greg? Perhaps, in a way, I always knew you would."

Her voice trembled. I thought, horrified, she's going to cry; if she cries I shall be lost, end up asking her to marry me after all. But she didn't cry.

I said something about feeling terrible, and that I was as fond of her as ever, which was true.

40

She turned towards me; I saw, momentarily, a flash of blue fire in her eyes.

"Damn you," she said softly, "don't patronize me," and walked away swiftly, back to the house.

I followed her more slowly, feeling bad, but relieved too at being let off so lightly. There was still one problem to be solved, the fact that Sarah worked for Hunter's; how was she going to feel about that? But she didn't mention it. Cross that bridge, I thought, when we come to it.

The children were in the garden with Helga when we returned; they greeted me clamorously and claimed all my attention. Maddy came out, and she and Sarah at once entered into an animated and entirely feminine conversation which naturally excluded me. After a bit I picked the children off me like burrs and muttered something about going down to meet Paul at the pub. The girls both looked at me and said nicely why yes, why don't you do that. "You can see he isn't late for lunch," Maddy called after me.

Paul was already sitting in a corner of the bar with a beer in front of him. He nodded at me, got up at once and went to get two more pints. Downing mine, I said, "I needed that."

Paul looked at me myopically, with a mild air of surprise.

"What have you been doing that's so strenuous?"

"Ending a beautiful friendship," I said.

"With Sarah? Have you been having a row?"

"Nothing so uncivilized."

"In other words, you're bailing out and she's letting you go gracefully."

"That's about it."

"Well, you know your own business best," Paul said peacefully. "Pity. A nice girl. Madeleine's always hoped you'd marry her."

"I know. Maddy's been trying to marry me off again for a long time. But Sarah deserves someone better than me anyway—"

Paul grinned. "That's the time-honored formula, isn't it? Have another?"

"My round," I said. That's all we said about it. A chap Paul knew called Rodney, and Rodney's friend, and Rodney's

41

friend's friend appeared, and came over to join us. The pub was filling up; the Rodney trio was noisy and convivial. It wasn't exactly the peaceful drink in a quiet corner I'd had in mind. Even so it was escape of a sort. I was not in the mood to talk much, and Paul never did anyway, but Rodney and Co. did enough for all of us and if they'd had their way we would still have been there at closing time. We left at last, not at closing time, but late enough, driving home straight into the teeth of a domestic squall.

Maddy was white with temper.

"Where have you been?" she demanded.

Paul said mildly, "Are we late?"

"Are you late! It's nearly two o'clock. Don't blame me if the lunch is ruined. You're going away tonight, remember? You were out last night, you've been out all the morning. If you don't care about me, or the lunch, or our guests, you might care about the children. They've hardly *seen* you, but you don't care, do you, you'd rather sit in the pub with that oaf Rodney and that crowd—"

Paul didn't say anything. He *really* didn't say anything; if I'd been in his place there would have been one hell of a shouting match going on.

Foolishly, I tried to intervene.

"Maddy," I said, "steady on, love," and, of course, she turned on me.

"You," she said savagely. "A lot of use you've been, I asked you to get him back here in time—"

"Oh, come on now, I'm not my brother-in-law's keeper—"

That didn't go down too well either. I should have known. Sarah, who hated scenes, had retired into the living room and was looking determinedly out of the window. Paul walked off upstairs. Jeremy ran in from the hall, fell over, and started to yell.

Paul appeared again. Above the racket Jeremy was making, he said in the most placid tone possible, "Madeleine, I can't find the camera."

"The what?"

"My camera."

"It's *packed*. Back left-hand corner," said Maddy loudly,

"and if you did your own packing instead of leaving it to me you'd know where everything was, wouldn't you? Jeremy, stop that noise, don't be such a baby. Helga, will you bring the vegetables, please?"

We sat down to lunch. You could have cut the atmosphere with a blunt knife. The children reacted at once to trouble in the air, the way kids always seem to do. Little Jane, enthroned in her high chair, blew out spinach on to the tablecloth. Jeremy, restored to good humor, thought this hugely funny and decided to imitate her; Lucy, the eldest, was smugly reproving. Told off by Maddy for interfering, she dissolved into indignant tears. Helga fussed in and out, mopping up children and tablecloth. Sarah made a well-bred effort to restore normality by talking to Helga, one of those how-do-you-like-England conversations; poor Helga, already agitated, lost her English in the middle of a sentence, whereupon Sarah moved off smoothly into her excellent German. Maddy said sharply, "Sarah, we're supposed to help Helga by talking English to her."

Sarah colored. She said meekly, "Oh, yes, of course. I'm sorry."

I could willingly have given Maddy a smart clip round the ear, it wouldn't be the first time either. I was exasperated with her. All right, so she was upset about Paul going away; did she have to behave like this?

I can't say the rest of the day went any better. I think we were all relieved when the time came to leave for the airport. Helga was left in charge of the children, and we started early, to allow for the heavy Saturday traffic. We did better than we expected, so there was more time to kill at the end. We all stood about in the upstairs bar, talking in the helpless and desultory way one does on these occasions, when all conversation becomes devalued. Paul bought a round of drinks; Maddy was behaving herself, being very bright, as if determined now to make some sort of festivity out of it. Most of the time she talked to Sarah, it made no sense really: if she was going to do that, what was the point of coming?

Paul was distraught as the one going away always is, wishing the good-byes were said, that he was safely launched, away from us all. Most of the other passengers around us were holiday makers, going on charter flights, I guessed. On a bank seat against the wall, a stout woman with a huge hold-all at her feet (surely she didn't think she'd get away with that as personal baggage?) was eating sweets from a paper bag: she munched steadily, one after the other. A girl sitting near her reminded me of Cass for a moment, because of her long fall of hair; but the hair was mouse-colored, the girl somewhat mousy too, pale and a bit doleful-looking as if she were waiting for somebody who hadn't turned up. She wasn't at all like Cass really, but it was enough to set my thoughts off in that direction, to wish myself miles away from where I was.

A woman's voice behind us said gaily, "Well, hallo there! Isn't the traffic terrible tonight? I thought I was going to miss the plane."

She was tall, striking-looking. Not pretty, not beautiful, but noticeable anywhere, with that indefinable air of confidence of the professional woman a good way up the scale. Attractive if you like the type.

Paul said: "Oh, hallo, Celia." Then he began to make the introductions: Celia Ross, from the Institute. Going to Africa too. "You've met my wife, of course."

"Of course," said Celia. "At the Hendersons' party, wasn't it?"

She had a brilliant smile, excellent teeth. She stood there smiling down at Maddy, who looked very small, shrunk back in her chair. Maddy murmured some sort of greeting. Then their flight was called, and we all began to say good-bye.

Maddy was very quiet on the return trip, sitting by herself in the back of the car. When we reached the house she went up at once to look at the children and have a word with Helga, who was in her room. Then she came down again. She said in a dry composed voice, "Well, that's that. What about a drink, you two?"

Sarah said quickly, "Not for me, thank you. I think I'll go on up to bed." She gave me a significant look, as if to say: over to you. She patted Maddy's shoulder and went away.

Maddy sat down on the edge of a chair. She stared in front

44

of her and didn't speak. I poured out a stiff drink and took it over to her. "Here," I said. "Have this and tell me what's up."

"Good heavens," said Maddy, "Don't you know?" She took the drink from me and downed it, something I had never seen her do before.

I said incredulously, "Paul—and that woman?"

"That's right."

"I can't believe it."

"I don't see why," Maddy said dryly. "She's attractive. Even I can see that."

"In her way. Not Paul's, I should have thought. And she works with him and she's gone to Africa with him. That doesn't have to add up to anything."

"It doesn't have to," said Maddy, "but it does." She held out her glass to me for a refill. I must have raised my eyebrows, because she burst out irritably, "Don't look at me like that; if I want another drink I'll have it, it's our Scotch."

But when I gave her the drink she didn't down it as she had the first one, but sat there turning the glass round and round in her hand.

I said uncomfortably, "Maddy, I'm sure you're cooking this up out of nothing, but even assuming it's true, it doesn't have to mean anything very much. A man can enjoy a little adventure, put it behind him and go on loving his wife just the same. More, perhaps—"

"We're not talking about 'a man,' Greg. We're talking about *Paul*. When you've been as close to anybody as I've been to Paul, you know when things have gone wrong."

"Well, could be you've got into a bit of a rut—"

"We don't make love," said Maddy loudly. "There."

"What?"

"Well, only very rarely, and then it's not like it used to be. Of course, he's always working, always tired. That's the time for the wife to take the initiative, don't they say? It doesn't work unless she's sure of herself—and him. I'm not sure of either anymore. I don't want to be rebuffed, and I have been. Oh, in the nicest possible way, of course."

I was *really* concerned now. "You haven't talked to him about it?"

45

"We don't talk. He escapes from me whenever he can; he goes back to the Institute even in the evenings. He's always disliked being telephoned there, so I've never done it. But a couple of times lately . . . I've felt so desperate, sitting brooding at home in front of the telly . . . I did. He wasn't there. Neither time. He simply wasn't there," she repeated dully. "Goodness knows where he was. Or what happened all the other times."

I exclaimed, "I still can't think why you let it go on like this—why didn't you have it out with him?"

"Well, I can't now, can I? I was waiting till I'd got my strength up. I didn't get my strength up in time and there it is."

"You could have told me before. I might have been able to do something—"

"Do something like what?" said Maddy. "Punch him on the nose? A lot of good that would do."

I was silent, and she exclaimed at once, "Oh, I'm sorry, Greg, I know you mean well and it's not your fault . . . my nerves are all to hell . . ." Her face crumpled into tears. I went over and put my arm round her and she cried silently into my sweater. I felt a dull heavy anger against Paul, not only on my sister's account, but on my own, for destroying one of the few illusions I had left: this ideal relationship, loving, united, loyal, the one good deed in a naughty world. Well, I should have known it couldn't be like that.

I sought words to comfort Maddy.

"Listen, love, Paul isn't irresponsible. He'd never leave you and the children—"

Maddy sat up, found a crumpled tissue and wiped her eyes.

"Oh, I know. He won't do that. He has a strong sense of duty, has Paul. He's got us all round his neck, like the old man of the sea. Sit tight," she said, biting the words off. "That's what you'd advise, of course. That way, I can hang on to my husband, the house, the car, the income, even the dishwasher. If I play my cards right. Whatever that means."

I said, stupefied, "You're not thinking of leaving him?"

"If I have to. Thinking, that's as far as I've got."

46

"My God, I can't believe it. That you could be so tough—"

"Tough," said Maddy. "Why do you think I had to go to the airport? To be with him up to the last possible moment. What's tough about that? But if he doesn't love me—I can't compromise, Greg. I love him too much. It's *because* I love him too much. Can't you see that?" She got up, and began to empty ashtrays. "Oh well. Time we went to bed, I suppose." She added over her shoulder: "If I were you, I'd fix up some golf or something tomorrow morning, keep out of the way. I'm sure Sarah would prefer that. I expect you would too."

"Has she said anything to you?"

"Not a word. But she doesn't have to. Heavens. What a shambles this weekend has turned out to be."

"Partly my fault. I'm sorry, love."

She grinned at me, a ghost of Maddy's old grin. "Oh, never mind. If you and Sarah were prancing around as happy as Larry, I daresay that wouldn't help me too much either. Besides, if you don't love her, you don't. You wouldn't be doing her any favors pretending you do."

"That's not what you said this morning."

"No. Well, this morning . . . it wasn't really you two I was thinking about. I'm fond of Sarah and I'm sorry for her, but I'm on your side really. The blood's-thicker-than-water bit, I suppose. What was it we used to say years ago, when Russell was throwing his stepfatherly weight about—"

"Solidarity forever," I said.

"Little beasts we were, weren't we? Always ganging up on the grown-ups. Solidarity forever, that was it. Don't tell them, will you? About me?"

"Mother and Russell? You must be joking. Anyway, I don't even know where they are."

"Somewhere in the Caribbean," Maddy said, "last I heard. They're coming to England soon. Then they'll want to come and stay here. A treat in store." Maddy sighed. "I sometimes think I wouldn't dislike Russell so much if he didn't take so many baths. Oh well, it hasn't happened yet." She leaned over to kiss me. "Good night, Greg. Thanks for listening."

"Will you sleep?" I asked.

"My dear, like the dead. I *escape* into sleep. It's getting up

47

that's the trouble. Facing another day. Turn the lights off when you come up, won't you?"

I sat on a while downstairs after she'd gone. One thing you can be sure of in this world is that you can never be sure of anything. I thought of myself driving down there with Sarah the night before, so smug, so complacent, everything sorted out: plans made, the expectation of a peaceful weekend—a peaceful future—in front of us. Then life or fate or whatever had neatly pulled the rug out from under us.

But for me, at least, this meant an astounding happiness. It was all very unfair.

Three

I DROVE Sarah back to London late Sunday afternoon. It was a silent, uncomfortable drive. We couldn't talk about ourselves, and we could not talk about Maddy and Paul: too near the bone altogether.

Outside her flat, I took her weekend case out of the trunk and carried it up to the porch. I waited for her to get out her key, so that I could take the case upstairs; but she said coolly, "Well, thanks for the lift, Greg," standing there on the doorstep with the key still in her hand.

"I'll take the case up," I said.

"There's no need. It's not heavy."

"Well . . . um. . . . I'm off tomorrow morning, as you know."

"Yes, I know. Have a good trip."

"See you Monday week then."

"I suppose so," she said. "Good night, Greg."

She turned her back on me, not rudely, put the key in the lock, opened the door, went inside, and shut it. I was free.

I wouldn't want anybody to think that I didn't feel badly about it. I did. But it didn't last. By the time I had reached the corner of the street, I had left Sarah behind.

I drove through the Park, in which Londoners were making the most of this splendid summer evening. In the mellow golden light children ran and shouted, fathers lay supine on the grass, lovers strolled hand in hand. I crossed the bridge over the Serpentine, the bright sliver of water shining in the long rays of the afternoon sun. In Kensington the hotels looked gay and Continental with their striped, colored awnings and flowers in tubs. By contrast the district where Cass lived had a sleazy sorrowful look, its grayness even more apparent on a day like this; there seemed little left of the lovely summer weather except dust, and heavy, humid London heat.

I parked outside the door in the wall and rang the bell.

Nothing happened. I rang it again, and all at once the elation and eagerness that had been driving me all day began to seep away into nervous anxiety. I'll be here, she had said; but that was two days ago. I couldn't hear the bell ringing. Impatience taking hold, I gave the door a shove and it at once swung open before me, admitting me to the yard she had spoken about. Walled with smoke-blackened bricks, floored with cracked concrete, it yet had a well-tended air, a small oasis in a gray stucco desert. The borders of earth next to the walls had been recently forked over, a climber on the opposite wall was coming into flower, and there were plants in tubs and pots. One corner was stacked with a few old and worn gardening tools, a bright-red, brand-new watering can, and an orange-striped deck chair propped against the wall.

The inner door didn't seem to have a bell or a knocker. I rapped on it with my knuckles and waited. Eventually I heard footsteps and the door opened, and there she was.

She wore a long cotton robe and was barefooted. Her hair was all over the place and she looked ill. She stared at me without speaking.

I said, "Hallo, Cass."

She said slowly, "I didn't think you'd come."

"Well, I have. Didn't you want me to?"

"Well . . . yes . . . I . . ."

"Aren't you going to ask me in?"

She pulled the door open wider and stood back so that I could enter.

"I'm afraid everything's in rather a muddle," she said helplessly. A divan bed in an alcove had obviously just been hastily covered up before she came to the door; various articles of clothing hung on a chair near it. She looked at these with dismay as I entered, and hurried across to snatch them up and thrust them into a drawer.

50

"Cass," I said, "leave it. What the hell does that matter? Come here."

She straightened up from putting the things in the drawer and turned to face me, and suddenly and marvelously her face bloomed into life and radiance. She came across the room in a stumbling run, straight into my arms. She buried her head in my shoulder and muttered awkwardly, "Gosh, I'm glad you've come."

I turned her face up toward me with a finger under her chin. She looked pinched, and there were blue shadows under those extraordinary eyes.

"What is it? Aren't you well?"

"I haven't been, not very. I just had a bad headache . . . not a real migraine, thank God, though I do have those. No, it's just reaction, I expect, from the bump on Friday. I've been in bed most of the day, but I feel a lot better now, honestly."

"I suppose you haven't had anything to eat."

She shook her head. "Didn't feel like it."

"But you ought to have something," I said, like an anxious parent with a sick child. With any other girl, I would have been resentful about finding her in this state. Oh, I would have made the sympathetic noises and hidden my irritation and disappointment, but they would have been there just the same. But seeing Cass looking ill only filled me with irrational fear. If she should be really ill. If she should die . . . my love, nothing must happen to you; I will hold you against the world.

It must have been all there in my face, because she looked at me with wonder, letting her breath out with a long sigh. This was not the time for the ready declarations, the words made banal by having been repeated so many times by so many people. I could only repeat stupidly, "You must have something to eat, Cass."

"I'm not really hungry, but I was just going to make some tea when you came."

Something simple and practical, something to be done for her. Tea. It recalled us to the world.

"Tea you shall have," I said. I pushed her gently into the only armchair. "I'll make it. Then, if you feel like it, we'll go and have a meal later. Would you like that?"

She nodded mutely, her eyes on my face with that look of wonder and astonishment.

"Kitchen through there?"

"That's right. But I shouldn't let you do it . . ."

"Why not?"

I went into the kitchen, which was hardly bigger than a cupboard, put the kettle on, found the tea things and the milk and sugar. I went back into the other room and asked, "How did it go last night?" How did it go, I said, but in the other dialogue, the dialogue of the heart, I said, I will love and protect and cherish you all the days of my life. Only very faintly, far back in my mind, came the recollection that I had once said these words, or some very like them, to another woman in the presence of many witnesses; I had not kept my promises. And she had not kept hers.

Cass's face became animated at my question and she cried quite cheerfully, "Oh, marvelous! They're terribly pleased. I've been asked to stay on."

"What did I tell you?" I said. "I must have brought you luck."

"Not *luck*. You helped me. That's different." She was looking at me rather shyly. "I suppose I should ask you how *your* weekend went."

I shrugged. "It's gone. That's all that matters."

"And . . . Sarah?"

"I drove her back to town this afternoon. She had a date. Or so she said."

"I see."

She didn't seem too happy about it. I said, "It's over, you know."

"Did you tell her?"

"I didn't have to," I said. The kettle boiled at that moment and I went back to make the tea. As I was bringing the tray from the kitchen, the telephone rang.

"Shall I get it?" I asked, but she shook her head, got up and walked slowly across to the instrument. She picked it up and said the number and let whoever it was talk. After a bit she said, 'No." More talk from the other end. Then she said, "No" again, and then: "Look, I'm going out anyway. There's no point. Yes, of course, all the evening—" The telephone went on quacking and right in the middle of it she said abruptly, "Good-bye," and put the receiver down. She looked up, met my eyes, and smiled, a brilliant, defensive smile, impenetrable as a fencer's mask. She said brightly, "Well, I'd better go and get ready, hadn't I?"

"Drink your tea," I said. "There's no hurry."

She picked up the cup obediently and drank. Her hand was trembling.

I said, "Something's wrong, isn't it?"

"No. No, really."

"Is somebody being a nuisance?"

"No. No, really. It's not important."

A man's voice on the telephone. Not important, she said. But it had upset her, that was for sure. A man's voice, and something wrong, and she wouldn't say. I felt jealousy and suspicion rise in me like gall.

She said uncertainly, "I'll go and change, I won't be long."

Now she was galvanized into feverish activity. She snatched clothing from drawers and cupboard and disappeared into the bathroom.

I stood in the middle of the room, listening to the taps running, and the most extraordinary thought came into my mind.

She was in the bathroom, she wouldn't come out for at least ten minutes, probably longer. I could walk out on her. Just go, without argument and explanation. Get in the car and drive away.

A cruel, heartless thing to do. But wise.

It was only a thought, of course, I didn't act on it. I had no more say in the matter than an iron filing attached to a magnet. But that I'd had the thought at all was the measure of my fear of her, of her power over me, the involvement, above all of the tenderness. That was when you were really hooked, not your own man any more; nobody knew the score about that better than I.

I wandered around the room, looking at it all. It was extremely plain, as if she had never had the time or money to collect possessions. I thought of Sarah's pretty little place; this spare white room was far removed from anything like that. The floor was the original bare boards, stained and partly covered with rush matting. There wasn't much furniture, except the divan and a table and one armchair, and an upright piano. On the piano was some music paper with part of a score penciled in. I can't read music and could make nothing of it. There was a poster above the empty fireplace, some shelves next to it filled with books, more music scores. I took out one of the books at random and found one of those plaque-shaped labels inside that they put in school prizes. That's what it was. "Middlebridge County Secondary School for Girls, form 3A. Kathleen Clayton, Form Prize, September 1964."

I thought of her, going up to get the prize, a skinny little girl in a white blouse and a tie and gym tunic. She would have looked shy, going up on the platform among the bigwigs, but she would pretend not to be, holding herself very straight, not looking at the sea of faces in the hall: mothers in their best clothes, bored fathers, about five hundred giggling schoolgirls, all clapping.

Middlebridge. It meant nothing to me except one of those signs indicating a turn-off on the M 1, a milestone to the traveler hurrying from London to the North: a small, Midland town. There, I supposed, she had grown up and gone to school, practiced the piano, and dreamed the long muddled dreams of adolescence. Then, at some time, had left and come to London; but what had happened since?

The bathroom door clicked and she came out. I don't know what she was wearing, I didn't notice that. Her hair hung smooth and shining and she had put stuff on her eyes and lipstick on her mouth, and she looked polished, armored against the outside world: armored, perhaps, against me?

I took her to a small restaurant I knew in the King's Road where we found a quiet corner. She didn't eat much, or talk very much either at first. So I did the talking, mostly about unimportant things, and after a bit I could feel she was relaxing and coming back to me. Afterward we drove out as far as

Hammersmith. I parked the car near the bridge and we walked along the Mall to the gardens where people were still sitting in deck chairs or on the grass, or just strolling about. The muffled roar of the Great West Road, just behind us, went on unceasingly, yet it seemed calm and peaceful there. We leaned on the river wall and watched a covey of swans making their way upstream to the Eyot, the muddy island off Chiswick Mall where most of them spend the night. It was high tide; the dirty Thames water looked smooth and silken, pearl-gray in the shadows, washed with gold by the setting sun. A crowded pleasure boat went by with a blare of music, people dancing on the deck.

Cass sighed, but it was a sigh of contentment. "Headache gone?" I asked.

"Completely. I feel fine.It's nice here. I'm terribly ignorant about London; I never even knew this bit existed. I just about know how to get from A to B on a bus or tube and that's all. I've always been too busy, I suppose."

"How long have you been here?"

"Five years, nearly. I was eighteen when I came first."

"From Middlebridge?"

"How did you know about Middlebridge?"

"I was looking at your books. I found a school prize."

"Oh, that!" She laughed. "Don't get the wrong idea. That's the only prize I ever got, for school subjects, I mean. After that, I was too much taken up with music. I was supposed to be quite bright and they were a bit annoyed about it. Anyway . . . I got some O and A levels, enough to get by. Then I got a grant and came down to the Royal College of Music, to study voice and piano. A regular little provincial I was, then. Scared of everything and terribly lonely."

"Homesick?"

She looked away from me across the river. "Oh, no, not homesick, really. That never worried me too much. Just lonely. Music students often are lonely. Tuition at music colleges is mostly individual; there are a few classes but most of the time you're on your own, studying, practicing, and wondering whether you'll ever be good enough. Then there's always the problem of where to practice, especially for pianists. In the end I teamed up with two other students . . . yes, in

55

that flat, all of us, goodness knows how we squashed in. One of the other girls was a drama student, the other a pianist. We hired the piano and took it in turns to work there, and if you didn't want to listen to somebody else's scales and exercises you went out and sat in the park or the public library or something. We used to get on each other's nerves a bit, but we never quarreled, not seriously." She smiled reminiscently. "It was a funny, muddled sort of time."

"And then?" I asked.

"Oh, yes, then . . . by the time I left college I knew I wasn't ever going to be a straight singer. I'm a mezzo for one thing; there isn't so much scope for them and I haven't got the range for opera. So there I was, wondering what to do next, just how to earn some bread for a start. I did some teaching, though I hate that . . . then it was waitressing, demonstrating in stores, the Post Office at Christmas. Then I joined up with a group, as a vocalist. That was a disaster; only one of them thought I was any good and he overruled the others for a while, but they were quite right. I'd started writing my own material but they didn't want to use it, it wasn't their style anyway. So we split up and it was about then I took a hard look at myself and decided that I'd got to do my own thing or give up altogether. Then my aunt Meg . . . my mother's sister . . . died. She had a house and some savings. She left the house to my mother and the savings to me, nearly two thousand pounds. Of course, at home they said I should put it away for a rainy day, but for me the rainy day was right now. So I kept the flat on after Karen and Julie left, and I'd always wanted a car so I bought that old Mini, and I've been using the rest to live on, as a sort of launching pad; I gave myself a year. I didn't think about what I'd do after that, if I didn't make it, I mean. It had to be a year or nothing. After all, I'm getting on a bit."

"You're what?"

"I'm twenty-three," she said with simplicity. "In this business that's quite old. The year's not up yet, so I'm hoping the gamble has paid off." She glanced at me and smiled. "You're not listening, are you? I expect I'm being boring, just chattering on—"

I said, "I love you, Cass."

She didn't speak, except with those speaking eyes of hers. A middle-aged couple went by, a woman with crimped gray hair in a button-through cotton dress, her husband wearing a shirt without a tie and carrying his jacket over his arm. They looked at us incuriously. A shouting child came skidding up to us to retrieve a ball right between our feet. I picked it up and gave it to him, the spell unbroken.

I asked, "You?"

"Yes . . . I mean, I think so."

"Only think so? You're not sure?"

She put her head down and muttered, "Well, I mean . . . we've only just met, really. We don't know each other. And there's an awful lot of living behind us."

"I'm not looking for a casual affair, you know. What's on your mind? *Other* girls? There just are bound to have been other girls."

"Of course. I know that."

"Then what? Sarah?"

"I suppose it's that. Oh, I'm not jealous of her. It's just the way it happened. It frightens me a bit . . . the way you disposed of her—"

"Darling, I haven't disposed of her. You make it sound as if I'd chopped her up and left her in the cloakroom at Victoria in a suitcase."

She giggled faintly.

"Listen. I never loved Sarah, and I never told her so. Before now, there was only one girl I loved. I haven't told you this before, there hasn't been time, but I was married once."

"What happened?"

"She was killed. In a car crash."

"Oh, Greg!" Her hand came out to clutch mine. "How frightful!"

"Yes. It was, at the time. But it's a long time ago and I've got over it. But it does mean I know what's real and what isn't. Doesn't that count for anything?"

"Yes. Yes it does." She was silent for a moment, then she seemed to make up her mind and turned to me and smiled and said simply, "Let's go home."

"Yes. Let's."

As we turned back the way we had come, we passed the boatyard off the Mall, where a notice, on a piece of blackboard in wiggly white letters, announced abruptly: "Trespassers Will Be DROWNED."

"Wow!" Cass cried. "Just look at that!" and we both fell about laughing; the moment of doubt passed, we were crazy with happiness.

"Race you to the bridge," I said, and we ran, dodging the people, like a couple of kids, not caring who stared at us. Nearer the bridge there's a gap in the river wall, leading to some steps which go down to the beach at low tide, and Cass hopped up on to these and began to walk along the top of the wall, laughing down at me; I was afraid she'd fall in the river.

"Get down, you crazy girl, you'll fall in in a minute." I held out my arms, and she jumped down into them, a flurry of scented hair and warmth and litheness, and I could hardly bear to let her go again.

In the car, in the snarl-up of Sunday evening traffic, I said: "I wish I weren't going away tomorrow."

"Oh! I didn't know you were—"

"Business trip. Amsterdam, Brussels, Milan. I'll be back on Saturday. Some time in the afternoon, I expect. Come and meet me at the airport. Will you?"

"Of course."

"I'll phone you, during the week, to let you know what time I'm arriving."

"I'll be there," she said.

Then, quite soon, we were back by the red door in the wall. As we pushed it open, the light struck us, streaming out from Cass's windows. We stood in the yard, looking at it.

Cass said quietly, "I didn't leave the light on, did I?"

"No. It wasn't dark when we came away. Look, you stay here. If there's something going on, I'd better—"

"No," she said. Her voice was quite dry and cold. "That won't be necessary. I think I know who it is."

The door into the flat wasn't locked; we went in.

A man was sitting there. He didn't get up when we came in; he leaned back comfortably, one leg hooked over the arm

58

of the chair. He was young, very thin, pale as if he didn't get out of doors much, with long dark hair reaching to his shoulders; a black lock of it hung down over one dark, bright, malicious eye. He had that sort of graceful animal magnetism that all other men dislike and mistrust, probably because it's too attractive to women. He looked us up and down and grinned.

"Well, here you are at last," he said.

Cass stood looking down at him, her face very white.

"How did you get in?" she said.

He gestured toward the door. "Careless as usual," he reproved her. "Left it on the latch. *And* the garden door. You'll have a break-in one of these days and serve you right."

"I told you not to come."

He looked at me. "And who's this? No need to ask, really, is there? Cass's latest man. Aren't you going to introduce us?"

She said, "Nick, please go. Please."

He didn't answer or move. He just looked from one to the other of us, grinning.

I went over to the door and opened it. "You heard what she said," I told him. "Get lost." I felt ridiculous saying it, as if I were playing a gangster in an old movie. Unimpressed, he stayed right where he was.

"All right, lover boy. I don't blame you for being in a hurry. Welcome to Cass's little nest. What more can you want, a lovely bird in a little nest. . . ."

He wasn't wearing a jacket. I went over and took hold of him by the front of his shirt and pulled him up out of the chair; I heard the shirt rip as I did it. On his feet he was as tall as I, our eyes met levelly; but he didn't try anything, though he said gently, "Man, don't get too rough with me. I'm a very dirty fighter."

"That I can believe," I said. "Out."

He grinned and said past me, in a plaintive, joking tone, "The man's spoilt my shirt, Cass. You'll have to buy me another one, won't you?"

But he didn't resist when I propelled him out of the door, across the yard, and out into the street. I slammed and bolted the yard door behind him and went back to Cass.

She hadn't moved. There was no expression on her face at all.

She said flatly, "There was no need for all that. He isn't violent."

"Maybe not. But I am. I suppose he was the chap on the phone."

"Yes."

"Who is he, anyway?"

"His name's Nick Edwards, he's a musician, a songwriter—quite a good one. Or he could be, if he put his mind to it."

"You know I don't mean that. What is he to you?"

"Nothing," she said. "Now. I was in love with him once. Or thought I was."

"With that nasty little character?"

"We all make mistakes," said Cass. "He's not quite what you think anyway. He does have his good moods. He's a bit . . . sick."

"And stoned as well, I shouldn't wonder."

"Sometimes."

"But you go on seeing him, associating with him—"

"Associating," said Cass wearily. "There's a stuffy word if you like. I'm not much good at ditching people when they need me. I owe him a lot, anyway. When I started writing my own material, he encouraged me. He's unstable and difficult. But he can be quite sweet sometimes—"

"Sweet," I said. "Sweet! But you were upset when he rang up—"

"Of course. I knew he would spoil things. And he has."

"What do you mean?"

"As if you didn't know! You think I go to bed with him, don't you?"

"I didn't say that—"

"But you're thinking it. It isn't true, but what difference does it make? We've had it, haven't we? The mood's gone, the way we felt—" She stared at me, and began to laugh without any amusement. "If you could just see your face! As if you had a bad smell under your nose—"

I didn't speak. I didn't know her, this girl. I didn't know her at all.

60

"Well," she said, "you've got a plane to catch in the morning, haven't you? We'd better call it a day. Thank you for dinner," she added politely, and turned away.

Her head was bent, and a strand of hair fell down across her cheek. Like that, she had the same helpless and vulnerable look she had had when I lifted her out of the crashed car and suddenly she was Cass again, I was alive again in a fury of desire and fear of losing her and I took hold of her, shouting, "Cass, for God's sake, what do we think we're doing?"

She twisted out of my grasp. "No. Don't touch me, please, it's no use—"

"Darling, don't say that. I know I reacted badly, finding that little bastard here, the things he said . . . it was a shock, that's all."

I wasn't getting through and knew it but I had to try. "You've got to listen. I love you, I meant it then and I mean it now."

"Love's a big word," she said. "You shouldn't use such big words. Of course, you still want to make love to me, I know that. That's got nothing to do with *accepting* me, as a person, understanding my life or the company I keep, or why I keep it. I tell you, the whole thing's been killed stone dead for me. Go away. Please go away."

Well. You can know that you're in some kind of emotional trap and still not see how to get out of it. Anyway, coldness and hostility are infectious.

"All right," I said. "So that's it, isn't it?"

She didn't look at me. "Yes. I'm sorry."

I found myself saying, "You'd better bolt the garden door after me," and she answered quite civilly, "Oh, yes. Thank you for reminding me."

I said, "Good-bye, Cass."

I went out to the car, shutting the outer door after me. In the car, with my hand on the ignition switch, I heard her footsteps across the yard, and briefly thought she was coming after me, to beg me to come back. Then I heard the bolt slammed home; and there was nothing left to do but to start the car and drive away.

Four

I DIDN'T sleep much that night, and for once I was in good time for the plane when it left next morning, glad to be off. There's nothing, I told myself, like travel, change, people to see and work to do, to cut one's personal moods down to size. It didn't work out quite like that, though. Traveling for business gives one little sense of displacement. I suppose there are some bits left of the old cities of Europe, of their beauty and antiquity, but only tourists get to see them. People like me go to places labeled Brussels or Paris or Milan, only to find the same pattern of things everywhere, the same airports, escalators, motorways, flyovers, the same office suites housed in glass and concrete towers, the neon signs, the roar of traffic, the nightclubs, the restaurants, and bars. In those restaurants and clubs and bars you entertain or are entertained by bland men in pale suits whose command of English often seems better than your own; and at the end of the day there's yet another air-conditioned hotel room waiting, with its smooth cold bed and silent, beckoning telephone.

It was then, in the late evening, having pushed it off into the corners of my mind during the day, that my obsession was at its height. It was then I would look at the telephone and remember she wouldn't be home at that time anyway; that there was never time or opportunity to telephone during the day; that such a call might end only in another brush-off. And having decided that, I got up to the usual rationalizing tricks: look, you've only met the girl twice. You want her, that's all, and while that lasts it's hell: but if you don't see her, it will pass off. It always does pass off. Leave it.

So I left it. But leaving it, I must say, didn't help much.

I ended up in Milan, hot and dusty in the height of the

summer weather, and made plans with Ricciardi, our agent, for the Furniture Exhibition due to take place there in the autumn. Ricciardi made himself agreeable, and invited me home to dinner in his apartment, one of those coldly formal apartments Italian businessmen always seem to have, not a piece of Hunter furniture in it anywhere, we'd have to see about that. I met his plump, meek wife and his two pretty daughters; I got on rather well with Dona, the younger one, and she distracted my mind for quite two hours. The world was full of delightful girls. It was ridiculous to feel that only one, out of all the millions there are, would do.

On Saturday I flew back to London.

It was raining when we landed. As we splashed across the tarmac in the airport bus and shuffled up the long rabbit burrow leading to customs, I wondered what to do next. Saturday afternoon and nobody expecting me anywhere, because of those other plans that had come to nothing. There wasn't anything to do except collect my case, find the car and go home. Or have a drink, and go home. Or two drinks.

Or I could telephone Sarah.

There would have to be a little scene, naturally. No woman in her situation, not even Sarah, would resist the temptation to make a little scene. And I would grovel a bit, and she would enjoy forgiving me, and then everything would be as it had been before; and as one really can't keep on doing that sort of thing, not to the same girl anyway, my boats would be irrevocably burned. There I would be, high and dry on the far side of the river.

My case appeared at last and I got through Customs and rode the escalator up to the concourse, looking around vaguely for the telephones. There was a crush of people outside Arrivals; a pretty girl who had been on the plane with me was just in front, looking around her eagerly. A man pushed his way forward, calling her name; they ran together, clung together, oblivious of everyone. I remember looking at them coldly, from a great distance. I began to shoulder my way through the crowd; and then I heard my own name over the loudspeaker. Will Mr. Hunter, recently arrived from Milan, go to the Information Desk?

64

I hurried over to the desk. There was a girl standing by the counter, wearing a shiny red raincoat, a scarf over her hair. She turned her head, our eyes met; it was Cass. She didn't move, waiting for me to come to her. She looked different, wearing the scarf. The expression on her face was timid and questioning. Fireworks of joy exploded in me, I couldn't get to her fast enough, to put my arms around her, make sure she was real.

She put her forehead against my chest and muttered, "I was so scared—"

"Scared? Of me?"

"Well, I thought you might just look at me and say, what have you come for."

"Well, you know better now, don't you? Why would I do that?"

The girl airline clerk, her face and hair neat as a doll's beneath her perky little cap, stared at us with interest. Neither of us cared a damn.

"It would have served me right if you had. By the time I came to and realized what I'd done you'd gone right out of reach. I thought you'd phone but you didn't, and I couldn't take any more of that, just waiting, thinking . . . so I came here . . . I've been here all the afternoon . . . I thought if I saw you, anyway I'd know for certain it was finished and then I could start trying . . ."

"Trying what, darling?"

"To get over it," she said.

That really shook me. I had thought about her, God knows; I had argued with myself about her, about what to do, but really, I suppose, I hadn't really thought about *her,* and what she was feeling while those days passed in a growing silence. Perhaps we all kid ourselves about what we mean when we talk about love. I love you, we say, when all we love is ourselves, seen in the mirror image in somebody else's eyes.

"I did try to phone. But you weren't there when I rang, and the rest of the time the pressure was on . . . it was just too difficult, love."

"It was all my fault," she said.

65

"Of course it wasn't, we were in it together. Let's get out of this place. How did you get here? Have you got the car back?"

"No, it's still being repaired. I came down in a hired car. The man's still outside, waiting for me . . . I had to have an escape hatch, you see."

"We'll go and pay him off. I've got my car here somewhere."

It was still raining as we drove back to town. They were doing a repair job on the motorway and London-bound traffic slowed to a crawl as it negotiated the single-line stretch beside the row of orange-and-white warning cones. As the queue came to a momentary halt, I leaned over and kissed her. The car in front crept forward and we followed; it is perfectly possible to drive a car at five miles an hour and kiss a girl at the same time. The driver of the car behind, who could, I suppose, see what was going on, let out an indignant blast on his horn as we reached the end of the bottleneck. I sat up hastily and pulled away but as soon as the road opened he edged out and swept by with another blast. Cass began to giggle.

"He's furious . . ."

"Envious, more likely. Poor sod's probably got ulcers and a nagging wife and can't bear seeing other people happy. Are you working tonight?"

"Yes. But I needn't be there till just before eleven—"

"What about dinner? Are you hungry?"

"Not specially. I had something to eat at the airport, to pass the time . . . not that I felt much like eating. What about you?"

"I'm okay for now. Anyway, there's food at home if we want it . . . All right?"

Out of the corner of my eye, I saw she was smiling.

"All right," she said.

I left the car parked in the forecourt of the flats and we made a run for it through the rain to the entrance. The lift was waiting, and we went up in it to the third floor.

I hadn't wanted to go back to her place and I think she felt the same way. That paralysis of feeling that had overtaken us

66

there, neither of us wanted to be reminded of it. Not that one is ever quite free of the wrong kind of memory anywhere. I wished, foolishly I know, that I was seventeen again, that she was my first love and I hers, with nothing behind us but our innocence, and in front of us the whole of the shining, promising, unknown world. Well, it wasn't like that for us, and could never be, but what we had was good enough.

I opened the door of the flat and Cass walked in front of me into the living room. She stood for a moment, in the middle of it, looking around: sensing the atmosphere, it seemed, rather like a cat when it delicately examines its surroundings before deciding to curl up and stay. It was an elegant, perhaps to her eyes even a formidable room. I had planned it like that, a show place, a permanent demonstration that the best of the Hunter furniture could make a harmonious marriage with beautiful things of any age: an old rosewood desk, an antique Shiraz rug hung on the wall like a picture, bits of nice old china picked up here and there.

I stood at the door and watched her while she unfastened her coat, slowly pulled off the head scarf and shook her hair free.

She said softly, amused and delighted: "Oh, Greg, it's all poshy and gorgeous, isn't it?"

I couldn't speak. She turned toward me, our eyes met, and she shrugged the coat off and let it slide to the floor.

Then she held out her arms to me.

Outside, it was almost like autumn, with heavy storm clouds darkening the sky and the wind throwing spattering gusts of rain against the window. Out in the streets people peered through streaming windshields, scurried under umbrellas, signaled vainly at taxis which tore heartlessly by with their flags down: in another world altogether.

I thought I knew it all: experience, what was that? You can go through the lot: love, or what one calls love at the time, not knowing any better; or the skilled exercises of two people, amiable and heartless, intent on using each other. The mistakes too, wrong place, wrong mood, wrong girl, and all there is to remember about those is the embarrassment and wondering why you had ever started it and how soon can you get away—all of this, grievous, useless, most of it, now just like images on an old film, unreal shadows, flickering by.

Oh, yes. I thought I knew it all. But what you know, faced with revelation, is that you didn't know anything before.

On Sunday morning the rain had stopped, leaving behind it one of those whitish-gray damp days which sometimes pass for summer in England, with a mean little wind sneaking up on you round the corners. I remembered that sort of day from other times, always associated with defeat and melancholy, the future like the cloudy sky, impenetrable as cotton wool and about as promising.

But today was not like other times. We were indoors in our own special world, the flat a fortress against the outside one. When the telephone rang we didn't answer it, and if the doorbell had rung, we wouldn't have answered that either.

We had got up late from sleep, from our love, and made coffee and let what was left of the morning slide past us in the indolent way of lovers. It was now past one o'clock; I was supine on the sofa in the living room, content just to lie there and watch Cass, who was wandering around the flat looking at things. Her hair was pinned up anyhow because she had been having a shower, she wore a white toweling bathrobe of mine that went round her about three times, and her feet were bare. The Modern Jazz Quartet was playing softly on my record player; the Sunday newspapers with their color supplements lay scattered on the floor around us, unread.

"They're like animals," said Cass.

"Animals? What are?"

"I meant the chairs . . . and that sofa. Like animals, lions perhaps, when they're crouching, or lying down. You know that sort of fluid look they have, as if they hadn't any bones . . . what are you looking at me like that for?"

"I was thinking that you're a very perceptive girl. We made a bit of a name for ourselves with these chairs."

"I'm not surprised. You must be very successful—"

"In a small way, yes."

"What started you off on it?"

68

"I don't know, exactly. Interests like that sort of creep up on you, I suppose. Anyway, when I left school, I did a design course, and the whole technical bit as well, cabinetmaking and all that, and then I did a couple of years with Pargiter's, the big furniture people, as a managerial trainee. The whole scheme came under a lot of fire at home; my mother and stepfather thought it was all rather infra dig. They wanted to be able to talk about 'my son at Cambridge' or wherever; they're like that."

Cass said thoughtfully, "It doesn't sound as if you like them very much."

"They're all right. I don't see much of them these days, they're abroad a lot. Maddy finds them a bit of a trial."

"Maggie? That's your sister?"

"Yes . . . it was her place I was staying at last weekend. It's not Maggie, by the way, it's Maddy, short for Madeleine."

"Madeleine," Cass repeated. "Madeleine what?"

"Gray. Husband's name's Paul. Madeleine and Paul Gray. Why, do you know them?"

She shook her head. "I've only been down to Stallington a couple of times; I don't know any of the local people, only the Barn Theatre Group. I worked with them for a fortnight at the beginning of the season."

I asked incuriously, "What was all the panic about last week, then?"

"Oh, that . . . a friend of mine, she's their stage manager . . . she rang me up in a bit of a state . . . there wasn't anyone in the company she wanted to talk to, and it sounded as if she might do something silly so I belted off down there in a hurry. She'll be all right now, I think."

"Emotional problem?" I asked. "A touch of the Samaritans?"

"Something like that." Something about the way she said this forbade further questioning. "Don't you think we ought to think about eating?"

"I suppose we should. Stop pottering about over there. Come here."

She came over to me, smiling. "What do you want to do? Get dressed up and go out to eat?"

"God forbid. I haven't even shaved yet."

"Don't bother. It's rather sexy. I like it." She passed her hand over the rasp of stubble; I kissed the palm as it went by.

"Shall I grow a beard?" I asked, grinning.

"Oh, no. I wouldn't like *that*, it would change you. I knew a boy once . . . he had a beard when I first met him and then he shaved it off; it changed his personality so much it was quite off-putting . . . what's the matter?"

"Nothing."

"I didn't sleep with him,you know," she said gently. "He was just a friend, a fellow-student. What have you got here in the way of food? Can't we manage? Let's go and see."

She was delighted with my kitchen, rummaging in the store cupboards, which I kept well-filled, and exclaiming over her discoveries: tins of chicken, ham, mussels, prawns and various sorts of exotic vegetables; onions in the vegetable tray, a bunch of garlic bulbs.

"There's everything here," she cried. "Let's make something with rice, paella, perhaps. You're awfully well-organized. Who does the housekeeping?"

"I have a very nice cleaning lady who comes in and keeps the place tidy, sees to the laundry, that sort of thing. I make lists and she shops. Of course, I eat out a lot. But I do cook sometimes, for myself and for friends. I'm not a bad cook, actually."

"Well, who's going to cook this? You or me?"

"We'll do it together," I said.

She was a bold and slapdash cook, the kind I am myself, so it worked quite well. We got in each other's way, and I made silly jokes, and we fell about laughing, and were at the same time, all the time, hampered by the intense awareness of each other which belongs to the early days of love. Even as she stood by the stove, spoon in hand, testing the rice, I could not forbear to touch her, and when I did, I saw her cheek burn.

The paella turned out quite well. We had some wine with it, and ate hugely; Cass, like many people with no weight problem, had an extremely healthy appetite. Replete, we couldn't even be bothered to make coffee, but collapsed onto the sofa to while away the rest of the afternoon.

After a bit Cass said, out of the blue: "Did your wife ever live here?"

"No."

"I thought you might have a photograph of her."

Taken off guard, I said shortly, "I detest studio photographs."

She looked at me gravely. "Sorry. You don't like talking about her much, do you?"

"I suppose not, really."

"Are you still in love with her?"

"You can't be in love with dead people. I'm in love with you, Cass. She was never here, you know. There are no ghosts here."

"No. No, all right."

I said, watching her: "But you don't like it much anyway, do you? The flat?"

"I didn't say that. I said it was beautiful—"

"Poshy and gorgeous, you said. I know. You mean it isn't a home, and it isn't. But we don't have to stay here. I've been thinking for some time about buying a house. Then we could start afresh, make things over the way you like."

"Greg, I don't . . ."

"When we're married," I said.

There was a brief, startled pause. Then: *"Married,"* she said at last; and then: "You don't have to do this, you know."

I laughed. "Idiot child, of course I don't have to. I want to, that's all. What's up? Don't you want to marry me?"

"It isn't that," she said soberly. "It's just that it's a bit soon and . . . I'm afraid of marriage, Greg. It does such awful things to people."

So it does, I thought, so it does. Aloud, I said, "To some people. It doesn't have to do it to us."

"We're not so different from other people. Don't you see, I'm afraid of spoiling it, what we have. People get married, and love gets all mixed up with law and money, signing a contract, sort of. It puts love in a straitjacket, ties it down. I don't want to tie it down. I don't want to tie you down. I'm afraid I'd lose you that way."

"You wouldn't lose me," I said. "And you're talking non-

71

sense." I took hold of her and shook her gently. "Now listen to me. *Are* you listening?"

She still looked a bit mulish but she said, "All right. I'm listening."

"Well, then. I don't agree with you about tying love down. I think some tying down is a good thing. I want to be committed to you, Cass. I want you to be committed to me. I want us to make promises to each other, and keep them. I want your children and I want us to bring them up together, and make a home together, and *be* together, for the rest of our lives. There."

She said quietly, "I *do* love you."

"Good. I love you too. So that's settled."

But it wasn't, of course. "It's not as easy as that. I'm not a suitable wife for you."

"Rubbish."

"I haven't got the background. You live in a different world from the one I know. Entertaining your business friends, that sort of thing, I wouldn't know how—"

"Of course you would. But you wouldn't have to, if you didn't want to."

"And then," she said, "there's me. I mean my career. Perhaps that's too big a word for it. But I have got started, and I want to prove I can make a go of it—"

"What's stopping you?"

"You. You don't want that. You said—"

"I said I wanted us to have children. One day. Nobody's yet found a way of making instant baby, so even if we started on one, which we won't, you'd still have a little time in hand. Anyway, I suppose you do want one, in time."

"Oh, yes, yes, I do—"

"Well then. It's easier with a husband, don't you think?"

She caught my eye and burst out laughing, and somehow or other, without her ever having said "yes," it was settled.

Later, in the evening, we went over to her place to pick up some of her gear; she hadn't anything with her except what she stood up in. We were standing in the yard and Cass was getting out her key, when a head popped out from an upstairs window.

"Is that you, Cass?"

"Oh, hell," I muttered. We both looked up. The face looking down at us might have belonged to an amiable and rather pretty monkey, its eyes being very large and its nose very small, and the hair on its head dark and shaggy.

Cass said, "Hallo, Liz."

Monkey-face, registering my presence, seemed embarrassed: "Oh, look . . . it doesn't matter. Another time."

But Cass said, "It's all right. I'll be up in a minute."

Inside the flat, she said to me, "Come up with me, Greg."

"Oh, lord, do I have to? What does she want?"

"Nothing special. A chat, perhaps. She didn't see you were with me at first. They're my best friends, Greg—Ben and Liz, they're sweet—I'd like you to meet them." I didn't say anything, and she shook her head at me and smiled. "Darling, we have to connect some time, don't we?"

"Yes. All right. Come on, then."

A door from Cass's flat led into the front hallway, painted dark brown at about the time of the Ark, the floor covered with ancient cracked linoleum. There was no carpet on the stairs. We went up them to a sizable room at the front of the house, which was wildly untidy. Like most rented flats in London these days, it was I suppose, let furnished; the furniture had to be seen to be believed: junk, not antique junk, but suburban high-street-store stuff many times removed from its original owners. The walls were painted a lumpy uneven white, books lay every which way on shelves propped on bricks. There was a table covered with painting paraphernalia and several canvases, brilliant and alarming, hung on the walls.

In the midst of the clutter one very small girl tottered around the floor, throwing her toys about. In some way that's hard to explain the general effect of the place, which sounds frightful, was rather pleasant.

Liz was small and thin and dressed in a T-shirt and jeans. Her husband was not much taller than she was but extremely solid. He looked, I thought, like a useful football player. They looked a bit like twins, something to do, perhaps, with the similarity of their open and gentle expressions. Cass was right, they were the sort of people who have instant appeal.

73

Cass introduced me to them and added, after a moment's hesitation: "We're going to be married."

There was quite a fuss then, with Ben and Liz both hugging Cass and wishing her joy. Liz, a bit carried away, kissed me as well and that was rather pleasant too. Ben shook my hand and told me I was lucky, and that we must have a drink on it and where had that corkscrew gone? "We've got some wine in for once, we're having a party tonight, it's Liz's birthday, and she sold a picture last week, how about that?"

"Oh, Liz, how lovely," Cass exclaimed. "How much?"

"Fifty quid, my dear, fifty lovely quid," Liz cried. "Of course it will all go on bills but who cares? It's the feeling that someone's responded to what you're trying to say . . . look, do stay, you two. We've got three things to celebrate now."

I thought, hell, that's our evening gone, but I could see Cass wanted to stay, or felt it would be churlish not to, so I said, a bit stiffly perhaps, that that would be delightful. I caught a quick, dark look from Ben, reading his thought, *oh, Lord, a gent.* I wondered then whether they weren't protesting a bit too much, rather suspicious, really, of this new man, not heard of earlier than a week ago.

I'd lost the thread of the conversation. Liz was saying, "Are you sure? It would be a help, I must say. I do get a bit worried about Mandy being disturbed—"

"Can't have that, can we, gorgeous?" Cass inquired of the baby, scooping it up off the floor. The child chuckled and grabbed at Cass's hair; I stared at them both. Cass with a child in her arms was a heart-stopping sight.

"But we'll have to let people know," Liz said.

"Put a notice on the door," Cass suggested, "with arrows and things. I'd better go and straighten up downstairs. Greg, would you mind?"

"Would I mind what?"

"Helping me get my room ready for the party. We're going to have it down there."

"Oh," I said. "Are we?"

Downstairs, Cass eyed me dubiously. "Are you fed up about this? Oh, I know, I know, it's the only night when I'm not working. I didn't think. Look, we needn't stay, if you don't want to—"

74

"But you do," I said. "Don't you?"

"Sort of. I mean, I don't care about the party. It's just something to do with being with people I know in a place I'm used to . . . something ordinary. Because everything else is so extraordinary. Can one be too happy, do you think? It's wonderful but a bit scary—"

"You think happiness is a big con, don't you?"

"No, of course not. It's just that it's all happened so quickly, I'm not sure I know where I'm at."

I put my arms around her. "Everything's going to be all right, love. I promise."

Then Liz was at the door with a heavy tray of food in her hands and had to be rescued, and after that there was little time for anything except shifting furniture and carrying food and drink down from upstairs. Cass rushed away to change and reappeared in a long dress, just as Ben and Liz's guests began to arrive.

The party made the usual slow start; more people came, their tongues were loosened by a drink or two, and it grew warm and noisy in Cass's room. The record player blared and there was dancing. I felt a bit as if I were going back in time, as I no longer got asked very often to this sort of party, which belonged to an age-group younger than my own. The hunks of French bread, cheese and salami, the beer, and the cheap red wine were all a far cry from the little dinner parties I usually went to, the atmosphere modish and moneyed, with the hostess showing off her Cordon Bleu cooking. No, this was not my scene. I knew I looked too smooth and prosperous among these careless, rather grubby young men and the girls with their young shiny faces, innocent and knowing at the same time, most of them rather curiously got up in clothes apparently culled from jumble sales. It made me very conscious of the ten years between Cass and me.

Still, I did my best to mix for her sake. I was introduced to people, chatted up girls I would not recognize tomorrow in the street. Cass herself was in her element, frolicking and carefree. Not that she ever forgot me, though. And I didn't mind sharing her with these people—for a little while.

Time passed, the tempo of the party slowed, the noise died down. Liz made coffee and passed it round in mugs. A few

75

people with a long way to go and no transport of their own departed. The rest sat around on the floor, leaning on each other's shoulders and drinking the coffee. Ben was tinkling idly on Cass's piano; somebody asked her to sing but she shook her head. "Too much like work, love. But I'll play for Ben, if you like."

"I'll sing," said Ben, grinning, "if you'll join in."

"I call that blackmail," Cass grumbled, but she sat down obediently on the piano stool. She didn't play the piano, though. A guitar was fetched and she protested a bit, it wasn't her instrument, she would make a mess of the accompaniment. But she cradled it in her arms confidently enough, tuning it, her head bent over it in the musician's intent and listening pose, while she plucked the strings softly and tightened or loosened the keys. I watched her, heavy with love.

Ben had a nice light baritone and clearly knew what he was about, leaving Cass the melodic line and harmonizing effortlessly, in the way all Welsh people seem able to do. Ben Morgan. I'd probably been right about the football player, too.

They sang "Scarborough Fair" and Tom Paxton's lovely song, "The Last Thing on My Mind," and finally a ballad called "Flora," which I had never heard before. It has a drumming, menacing accompaniment and a poignant melody, and tells the story of the young man who came to Louisville, his fortune there to find, and met a fair young maiden there, whose beauty filled his mind. But Flora, the Lily of the West, was faithless and her lover crazed by jealousy:

> I stepped up to my rival
> My dagger in my hand
> I seized him by the collar and
> I ordered him to stand
>
> All in my desperation
> I stabbed him in his breast
> I killed a man for Flora
> The Lily of the West. . . .

The room suddenly seemed intolerably stuffy. I muttered

something about it to Liz, who was standing near me, and pushed open the French door onto the yard and walked out there, looking up into the starless, cloudy sky. The brick walls of Cass's yard seemed very high and close. I stood there, my mood shattered.

They put me in a prison dark . . . the voices followed me; Ben and Cass were giving the song the full treatment. *Although she swore my life away and robbed me of my rest, I'll love my faithless Flora* . . .

It was over and they clapped, and then Cass came out after me.

"Greg," she said, "what is it?"

"Nothing," I said. "I came out to get some air."

She put her hands on my arms. "It isn't just that. There's something the matter, isn't there?"

The light from the door made it as light as day out there. I looked down at her; I saw her, and I didn't see her. The enchanting irregularities of her face were blotted out to make way for another face, heart-shaped and invincibly photogenic. The whole thing was over in a second and she was Cass again, thank God.

But it didn't pass quickly enough, even so, because she exclaimed, "What are you looking at me like that for?"

"It's nothing, Cass. It's all right. Honest."

She put her head down and muttered, "You scared me. You looked . . . sort of . . . terrible. As if—"

"As if what?"

"As if you'd killed somebody," said Cass.

Well. I laughed it off, of course.

Five

MONDAY MORNING. Hunter's again, after a week away, and in some ways that week seemed about a million years. I went down to the factory first and had an hour or so's conference with Jim Cotton, the works manager. Never a very enlivening thing to do, this. Jim, though very good at his job, was incurably pessimistic, the prospect of expanding to meet new export business filling him with gloom. "We'll need more craftsmen, Mr. Hunter. And where are we going to find them, that's what I'd like to know."

"We'll find them," I said.

"Well, if you say so. But these trainees, you know, they hardly earn their keep yet."

This was a sideswipe at the training scheme I had initiated; when the lads we had taken on under the scheme disappeared once a week on day release to the local technical college, Jim could never really dismiss the idea that the firm was being robbed.

He said now, as I knew he would: "God knows what that college does for them, except make them think they know it all. Cheeky little buggers, too, they are. I don't know what kids are coming to these days."

"Nobody ever did know what kids were coming to, Jim. But they're sticking to it, are they? They take an interest in the work?"

"Oh, yes, I suppose so," he said, grudgingly. "Young Philip, now. He's not bad. Take a look at him as you go by."

"I already have," I said with a grin.

I'd arrived down there when the chaps were clocking on and didn't get back to London until midmorning. Our London office was not far from the gardens where I had taken Cass the week before, a tall Regency house with a blue plaque outside: "Joseph Brayton, designer, author and philosopher, lived and worked here, 1880–1919." It was this which had made me want to have this place as our headquarters; Joseph Brayton did more than anyone except William Morris, I suppose, to transform people's ideas about their surroundings.

Inside the house, on the ground floor, was the show room and a square hall where Carol, our receptionist, sat at a semicircular desk, her switchboard disguised by a bank of flowering plants. Chairs for waiting visitors were our own chairs; the walls were papered with a Brayton design, the high ceiling adorned by an earlier hand with plaster moldings of flowers and fruit. A curving staircase led to the floor above where our offices and the studio were. It was all very pretty, including Carol, who had been chosen for looks as well as competence. She greeted me now with her friendly smile and I nodded at her absently, being absorbed by the fact that Sarah was coming down the stairs, on her way out.

Well, it was as good a place as any to meet her again, with Carol there in the background, the business atmosphere enclosing us, Sarah perfectly self-possessed, perfectly friendly; setting the tone at once by asking how the trip had gone.

"Fine. I must tell you all about it later."

"Yes . . . well . . . I've some layouts I want to show you. This afternoon?"

"Sure." Really, there might never have been anything. It was a great relief.

Sarah lingered. "Oh, by the way. Your stepfather's here."

"Here? In London, you mean?"

"I mean right here," said Sarah. "This minute. He's with Hugo. They're both in your office, actually. Waiting for you, I suppose."

"Jesus," I muttered. Sarah regarded me with amusement and some genuine sympathy.

"Never mind," she said kindly. "He never stays anywhere for long, does he?"

"Not as a rule, thank God. Well, I'd better go and see him. Thanks for warning me."

80

"My pleasure," said Sarah, and went away. I stood there for a minute, looking after her and wondering what, if anything, I should have to do about her, until I realized that Carol at her half-moon desk was watching me under her eyelashes. Then I went to find Russell and Hugo; it was, I could see already, going to be one of those days.

Approaching my office I could hear already the familiar boom of Russell's voice. When I opened the door, I found him sitting in my chair; damn it, he was actually sitting behind my desk, in my chair, as if he owned the place. Well, so he did, some of it, anyway. Hugo was there, too, standing in the middle of the room rocking on the balls of his feet, a habit of his. I looked at them both with an irritation which I tried, not too successfully, not to show.

To do him justice, Russell didn't continue to sit in my chair, bounding up out of it in his usual energetic way. Although on the far side of fifty, he was remarkably fit and youthful looking, with his thick iron-gray hair, face ruddy-brown from much exposure to Caribbean sun, and no trace of a belly. He rushed at me, shook my hand painfully, hugged me, punched me playfully in the biceps; I knew quite well that all this was supposed to mark a close, affectionate relationship between us, as it were of a father and son.

"Well, well," I said, extricating myself from the paternal embrace. "This is a surprise. How are you, Russell?"

"Very fit, dear boy, very fit. Had a little trouble with the weight, recently, but I've got the better of it. As you see." He slapped his flat stomach proudly. If you asked Russell how he was, he always told you, in some detail. He was as much concerned with the preservation of his health and appearance as my mother was. I imagined them sometimes, solemnly exercising, communing together over diet sheets and weight lost or gained, counting calories. I wondered if it were worth it, to concentrate so hard on remaining lean and handsome, for whatever they did, youth was gone forever, and only its illusion remained.

"When did you arrive?" I asked.

"Last week. Hugo said you should be back by yesterday and we tried phoning, but no luck. Good trip?"

81

"Quite fruitful, yes."

"The competition's steep though, isn't it?" said Russell, looking wise. "The Scandinavians and the Italians have really got the European market to themselves . . ."

I didn't answer. What Russell knew about designing, making or marketing furniture was negligible. Money only he understood, and had made most of his own on the stock market. But money he certainly had, and when Hugo and I started Hunter's we saw no reason, at the time, to keep him out; we needed capital too much for that. Hunter's had grown and prospered, Russell got a good return on his investment, and so long as he kept out of the way his association with the business didn't worry me. So long as he kept out of the way—which fortunately he did, most of the time.

"How is Mother?" I asked.

"Blooming, old chap, beautiful as ever." He was an uxorious husband. "Left her at the hotel still asleep." He chuckled indulgently. "As time passes, she gets no better at getting up in the morning. Not like me. I've always believed in the early bird and all that."

And what worm, I asked silently, are you aiming to turn up this morning? We were all still standing about. Hugo, who had said nothing since I arrived except a muttered greeting, was still teetering back and forth in that exasperating way. When I entered the room, there had been a hint of embarrassment, an atmosphere of collusion, of a discussion hastily broken off. Collusion, I thought. About what?

"She's longing to see you," Russell said, still talking about Mother.

"Yes. Well, I'm looking forward to seeing her, of course. But I wish I'd known earlier that you were coming. I'm pretty much tied up today, unfortunately."

"You can't manage lunch?"

"I'm afraid not." I was meeting Cass for lunch.

"This evening, then. We're off to the country tomorrow. To stay with Madeleine and do some house-hunting."

"House-hunting?"

"Time we settled down," Russell said. "Find a cottage

82

somewhere to end our days in. Not too far from Madeleine and the children. Keep dogs," he said vaguely. "Garden. Golf."

I laughed. "You'll both be bored stiff in a month. And you know you hate it in England."

"I don't know about that," he said genially. "When you come back from being away for a while, you feel rather attached to the ramshackle old place, weather and taxation notwithstanding. We shan't be bored. Lydia will have her grandchildren. And I . . . well, I could start taking a bit more interest in Hunter's. I've been no more than a sleeping partner up to now, I'm afraid."

Hugo said with unnecessary cordiality, "That's very welcome news, Russell."

I didn't say anything. I was thinking too hard about Russell at a loose end in England, the charms of country life soon palling, finding unnecessary and interfering work for his idle hands to do.

Hugo muttered some excuse and went back to his own office. I sat down at my desk. Russell sat on the edge of it and eyed me.

"How are things?" he asked.

I was not sure what things he meant, but I said, "Fine, thanks." It had to be said sometime so I said it. "I'm getting married again."

"Are you now? Anyone we know?"

"I shouldn't think so."

"Well, congratulations. When are we going to meet the lady?"

I said, without thinking much about it: "I thought I might bring her along tonight."

He looked doubtful. "Well . . . you know how it is. Your mother sees you so seldom. I expect she'd like to have you to herself for a bit."

It might, I thought, be as well to accede to that, to make some sort of preparation for Cass's appearance.

"I'll come along early," I promised. "I'll ask Cass to meet me there, then I can have a talk with Mother first. Give her

83

my love," I added—a dismissing phrase, which Russell ignored.

"I've been having a chat with Hugo. He seems rather worried. But then he generally does. Such a good chap," Russell pronounced, "but I always feel he lacks nerve. That must be quite a problem for you, sometimes."

I waited. I knew all Russell's little ways. He was playing both ends against the middle as usual. Just so, no doubt, he had been communing with Hugo, condoling with him over my recklessness and ungovernable behavior.

"Still," he began again, "there's something to be said for his point of view—"

I said pleasantly, "There's always a lot to be said for Hugo's point of view, Russell. Look, there's nothing I'd like better than to have a talk and put you in the picture about everything. But this morning's quite impossible, I'm afraid. I've just got back, and you know how it is. Let's fix something in a day or two, when I've caught up with myself a bit."

He did get the message, then, and soon after went away. Russell had no real power to intervene in the firm's affairs, he hadn't a controlling interest, which remained mine by a combination of Maddy's shareholding and my own; but his nuisance value was certainly high.

I said this last to Hugo later on, to see what his reaction would be.

Hugo looked into the middle distance and said, "If you felt like that about him, you should have fenced him in from the start. He didn't have to be on the Board—"

"He wouldn't come in without."

"There you are, then. And if he wants to do what he's entitled to do anyway, surely that's all to the good? He might bring a fresh eye to things."

"Do you," I asked, "feel in need of a fresh eye?"

"Now and then."

"What Russell knows about our business could be put on the back of a postage stamp."

"He doesn't have to know," said Hugo dryly. "Making furniture or washers, the principle's the same. Making the

books balance and showing a profit at the end of the year."
I said with a grin, "And don't we do just that?"
"Up to now. We've had it easy, you know. Those days are over. The way our costs are going, we could have a cash problem before long."
"So? What are we doing about it?"
"I've done a cost analysis. And worked out some proposals for economies . . . I'll let you have them this afternoon.'
"Tell me the worst," I said.
Hugo sighed. "Here we go again. Anything rather than actually study the figures—"
This was a reference to a perennial dispute between Hugo and me. In one of his rare outbursts he'd told me that I had drive, creative flair, and could sell iced water to an Eskimo, but totally lacked a financial sense; I retorted that that was his department. The trouble from his point of view was that I was the one in control.
Hugo's economies were much as I expected: among them the London office, which he thought a gross extravagance we could well do without, and a cut in office staff.
"As Sarah's going," he said. "I think we shouldn't replace her."
"She's going? Did she say why?"
"Don't digress. What the hell does it matter why she's going? Anyway, she didn't have to say. It was obvious." He eyed me irritably. "Couldn't you have avoided that situation? Mixing business and pleasure never works. I thought you were serious. Never dreamed you were just amusing yourself—"
"Do leave off, Hugo. You go on as if I were an Oriental potentate toying with a slave girl."
"Well, it does rather express your attitude, I think. Anyway, she *is* going, and we shall have to take a decision about keeping up the department—"
"She hasn't gone yet," I said.
In the end, I made a lot of concessions to Hugo. Whatever our disagreements, we had to stick together. Hugo knew that without me there would be no Hunter's at all. I knew that I couldn't do without Hugo, or another Hugo-type, a neces-

sary evil. Perhaps he wouldn't have been so forthright if he hadn't had Russell there in the background. But I knew, too, that he was genuinely sounding the alarm.

I met Cass for lunch, and told her about the parental invasion and my plans for the evening.

"Tonight?" she exclaimed. "Have I got to come?"

She looked so comically dismayed that I laughed.

"You haven't got to do anything. But it would be a bit odd if I said I was getting married without producing the girl. Darling, don't look so worried; the bloody old world will keep breaking in. You said so yourself last night."

"So I did. All right. I'll be there . . . do you think they'll want to come and see us married?"

"I shouldn't be surprised."

"Oh, well. In that case, I'd better ask my parents as well. Goodness knows what they'll all make of each other—"

"I'd like to meet them," I said.

"Would you? Yes, I suppose you would."

"We could go up on Sunday," I said. "Give them a ring during the week."

"I'll write," said Cass. "I can't telephone. They don't have a telephone. My father thinks there's no point in it. You see what I mean."

I was not sure that I did.

Sarah came to my office in the afternoon, crisp and businesslike, a folder with the layouts in her hand. It seemed as if nothing had changed, but of course everything had. We spread the layouts on my desk and stood side by side over them, discussing, discarding. I thought when we'd finished that she might simply put the papers back in the folder and go away again, but she said in a friendly way, "How was Russell this morning?"

I gave her a brief rundown on the conversation. I had always confided in Sarah. "They're going to settle here, and I'm going to have him on my back the whole time. You see."

Then she said it. "Well, Greg, I won't be here to see, I'm afraid. I suppose Hugo told you."

86

"Yes. He told me. I suppose you have to do this, Sarah."

"I think so," she said. "Don't you?"

I understood. She was giving me an opening to deny everything that had happened, to beg her not to go. I didn't say anything, because there was nothing to say, and she added coolly, "I rather gather Hugo doesn't want to keep the department up. If you want to let Ginny go, I can probably take her with me." Ginny was her secretary.

"You've got another job in view?"

"Oh, yes. At Pargiter's. Well . . ."

She turned toward the door with a little nod and a rather pinched smile, and briefly I saw beyond the conveniently calm exterior to the real Sarah, quietly grieving inside herself. I felt terrible and wanted to comfort her, but of course there was no way of doing that.

I said, knowing I shouldn't. "I shall miss you, Sarah."

She shook her head. "Oh, no, you won't. Just now you're not very happy with yourself. I know that. But soon you'll just be glad I've gone quietly. You're going to marry her, aren't you?" and I said foolishly, taken off balance: "How did you know?" and she smiled that little cold smile again and said, "Instinct."

With her hand on the door, she added, "I hope you'll be very happy," and was gone.

I thought that evening, as I entered the hotel lobby and asked for Mother and Russell at the desk, how typical this was of the pattern of things where Mother was concerned. I met her off planes, I asked for her in hotel lobbies. I did not knock at a door and hear her running to it, to open it and embrace me, with the smells of welcoming cooking wafting by. That was not at all her style, not anymore anyway. Come to think of it, it never had been, much.

When I knocked at this particular door I heard her voice calling to me to come in, it's not locked. I went in. It was a suite, of course; they always had a suite. The sitting room was empty, Russell didn't seem to be there. Mother cried, "Is that you, Greg? Come through here, darling."

She was in the bedroom, doing some last-minute thing to

87

her face. She was wearing one of those elaborate negligees beloved of film stars in the thirties. Her hair was a pale, pale blond, and she had had her eyes picked up, I think, since I last saw her.

She put the eye pencil or whatever it was down on the dressing-table, whirled about, stretching herself up from the waist like a dancer, and like a dancer with her partner, lifted her graceful arms and placed them gracefully around my neck; there seemed, as usual, to be a lot of expensive perfume about.

I said, smiling, "Well, Mother."

We kissed. She clasped her hands together behind my head, leaned back a little to inspect me.

"Darling! It's so wonderful to see you! How enormous you are, I'd forgotten. And so handsome! You get more like your father every time I see you. I like your hair cut like that, sort of Byronic, it's very fetching." She ruffled it with her fingers. "How are you, dearest?"

"Well. No need to ask how you are. You look, as Russell said, blooming."

"Did he say that? Bless him." She glanced complacently at the mirror. "I don't do too badly for such an aged lady, do I?"

"Now, I've paid you one compliment," I said, grinning. "Don't fish."

It was true, though, that she was still astonishingly good-looking and her charm still cast a powerful spell. As always at the first moment of meeting, I felt very fond of her, delighted to see her. The feeling wouldn't last, it never did, but it was nice while it lasted.

"Look, sweetie"—she was fond of this outdated endearment—"I must just get my dress on, and then I'll be with you. Help yourself to a drink, hm? And make one for me."

I went out to locate the drinks. "What are you having?" I asked.

"Gin, please, darling, and some tonic and lots of ice." I waited for her to ask me about Cass, but I had forgotten that Mother was sometimes a little devious. That subject would come up later. "Have you seen Maddy lately?" she asked through the door.

"A week or so back."

"How did she seem to you?"

I said carefully, "All right. Why do you ask?"

"She sounded a bit down in the mouth, I thought, over the telephone. There's nothing wrong there, is there?"

"Not that I know of." Maddy and I had a pact going back into childhood: never discuss each other with Mother.

"Oh, well," Mother said, "we're going down tomorrow. I'll be able to see how things are for myself. Oh, by the way, I must tell you while I think of it. Do you know who I ran into last week? Guess!"

I couldn't guess, and said so.

"Neville!" she cried triumphantly.

I was silent.

"Greg! Did you hear what I said?"

"Yes, I heard. I didn't know you were in touch. How is he?"

"Oh, fine—"

"He's not married again?"

There was a brief pause. Then she said, "No. No, he hasn't married again. He's been living abroad for the past few years; he retired early, I think he had some money left him. But he's back now, he's got a cottage in the country somewhere."

Mother came tripping out, holding her dress together at the back. "Zip me up, dear, will you?"

I zipped her up, handed her her drink.

"Well," she said. "*Isn't* this nice? Cheers."

"Cheers," I said. We smiled at each other fondly, and drank.

As I'd told Cass, I hardly remember my father. I can just remember being told he was killed, not really knowing what it meant, and Mother crying a lot.

Mother's tears were soon dried. She was young and lovely and a magnet for men and there always seemed a lot of them about. I hated them all until Neville came. I don't suppose they liked me too much either, the jealous, glowering little boy, always hanging around and getting in the way. We shared a London flat for a time with a friend of Mother's called Freda who had a little girl about my age, a whiny child whom I detested. Freda's marriage had broken up, and I imagine the two young, husbandless women found the setup a convenience, sharing the responsibility of the children and taking turns at baby-sitting while the other went out. Mother had a job, Freda kept house. It wasn't, I think, a very happy time. Freda had no time for me, and in retrospect I don't blame her, I was a cussed, destructive child. That boy needs a father, people said, in the ominous tone which implies a father is something unpleasant; and I suppose in the unconscious way children do, I made sure, by my behavior when Mother's men friends were around, that none of them would volunteer for the job.

Anyway, quite suddenly Mother married Neville, Freda and her daughter disappeared from our lives, and everything was changed.

Because Neville loved us, Maddy and me; he really did.

A simple soul, really, Neville, not the sort of man one might have expected Mother to marry. He had been in the RAF, too. He was big and jolly and rather noisy, and he had one of those huge moustaches the Air Force chaps affected at that time, and all the time I knew him he never gave up all that wartime slang. He talked about gremlins and wizard prangs, and, more sadly, about friends of his who had Bought It, or Gone for a Burton; he kept us entranced for hours with stories of the war in the air, when, I am sure, he lived more intensely than at any time before or since. After a bit he bought a car and we used to go for picnics in the country; he taught me to play cricket, and when we went to the sea for our holidays, he hired a beamy cumbersome dinghy with a lugsail and taught me to sail it, thus beginning a passion for sailing which has lasted all my life.

Yes, we were happy during those years. We had a father, the only one, really, we ever had. Then, just as suddenly as she had married him, Mother took him from us.

I was fourteen. It seemed at first as if he were leaving her. He came up to my room one evening, when I was doing my homework, and told me he was going, he was sorry, things hadn't worked out, Mother would explain. I remember his face, a pasty mask with the big moustache stuck on, and the way he wouldn't look at me.

Bewildered and dumb, I wanted to ask a lot of questions and never got them out. I can see us now, me springing up from the table where I was doing my maths, my throat thick with the tears which, of course, I was too big to shed. And then, strangely, he put his arms around me, and as if I had been a girl or a little child, he kissed me. Then he went off down the stairs, and I never saw him again.

Then there was Russell. Mother explained it all: how you loved one person and then you sort of grew out of loving them and loved somebody else. And this somebody else was Russell. It made no sense to me. All I could see was this marvelous car, and Mother wearing a fur coat she could never have bought for herself, and it seemed to me that Russell had bought *her*.

Of course, it can't have been easy for Russell. I can see now how we must have seemed to him, Maddy and I; Maddy was only ten, but she loved Neville too, and anyway was much under my influence. I can imagine the four round blank eyes and the two glum pudding faces, and neither of us with anything to say. I did mutter something hostile to Mother once, I can't remember what, but I do recall her fury: "My God, what a little prig you are! I don't know how I managed to give birth to anyone so stuffy!"

It was all smoothed over eventually. We grew up and became more civilized; and, I suppose, more tolerant.

"*Greg,*" Mother said.

"What?"

She looked at me sharply. "You've gone broody again. I didn't know you still did that. Before she comes, hadn't you better tell me something about this girl?"

So we had got around to that at last.

I said nicely, "Look, love, I'm going to marry her, so let's not start by calling her 'this girl.' Her name's Cass—"

"Her name's what?"

"C, A, double S. That's what she's called. She's twenty-three, and she's a singer."

91

"Oh. An opera singer?"

"No, no, not an opera singer—"

"What, then? Clubs, that sort of thing, a pop singer?"

"Not pop, exactly—"

"Oh," said Mother again. "How long have you known her?"

"Oh, a while," I said mendaciously. "Anyway, why don't you wait and see? She'll be here in a moment, anyway."

Mother sighed. "What happened to that other nice girl? Sarah, wasn't it? Didn't she work for you?"

"At this moment in time, still does."

"Isn't that very awkward?"

"It will sort itself out, I expect," I said.

"A bit ruthless," Mother murmured, "aren't you?"

I nearly said, hark who's talking, but restrained myself. To divert her attention, I said, "Before Cass and Russell come, I wanted to ask you a bit about Neville."

"Neville?" Mother said, as if she had never brought the subject up. "What about Neville? I've told you all there is to tell. He's older. Fatter. He's got quite a corporation," she added with a faint flick of spite.

"Did he ask after me?"

"I don't remember. I suppose so." A look of sulky, childish obstinacy spread over her face. "I didn't think you'd be so interested."

"Is that why you didn't mind telling me?"

Mother looked baffled as well as obstinate. "It's twenty *years*," she said.

"I loved Neville," I said. "You never knew that, did you? It broke my heart when you threw him out."

"I did not throw him out," said Mother furiously. "He left me, you know that perfectly well—"

"He didn't want to go, though, did he?"

"You think he's so marvelous," she cried. "You don't know a quarter of it. You don't know how he treated me—"

I said, "Did you get his address?"

Mother looked as if she might be about to cry. "I haven't got it."

"Oh, come on, Mother. He must have given you some idea where he's living."

"Somewhere near Marlow," Mother muttered. "A place called Polney. I expect he's in the book."

"Good enough. I'll find him. Thanks."

She stared at me. "It's always the same," she cried. "Every time I looked forward so much to seeing you and it's always like this, you're nice for about five minutes and then it seems as if you just *have* to start something. You can't resist being unkind—"

I most certainly didn't want to start a row with Mother just then, with Cass about to arrive. I said mildly, "Now come on, Mother. What have I said?"

"My God," she said. "Perhaps you don't even know you're doing it. You always were difficult," she added bitterly. "But it's worse now. You've got so hard. Ever since Tessa died."

"Mother, please—"

"Oh, you don't want to talk about that, you never do. That's what's the matter with you. You bottle it all up—"

I can't take this sort of thing, never could. I said loudly, "For God's sake! Don't keep on about it!"

There was a sudden, ominous silence. Into this silence came one of those artificial, attention-catching coughs. I turned, and there was Russell, with Cass beside him, standing just inside the door.

We were all trapped in the moment like flies in glue. Mother stood there with her hand at her breast in a theatrical gesture of distress and surprise. Cass looked as embarrassed as I felt, and I was at once filled with an angry concern for her. Christ, what an introduction. Even Russell looked a bit taken aback, but he recovered first, grinning amusedly, not altogether sorry, I daresay, to have it once more demonstrated that my mother and I did not Get On.

He said cheerfully, "Well, here she is. Heard her asking for us at the desk, so I introduced myself and we came up together."

I said, "That's very helpful of you, Russell." I went over and put my arm around Cass and said quickly, "Let me introduce you to my mum, darling. Mother, this is Cass." I could feel Cass's shoulder, rigid with nervousness, under my hand.

One thing about my mother, she can rise to an occasion

faster than anyone I've ever seen. Tears and resentment all forgotten, she came across the room in a little graceful run, and took Cass's hands in hers. The charm was turned on like an arc light. "My dear!" she said softly. She drew away a little, still holding Cass's hands, so that they looked as if they were about to begin some sort of country dance; she gazed at Cass with every appearance of delight, and said in a gentle wondering tone, "Greg, she's lovely. She's absolutely lovely." She drew the unresisting Cass toward her—the next step in the dance, so to speak—and kissed her on the cheek. "Welcome into the family, my dear."

Cass said, "Thank you." She looked a bit dazed. In the background, Russell was phoning room service for champagne.

Six

WE SPED through the northerly suburbs in the silence of a Sunday morning, shops shuttered for the day, the streets yet empty of the mass exodus still to come. We were on our way to spend the day in Middlebridge. Cass sat beside me with a dazed early-morning look, wearing, surprisingly to me, the most conventional of summer dresses, and with her hair pinned up; like that, she looked neat, modest and unremarkable, the way ballet dancers do offstage, all their grace and dynamism diminished.

A dull trip; a long stretch of the motorway, and then a meandering drive through flat scarred countryside to Middlebridge. We had miscalculated, it was too early to arrive anywhere for Sunday lunch. "Shall I drive around for a bit?" I asked.

"There isn't much to see, you know." This seemed to be true. Middlebridge was an ugly little town, with no historic or aesthetic significance whatever. There was a main street which had recently had a face-lift with a lot of plate glass and concrete, housing supermarkets and chain stores; regiments of red-brick, Victorian terrace houses; a cinema converted to bingo; a chapel, a church, both hideous; and a lot of uninviting-looking pubs. I tried to imagine Cass growing up here, and failed.

A gray-brick building loomed, surrounded by asphalt tennis and netball courts. "There's the school I went to. Used to be grammar, gone comprehensive now. Oh, there's the Running Horse—they used to run a jazz club on Saturday nights, in a room at the back of the pub. I was there every week at one time." She spoke as if it was a lifetime ago. A woman washing her windows stared at us as we went by: citified

95

strangers in a large car, looking Middlebridge over like tourists.

"Would you turn left at the end here? I want to look at Aunt Meg's shop. Mother said it had changed hands again— oh, heavens, they've made it into a launderette. Could you stop a minute?"

I pulled up and we stared at the unremarkable little building on its corner site.

"What was it before?" I asked.

"Grocery, general stores. It was Grandpa's, of course, and then he got too old, and Meg ran it and looked after him as well. She had a piano in the room behind the shop and I used to go there every day from school and practice. Customers would come in and say, 'Is that your niece, Miss Thornton? Doesn't she play nicely!' and dear Meg would be all puffed up with pride."

"Didn't you have a piano at home?" I asked.

"No. The whole music thing was Meg's idea. I owe her a lot, really." She touched my arm. "I should think we could go now, don't you?"

At her direction I drove through the town to a newish housing estate on the outskirts. This was a great improvement on Middlebridge itself. On this bright morning the men were busy with their cars or their gardens, the air filled with the sound of lawn mowers and hoses hissing. The grass verges were well clipped, everything was neat and same. Cass's home (had she ever really lived here?) was exactly like all the others. The front door was white painted, the brass knocker glittered. Two perfectly clean empty milk bottles stood by the front door. From an open window overhead a pop group, on radio or record, was shouting its head off. There was a faint smell of roast dinner.

There was that little gap in time which told you that the woman who opened the door had shed an apron, wiped her hands free of flour, peered at herself in a mirror.

I don't quite know what I expected, some sort of older version of Cass I suppose, but in Mrs. Clayton I could see no likeness to her daughter. But there was something about her

96

flustered timidity that made me warm to her, and when she smiled she looked like Cass after all.

She said, "Well, hallo, stranger," to Cass, but her look robbed the words of bite. They hugged each other, the flowers Cass had brought were accepted and exclaimed over; then she turned, rather shyly, to me. Cass introduced me, we shook hands; behind her shyness she was measuring, judging me. Well, that one expects. The music continued to blare away upstairs. Mrs. Clayton called, "Michael! *Michael!*" There was no response. "He doesn't hear," she said apologetically. "With all that noise. Will you excuse me a moment, there's something I've left on the stove. Your father's in the garden, Cass, take Mr. Hunter out there and I'll bring some coffee."

I said, "Please call me Greg, Mrs. Clayton, everybody does," and she gave me her fleeting, unsure smile.

We went out into the garden. It was very small but looked bigger, with a lawn which curved around a young magnolia tree; flower beds rioted with color. In its tiny compass it was a work of art.

"Good heavens," I said.

"It *is* heavenly," said Cass, "isn't it? My father is a very good gardener."

He was on his knees with his back to us, clipping the lawn edges.

"Dad," said Cass.

He got up then and turned toward us. Cass's eyes looked at me out of a male middle-aged face; the effect was rather odd. He said in a dry voice, not especially welcoming, "Well, Kathleen."

She went up to him and reached up to kiss his cheek. He didn't kiss her back, he didn't put his arms around her. To be sure, he was still holding the shears. Cass introduced us. He nodded. "How d'ye do. I won't shake hands, mine are rather grubby." He turned to Cass, and added, "Well, what have you been doing with yourself, eh?"

"Oh, I don't know. This and that," Cass said. She seemed ill at ease. "I mean—I've been pretty busy, really."

97

"Must have been. Not a squeak out of you since Christmas."

"Dad!" She was laughing, protesting. "That's not true! I came up in March. I've written—"

"Your mother thought you'd come for Easter."

"I didn't say I—"

"She frets."

"Yes, I know, I'm sorry . . ."

I said quickly, "I've been admiring your garden, Mr. Clayton. It's beautiful."

He looked around at it and his face softened. But he only said grudgingly, "It's not bad. Makes a lot of work."

End of conversation, I thought. Cass's mother came out carrying a tray. She looked anxiously at her husband. "Are you going to have coffee, Sam?"

He shook his head. "Not for me. I'll have a beer, if there is any. No, all right, all right, I'll get it myself . . ."

He went into the house, kicking off his gardening shoes on the mat, came out again. "There's none left. I'd best go and get some from the pub, must have something to drink with our dinner."

"I'll run you down there," I said.

He accepted the offer and we went out to the gate where two fourteen-year-old boys were staring with rapt attention at my car. One, apparently, was speeding the departure of the other, who mumbled something and made off. The first boy remained, shuffling his feet and looking from me to the car and back again.

"My son Michael," Clayton said offhandedly, but you could hear the pride in his voice. "A friend of Kathleen's, Michael—Gregory, is it?"

"Hi," said Michael. He had Cass's eyes too. He grinned at me cheerfully. "I *say*, is this your car? Are you going out in it? Can I come?'

I was going to say yes, but Clayton said shortly, "No, you can't. We're going to the pub."

"I can wait outside—"

"I daresay. You're still not coming."

"Oh, *Dad*—"

98

"Michael, you heard me the first time. I said, 'No.' You haven't seen your sister yet. Go and say hallo to her."

Michael looked disgusted, but he turned obediently enough and went into the house. As we drove away, Clayton said with a sort of gloomy humor, "Who'd be a father? Bloody awkward age, fourteen. They grow up so fast these days; don't know anything, think they know it all, and whatever you do it's wrong. Play it by ear all the time and you find yourself making a stand about something that doesn't matter a damn, like now."

I laughed, suddenly liking him better. "I shouldn't worry. I expect he'll turn out all right."

"I hope you're right," he said, worrying away at it. "This is a small place, a bit slow for the youngsters, not much to keep them occupied. But the big cities are worse, it seems to me. I'm thankful Mike's not in London—all those clubs, kids of fourteen taking drugs and that—it's shocking."

"They're the ones who make the news," I said. "It's easy to get the drugs scene out of proportion. There are a lot of ordinary people about, even in London."

"Well, you should know, I suppose . . ."

"Very like Cass," I said. "Isn't he?"

"Yes. They both favor their mother."

"I wouldn't have thought so. I should have said they take after you."

"Would you?"

We drew up outside the pub.

"Feel like a pint now?" Clayton asked.

The pub, like pubs everywhere, was crammed with Sunday morning drinkers. We fought our way through to the bar. One or two people nodded at Cass's father and said, 'Hallo, Sam,' and he nodded back and mumbled something. Clearly, he was not a convivial man, nor one that was easy to get through to. I wasn't sure if it mattered whether I did or not, but thought I had better try.

I got the beer, and we found a corner where we could lean up against the wall with it. I said, "You know Cass and I want to get married?"

"The wife said something about it."

99

"I hope you approve."

He looked at me with his small, unwilling grin. "Not my business, is it? She's of age. Don't know much about you, anyway."

"I can look after her, you know. I mean, I'm not badly off."

"I reckoned you must be doing all right—the car and that. Not that you can always tell, people get anything on the glad and sorry these days. What's your job?"

I explained about Hunter's; he nodded, unimpressed. "Good bit older than her, aren't you?"

"I'm thirty-three."

"Hm. Ten years. Not a bad thing in some ways. You'll be good for her, I daresay. She needs a man who knows his own mind, let's her know who's boss."

I made no comment on this. I still had a feeling of puzzlement, of something not quite right.

Then he said, "Taken your time about getting married, haven't you?"

"I've been married before."

"Ah. I thought that would be it. You're divorced, I take it."

I let a little pause elapse. Then I said deliberately, "My wife died four years ago."

"Oh. Oh, I see. I'm sorry."

"That's quite all right," I said smartly.

We contemplated our beer. After a bit I tried again.

"Cass and I are planning to be married quite soon. Just a quiet wedding in a register office. I hope you and your wife will be able to come down for it."

He pursed his lips. "Don't know about that. Taking a day off. I don't know about that."

"We can arrange it for a Saturday, I expect. Perhaps you and your wife would like a weekend in London; I mean, if you'd like to come up, stay at a hotel . . . as my guest . . ."

He stared at me. "You trying to patronize me, young feller?"

"No, no, of course not . . ."

"If we come," he said, "*If* we come, I'm not short of the price of a hotel room."

"No . . . well, of course I didn't mean to suggest . . ."

"That's all right then. Soon," he said suddenly. "What do you mean, soon?"

"I've applied for a license."

"In a hurry," he said, "are you?"

I said shortly, "She's not pregnant, if that's what you mean."

I thought at once, that's torn it, but he did not seem provoked, taking a long swallow of his beer and looking at me noncommittally over the top of his glass; he didn't say anything. The silence seemed awkward and I plunged on. "Look, Mr. Clayton, I'm well established in life and I've a perfectly adequate flat. We haven't got to save up, get a home together. There's no reason to hang about."

"Seems not," he agreed. Arguing with him was like punching a punch ball; it always came back but didn't hit you. "Known each other long?" he asked.

I was making no more efforts to win him. "Long enough," I said, looking him in the eye.

He took that, nodding placidly at my empty glass. "Have another?"

"Not for me, thanks."

"We'll get back then. Well," he added reluctantly, "if it's all settled, I'll wish you joy."

We returned to the house. A rather battered estate car was standing outside; this proved to belong to Audrey, Cass's sister, and her husband, Len. Len, a large silent young man with hands that looked as if they could have felled an ox, was in the living room with his two small children; Michael was there, talking about model airplanes, a monologue punctuated by Len's monosyllabic replies. There was a clatter of dishes and a lot of feminine chat and laughter going on in the kitchen; a comfortable, familial sound. Then Cass appeared, followed by her sister, and introduced us.

Audrey, enormously pregnant, her head topped by a mop of improbably bright red curls, seemed ordinary enough until she raised to my face a pair of pale green, acutely shrewd eyes. I felt I was being rapidly taken apart, put together

101

again and docketed in some tidy compartment of Audrey's mind; it was a bit chilling. Then she grinned disarmingly, and said gently, "Cor."

"Well," Cass said, "I did tell you, didn't I?"

"Told her what?" I asked.

Audrey giggled. "As if you didn't know. Hallo, Dad, how's tricks?"

Her father was gazing at her in astonishment and disapproval.

"Stone the crows. What *have* you done to your hair?"

"It's a wig," Audrey said. "I wanted something startling, to distract attention from the hump. Still, if you don't like it—"

She plucked the wig from her head, revealing her own hair, cut short, mouse-colored and fine as a baby's. "There you are. Now I look like nothing, as usual."

"You look all right to me," Clayton said. There was the same note in his voice as when he spoke of Michael; pride and tenderness, imperfectly disguised by his disgruntled manner. "That carroty thing's horrible, a waste of good money I call it."

"You know what you are," said Audrey affectionately, "a grumpy, critical old bugger—"

This was going a bit far, surely; but he took no offense, grinning dourly and making a mock-threatening gesture toward her while she squealed and dodged away, crying, "Now, no rough stuff, remember your grandchild! Mum's just dishing up, Len, give me a hand with the kids, will you?"

Len lumbered obediently to his feet, fetching a high chair from the car, strapping the younger child into it, tying a bib round his neck; a well-trained husband, that, if ever I saw one. I was a bit troubled. While that cheery family horseplay was going on, I had seen a stiff, strange little smile on Cass's face.

We sat down to the traditional Sunday roast, Yorkshire pudding, cabbage and potatoes, followed by apple tart and thick hot custard. The men drank beer, the women drank water. It wasn't very merry. I am not well up in this sort of family gathering and I don't know exactly what I had expected: a bit of an ordeal-by-family for me, perhaps; a celebration of our engagement, or just of the fact that Cass was there visiting them. I looked around the table at them all: Mrs. Clayton, flushed, a bit harassed, plied us all with food, forgetting her own. Michael just ate with the relentless appetite of the fourteen-year-old. Len, silent as ever, likewise plowed his way through an enormous plateful. Audrey dominated the scene, Audrey with her red wig and her pumpkin figure, Audrey spooning gravy and chopped up meat and potato into the toddler's hungry little maw while she chattered, gossiped, giggled, bantered with her father, who had a deadpan humor of his own. Her mother deferred to her, seeking instructions about the feeding of the children. She might have been the one who had been long away.

In the face of all that relentless vivacity Cass was very quiet. I caught her eye once across the table, and winked when the others weren't looking. She smiled faintly, and looked away.

After the meal, Mrs. Clayton retired to wash up and Cass said she would help her. The other men in the party retreated to the garden where Clayton settled in a deck chair with the *Sunday Express* over his face. Len lay on the lawn with the children crawling over him. Audrey and I were left.

I offered her a cigarette. "I shouldn't," she said, patting her swollen belly, "but now and again, I just must . . . thanks." Leaning awkwardly forward to take a light from me, she added, "I thought you did very well, by the way. Considering."

"Considering what?"

"Well, meeting prospective in-laws is always rather an ordeal. My parents more than most, I should think."

"Would you?"

Audrey looked at me out of the corners of her eyes. "*Cagey,*" she murmured. Then she added pleasantly, "You don't like me, do you?"

"I beg your pardon," I said stiffly, and she burst out laughing.

"Don't look so shocked. There's no reason why you should. I know why it is, anyway. You thought I hogged the conversation over dinner."

"Well—"

103

"What you don't understand is that if I didn't, there wouldn't *be* any conversation. We're a funny lot. I suppose Cass told you."

"Told me what?"

Again there was that sideways flash of her pale cat's eyes.

"Well, that we're a funny lot."

"Most families are a funny lot," I said. "You should see mine."

She looked straight at me this time. "Look, Greg. There's a big age gap between Cass and me, and we're not as close as we ought to be. But I'm fond of her. She's a smashing kid, and she deserves the best—"

"You don't have to tell me that."

"I hope not," Audrey said. She hauled herself up out of the armchair. "I'd better go and see what they're up to in the kitchen, and show willing, I suppose." She paused by my chair. "She hasn't had an easy time of it, you know."

"How do you mean?"

She shrugged. "That's for her to tell you. I've said too much already, I expect." She hesitated. "This sounds soppy, I know, but . . . she needs love, does Cass. Lots of it. Mind you give it to her, that's all."

"I do," I said, "and I shall."

"Good, because if you ever let her down, I shall engage Len to come and wring your neck. That's a promise," she added cheerfully, and went away.

As we were driving back to London, Cass said, "Audrey thinks you're gorgeous. A dreamboat, she said."

I thought this showed a certain duplicity on Audrey's part, but I only said, "Did she now? That's very nice of her."

"Mother likes you too."

"I liked her. She's sweet."

"Isn't she?" Cass said eagerly. "I feel awful that I don't see more of her. She misses me, I know that, but . . . I keep asking her to come up to London and stay with me, but she never can. My father isn't the sort to manage on his own. He thinks she always ought to be there."

"Yes. I can imagine that."

104

Cass stared through the windshield for a few minutes and then asked suddenly, "How did you get on with him?"

"Your father? All right, I suppose. He isn't easy to get at though, is he? A rum sort of character."

"Yes," said Cass, and sighed.

"I expected him to be a lot more on the ball about who I was and what my prospects were. You know how fathers are—who is this chap who is going to take my daughter away from me and all that. But it wasn't like that. He seemed, so, well, detached. . . ."

"Yes. He would be."

I glanced at her, at the delicate composed profile, with its lifted chin. "What's the matter? Don't you get on with him?"

Cass said quietly, "He hates me."

"*What?*"

"It's true."

"But that's ridiculous. Unless they're sick or something, people don't *hate* their children—"

Cass said, "Greg, I can't explain this while you're driving at seventy miles an hour. Let's stop and have a coffee at the next diner; there's one coming up quite soon now."

"All right." I eased over into the slow lane. The café, bleakly glassy, neon-lighted, crowded with people refueling themseves at speed with about as much enjoyment as they refueled their cars, had that same anonymity and impermanence of an airport lounge and had, for me, the same brand of melancholy. I shuffled along a counter and collected the coffee, and took it over to where Cass was sitting.

She looked up as I approached and murmured, "Don't look so put out. I'm used to it. It's been going on all my life, really."

"Why didn't you tell me before?"

"I don't like talking about it, I suppose. And perhaps I thought you ought to see them for yourself. Without prejudice."

"Audrey said you hadn't had an easy time of it."

"Did she? Poor old Audrey—she feels guilty. Goodness knows why; it's not her fault. But you can see how he is with *her.*"

105

"Yes. I noticed that. And with the boy . . . but what's it all about?"

"He thinks I'm not his child."

"But that's absurd," I exclaimed. "You're so like him!"

Her lovely smile broke out, like sunshine, and she said softly, "Thank you, darling. That's the nicest thing—"

"I told him so, too."

"*Did* you! What did he say?"

"Nothing much. Of course, as I didn't know anything, I wasn't watching for a reaction. But I still don't get it. There's the evidence staring at him every time he looks in the glass."

"He won't recognize it. It's a sort of obsession—"

"Was he unkind to you?"

"If you mean, did he beat me or anything, no. But there are other ways of being cruel. No love. Just no love, and knowing that you're different, you don't really belong." She sighed. "I never learn, you know. I have these fantasies . . . like in a Christmas story, bells ringing and lights twinkling, carol singers in the snow, and my father coming to me with some marvelous present, putting his arms round me and saying he's sorry and everything suddenly being all right. Daft, isn't it? I should know better by this time."

"God," I muttered. "How bloody."

"Never mind. Now I've got you, it doesn't matter so much."

"But I don't get it," I said. "Your mother seems the last person . . ."

"She does, doesn't she? But Dad was away when I was born. In the army."

"But you're not old enough to have been born when the war was on—"

"No war," said Cass, "just service abroad. Dad was in World War II as well, he was a Commando then. That was when he and Mother got married. I've often thought they couldn't have known each other very well, that it was an instinctive thing, let's mate and make a baby before the holocaust comes. Well, anyway, they had Audrey in 1944, and then when peace came he couldn't settle to civilian life. I suppose he missed all the excitement and the danger and the killing. Hard to imagine, isn't it, seeing him now?" She spoke coldly. "So he joined up again, and Mother and Audrey went to live with Grandpa and Aunt Meg, and she got a job. Anyway, she met this other man there, and they fell in love."

"Oh," I said. "I see."

"I don't think you do, not really. It was all quite innocent, that's what she told me, and I believe her. Then Dad came home on embarkation leave . . . they were going to Singapore or Aden, somewhere like that . . . and she got pregnant. Directly she knew that, she gave the other man up. Everything might have been all right, but this is a small place, and when Dad eventually got home again, someone had to pass the glad news along to him."

"Poor devil," I said.

Cass stared at me. "You could say that. You could say, poor all of us."

"But he stayed. He looked after you, materially at least. That's to his credit—"

"Oh, yes, he did that. He could hardly do anything else. He had no proof."

I said mildly, "You're a bit hard on him, love, aren't you?"

"He was hard on me."

"Yes, I know. That was cruel and unfair. But look at it from his point of view. Coming back to learn that his wife was in love with somebody else, his neighbors laughing at him, a new baby. At that time he couldn't have been sure whose child you were." Unwarily, I warmed to the argument. "There's a lot of excuse for him, isn't there? This is really your mother's fault, not his."

Cass said dangerously, "Are you suggesting she was lying?"

"Not necessarily—"

"Not necessarily! You're talking about *my mother*."

"Darling, people do lie, even the nicest of them. I told you—I like your mother very much. But it could still have been the way your father thought. I mean, you're his child all right, that's obvious now. But she could still have been unfaithful—"

"I wish she had been."

"What!"

"I wish she had been. I wish she'd had a proper love affair, something to remember. She's been paying and paying all these years, for something she never had, and so have I. I tell you, I wish she'd had it."

"What an extraordinary thing to say."

"You wouldn't think it extraordinary if you understood," said Cass, "but you don't. You're on his side. You're as worked up about it as if it were you it had happened to. You're *angry*."

"Yes," I said, "I suppose I am. That sort of thing makes me sick. If a woman can't stick to a man when he's away fighting—"

"He wasn't fighting. And he needn't have gone. Look. My mother fell in love. She couldn't help it. People *can't* help it. Could we help falling in love?"

"It's not quite the same—"

"Why? Because we're not married to other people? I don't see that it makes any difference."

"Oh, you don't. You don't think faithfulness matters."

"*I didn't say that!*"

"Don't shout," I said. "People are looking."

"Let them look, I don't care." But she lowered her voice, saying furiously, "Of course I think faithfulness matters. I'm just saying nobody can help falling in love, married or not."

I said, "I see. That makes a beautiful augury for the future, doesn't it?"

We faced each other across the table like enemies. Cass had gone very pale. She pushed her coffee cup away from her; she had hardly touched it. She muttered, "I hate this place. Let's go."

We had a rather silent journey home. It was almost dark when we got back to the flat, which looked alien and forbidding in its orderly, elegant emptiness. I thought, not for the first time, how it never really looked lived in, it was just a show window for my wares, that's all. The living room, with the curtains undrawn, was illuminated by the streetlights and neon signs outside. Cass went over to the window; she didn't draw the curtains, but just stood there, looking out into the

108

spangled dusk. I touched a switch, and she flinched as the light came on.

"Cass," I said.

"What?"

"I love you."

She turned at once, and her face came alive again. "Oh, darling, I know, and I love you too. I didn't mean to be horrible, it's just . . . well, I hoped for too much, going there with you. I thought things would be different, that I'd stop feeling bad about it. You see, I've got this thing about *belonging*, of being loved and trusted. I thought when you saw it all for yourself you'd be on my side. If I've got that, nothing else matters. I can even be generous, say poor old Dad, he can't help it, I understand. But *I've* got to say it, myself, don't you see that? If someone else says it for me, especially you . . . it just leaves me where I was before, out in the cold."

"Yes," I said. "I can see that. You think I've let you down, don't you? I didn't mean to, you know. We just had an argument, and it got away from us—"

"I know. It's some hang-up of your own, isn't it?"

I was silent. I did not want her perception, as she so much wanted mine.

"Two hang-ups in collision," she said soberly. "Perfect recipe for a fight. But there's a bit more to it, anyway. Nothing to do with you. Something I hate myself for."

I waited.

"I wanted to show you off to them."

"Show me *off*?" I was bewildered.

"My father's always believed I'd go what he calls to the bad. Living alone in London, singing in clubs . . . I mean, in his book, I'm half way there already. So I was bound to end up on drugs, or as a call girl, or having an illegitimate baby at the very least. So I wanted to impress him. I knew you would. You're so well-spoken, and you've obviously made it, with the expensive gear and everything. And I'm going to *marry* you . . . that's the important part, of course. Ridiculous, isn't it? After what I've said about marriage? And despicable, too. I'm ashamed," she said sadly.

109

I burst out laughing, and hugged her. "Darling, you are a funny little girl. That's a perfectly natural reaction, nothing to be ashamed of—"

"You really think so? Oh, well. I suppose the whole business always does tie me up in knots." After a moment she began to laugh too, though there was a hint of tears in her eyes. "Oh, dear. You have got a crazy mixed-up kid on your hands, haven't you? I only hope you won't regret it."

Seven

MADDY came to see me one day the following week. She turned up unexpectedly at the office toward the end of a busy morning and I wasn't best pleased. Still, I did have a bit of conscience about her. Absorbed in my own affairs, I hadn't been in touch with her since the Sunday Paul went away.

She seemed thinner than ever, dressed with the self-conscious smartness affected by women who visit London only rarely and feel somehow that they have to live up to it when they do. She had a sort of sharp-edged look.

"This is very nice, love," I said, "but I wish you had let me know. I could have given you lunch, but I've a date I can't get out of, I'm afraid."

"That's all right," said Maddy. "I should have telephoned. I've got a dental appointment today. Nearly forgot it and only just made the train so there was no time to phone." She sat down and pulled off her gloves—another countrywoman's touch, none of the girls I knew wore gloves—looked about her and said abruptly, "Heavens, what a very lush office this is. You do believe in doing yourselves well, don't you?"

This sounded like an echo of Hugo.

"My dear, we make furniture. We could hardly—"

"All right. I didn't come here to criticize. I want your advice, Greg. And help. I didn't want to phone you at home in the evening, I mean, you're not alone now, are you?"

"No. We're making it legal soon, by the way. Did Mother tell you?"

"She said you were getting married. I don't know whether

she knows that there's anything to make legal, but she acts as if she doesn't. You know Mother's attitude: do what you like, but always pretend you don't." She eyed me, and added politely, "Well. Congratulations, anyway."

I grinned. "Thanks. Well, what's doing? Are they still with you?"

"Mother and Russell? Not now. They took off again yesterday. I'm just getting my breath back."

I knew just what this meant. When Maddy had Mother and Russell to stay, she seemed to feel that she must provide the same standards of comfort, service and cooking that they would get in a first-class hotel. They accepted this graciously, as no more than their due, and Maddy would nearly run herself into the ground. I thought this ridiculous and had often said so, but it made no difference.

But of course, Maddy had not come to talk about them.

"How is Paul?" I asked.

"All right. I've heard. Just an air letter." She rummaged in her bag and came up with the letter. "Here."

"Do you really want me to read it?"

"There's nothing in it," said Maddy flatly, "that anybody couldn't read."

The thin blue sheet was crumpled, as if Maddy had crushed it in her hand. I smoothed it out. "Dear Madeleine," I read. "Just to let you know we arrived okay and are settling in. Everything very much a shambles at the moment but I daresay it will be sorted out soon. Don't forget to take the car to Cossors to have the brakes done. Hope the kids are well and being good. It's bloody hot here. Love Paul."

I handed it back to her. There were things I could have said: that thousands of perfectly faithful and affectionate husbands habitually wrote such letters to their wives; that it proved nothing, except that they weren't very good at writing letters.

I didn't say them. "You've heard again?" I asked.

She shook her head. "I wrote to him. It took me ages to put the letter together. I didn't exactly put all the cards on the table. But I did say I loved him and missed him and I was unhappy about the way things had been between us lately and was it my fault and . . . well, you know, the sort of letter that asks for a response. Well, I waited. I know I had to allow time for the letters to go to and fro . . . but it doesn't take long, airmail. Then I thought, maybe he's gone off somewhere, on safari, don't they call it? Then, yesterday, I had a phone call. From Dr. Frith, the head of the Institute. Paul had been through to *him.* On official business, I suppose. Anyway, he was very affable, Dr. Frith was, rang me to say Paul was fine, everything was fine, but he thought Paul a bit worried lest I was feeling lonely, and he and Mrs. Frith wanted me to come to dinner."

"That was nice of him," I ventured, "wasn't it?"

Maddy laughed without amusement.

"Ever so. It's clear you've never met the Friths, or been to one of their dinner parties. I expect he meant to be kind, but what's that got to do with it? I asked for bread, Greg. I was given a stone."

I was silent. Rather meanly, I felt a certain sympathy for Paul creeping up on me. I could imagine him, coping with a host of new problems, sweating in unaccustomed heat, reading Maddy's letter with dismay. Of course, all he had to do to make her happy was to write the words "I love you" on a cable form and give it to a clerk to send. Some men would do just that, fending things off for the time being. But not Paul. If he didn't mean those words he wouldn't send them. And in the same circumstances, neither would I.

I didn't know what I was supposed to do about all this. Apart from getting her feelings off her chest, I couldn't think what Maddy had come for. There wasn't much she could do except wait, as women usually have to—wait for time to sort things out, as it often does; or, perhaps, for the final, the irrevocable blow. Surely it wouldn't come to that? I thought gloomily about the children, of whom I was extremely fond.

I began, searching awkwardly for words, to counsel patience, but I didn't get very far.

"*Greg,*" Maddy said, "spare me that guff. It's practical help I want. If it's finished I have to think what to do next. I told you. I won't live with Paul, or live *on* him, if he doesn't love me."

For a moment, as she said this, that blindness that afflicts us all about the people nearest to us was lifted. I saw her as she really was, I recognized it all: the high temper, the chafing at inaction, the drive and will to act. I saw, of course, myself. We shared the same blood and the same inheritance, Maddy and I.

"So I have to be ready," she was saying.

"Ready for what?"

"For when he comes home. Don't think I shan't give him a chance. I love him. I still have a bit of hope, not much, but a little . . . but if we have to split up," she added with that terrible energy which was beginning to alarm me, "then I want it to be *clean*. No temptation for me to blackmail him about his responsibilities. No arguments about money. No horrid business about Celia Ross helping to pay the alimony. It'll be hell, I know, but at least I'll come out of it with some dignity—"

"You mean you'd just go, and take the children?"

"Just that."

I said gently, "Maddy, they *are* his children too, you know. He loves them. And they love him."

A tremor passed over her face and was gone. "They'll see as much of him as they do now, which isn't much—"

I said, "Look, Maddy. It's time we brought a bit of common sense into this. You haven't thought it out, love, the legal position, everything. Do you really realize what it means to leave Paul, get a place of your own, support the children?"

Her face was closed, stubborn. "Of course I have. I just need some money to get started."

"Well," I said. "There's always Mother—"

"Are you mad? You know I'd never go to Mother for help, I haven't even told her. They wouldn't help anyway, just interfere. Can't you imagine what Russell would do? He'd be doing the stuffy father act in no time, writing what he'd call a 'stiff letter' to Paul, something awful like that. I won't have them brought into it, I won't . . ."

114

"All right, all right. But what's the alternative?"

"There's Grandma's money," Maddy said, "my shares in Hunter's."

"You mean, I could buy you out? But I couldn't love, not at the moment. Well, I suppose I could if I had to; if I were convinced you were doing the right thing. Which, at the moment, I'm not."

"So you won't help me."

"I didn't say that. But it doesn't make sense to help you do something you'll probably regret. You're not even really sure yet what's happened, or what's going to happen. Paul will be away for some time yet. Surely there's no frantic hurry? Can't we leave it, wait and see for a bit?"

Maddy gave me a look which I couldn't interpret, and seemed, suddenly, to surrender. "Yes. All right." She began putting her gloves back on again. "I'd better go. Sorry I've taken up so much of your time."

"*Maddy,*" I said.

"What?"

"Don't be like that."

She smiled faintly. "I'm not being like anything. When's the wedding going to be?"

"A fortnight on Saturday. Will you come?"

"If you'd like me to. I thought maybe you wouldn't want anybody."

"We didn't, really. But it got away from us and now it's turning into the usual tribal rite. On a small scale, of course. Register office, lunch afterwards. Mother and Russell are coming, and Hugo, and Cass's family, if they make it. I'm not sure about that yet; they're an odd bunch. If you could manage to come I'd be glad. It would help things along a little."

"Yes. All right. I'm not very good company just now, but I'll come."

I went downstairs with her. I felt uncomfortable, wanting to get rid of her and yet reluctant to let her go. On impulse I said, "Maddy, don't go back tonight. Come to dinner at the flat and stay over. I'd like you to meet Cass—"

"I can't do that. I'd love to, of course, but I can't. Helga's

115

scared of staying alone in the house at night, just with the children. Greg," she stopped on the stairs, and added in a rush, "I'd rather you didn't tell her—Cass, is it?—about Paul and me. I haven't met her yet, I'd rather it wasn't the first thing she knows about me."

"All right, if you want it that way. She's a very sympathetic girl, you know; you'll tell her yourself sometime, I daresay."

"I shall probably have to." She regarded me gravely. "You're very happy, aren't you? I'm glad somebody is."

At that moment Hugo appeared, and greeted Maddy enthusiastically: "My dear Madeleine, how nice to see you. And how lovely you look."

I looked at my watch. I was due to leave for my appointment, and anyway I couldn't stand Hugo when he was doing his chatting up the birds bit—he tried so hard and so ponderously that it was embarrassing. Still, it seemed to work with Maddy, who visibly perked up a little. She needed some masculine fuss made of her, poor Maddy, something that brotherly affection couldn't provide.

"I suppose you two are going out to lunch," Hugo said.

I shook my head. "I have an appointment. Maddy came unexpectedly."

"Well, that's a pretty miserable state of affairs," Hugo exclaimed. "You'd better come out to lunch with me, Madeleine." Maddy cried that that would be a wonderful idea and she'd just love it. I looked at her with astonishment while she transformed herself instantly from the tense unhappy creature who had been sitting in my office into a woman sparkling with charm for a man's benefit. They went off together very merrily, Hugo's hand on Maddy's elbow as if guiding her tiny steps.

Watching them go, I felt rather uneasy; but I hadn't the faintest idea why.

This episode wasn't the only thing to make me uneasy along then. The night before we were married, Cass and I met Jay Fisher.

I had been taking her to the club every night during the

past weeks, and, against her protests, picking her up again when her second spot was over. It was not a way of life I could have kept up for very long, but fortunately I didn't have to. Cass was leaving the Silver Rhino, and tomorrow, after the wedding, we would leave for Scotland, where a friend of mine had lent me his cottage in the Highlands. I didn't usually take holidays, just snatching a few days off now and again to go sailing, but that would hardly do for Cass. I had thought she might want a holiday in the sun, complete with palm trees and tropical beaches, but she only said, "I don't care where we go, so long as I'm with you."

"It's pretty primitive," I warned her. "A bit like camping. Miles from anywhere, and it just might rain all the time."

"So long as the roof doesn't leak, I shouldn't think that matters. And miles from anywhere—that's just what we want, isn't it?"

So it was with a sense of relief and peace that I took her down to the club that last evening, and stayed to listen. She was great that evening, radiant with her newfound joy and confidence, and I was full up with pride in her. Then I noticed this man, sitting alone at a table not far from me. He was giving Cass his full attention; well, so was everyone else, but the quality of his attention was different, detached, judging, the look of a connoisseur. He applauded vigorously when she had finished, then he called the waiter over. Presently I saw Dominic, the manager, leaning over his table. They both glanced a couple of times in my direction and presently the man at the table got up and they both came over to me. Dominic introduced us. I remember we both laughed over the comical juxtaposition of our names—Hunter, Fisher—and that broke the ice a bit. He was a squat, dark little man, fortyish, beginning to run to fat, with a mobile ugly face and an engaging grin which made him oddly attractive. I had a feeling I had seen him before somewhere.

He started off by saying he'd been told we were going to be married. "May I congratulate you, Mr. Hunter? You're a lucky man, if I may say so."

"I know it," I said.

117

"This young lady of yours has a very unusual talent. And a great future, I'd say, and believe me, I know what I'm talking about."

"It's nice of you to say so. Cass will be flattered."

He stared at me, and laughed softly. "You don't know who I am, do you?"

I said nicely that I hadn't that pleasure, and he chuckled again and said, "It's easy to see you're not in show business. I'm a manager. Among other things."

"Oh, I see." Now I remembered: an article in a Sunday color supplement. Of course. The title of the feature had been "The Star Maker." So that's who he was.

"I've taken the liberty of asking your little girl to come out and talk to me. But I thought I'd like a chat with you first. Seeing"—the engaging grin flashed on and off—"you're now the most important person in her life. And the biggest influence."

"Well," I said, "I hope so."

"You're not going to take her away from us? She won't give up her career?"

I started to say that we hadn't thought about that yet, when Cass appeared. She looked both excited and a bit shy. If I hadn't known first go who Jay Fisher was, she certainly did. I watched and listened while he talked to her, drawing her out. His attitude was a nice blend of flattery and serious, constructive criticism. He made her feel important, that he was eagerly interested in her, and at the same time—don't ask me how he did it—contrived to convey that his interest in her was a great honor. He didn't ignore me, either, I was drawn into the conversation, my probably worthless opinion asked. At one point Cass began to tell him what a help I had been to her the night we first met. He turned to me and said amiably, "You're too modest, Mr. Hunter. Gave me the impression you didn't know anything about this business."

"I don't," I said shortly. "I'm in the furniture trade." God, why did this have to happen, tonight of all nights? Fame and fortune, here they come, I'd said to her that first night, but it was just a flattering, nice thing to say, something to please her. I hadn't wanted to believe it. Now, on the night before

118

we were to be married, here he was, this ugly, powerful little man. He could make her dreams come true, and alter the course of both our lives. Enter the Demón King; I could almost smell the brimstone.

"The fact is, Mr. Fisher," I said, "I haven't really much idea what people like you do."

This wasn't strictly true, but I wanted him to spell it out, what he was going to do to us.

"Call me Jay," he said. "Well, let's put it this way. You must know that in entertainment these days, anyone who makes the big time counts their audience in millions. So the days of going it alone, hoping for the lucky break, are over. Talent's a commodity. To sell it you must develop it, package and promote it, find outlets for it—"

"Like detergent," I suggested dryly.

He nodded good-humoredly. "If you like. The method's a bit different, but you can put it that way. Now take"—he mentioned a pop singer whose name was a household word—"five years ago that girl was a nice little bundle of puppy fat with a good rhythm sense and a big noisy voice. She belted out every number at the top of her lungs because that was the only way she knew. She had personality, but left to herself she would have been a rocket, up one day, down the next. As it is, because she's been handled right, she's at the top and staying there, she's a real pro, a real artist—"

I said, "Cass is a real artist now."

Jay Fisher smiled and said of course, of course she is, he wasn't suggesting otherwise; but he looked rather hard at me just the same. It seemed as if we had both forgotten Cass, that she was there, I mean, in the way in which two men fighting over a woman might easily forget her in the heat of the battle, in the blows given and received.

But Cass was still very much there. Her hand stole into mine under the table and she turned on me a look of such love and trust and candor that my anger and anxiety were immediately dissipated. Then she leaned forward and said gently, "Mr. Fisher—"

"Jay," he said genially.

She smiled and repeated, "Jay—there's something I want

119

to say. I don't know whether I'm a real artist or not. I know I have a lot to learn, and I'm grateful for your interest in me. But"—she looked up at him, very directly—"I still have to do my own thing my own way. And if I thought I was likely to be, well, manipulated, I'd have to get out from under before I ever got started."

I thought, that settles it. He will now dismiss her from his calculations and say amiably that it was nice meeting us.

But in fact he was looking at her with an amused and wary respect. He said softly, "Character, I see, as well as talent. Message received loud and clear. All right, my dear."

Cass's sudden access of fluency seemed to have left her. She murmured awkwardly, "I'm sorry—"

Jay Fisher laughed. "There's nothing to be sorry about. I suppose you're off on honeymoon tomorrow. Come and see me when you get back. How long will you be away?"

"Three weeks," I said quickly. Cass opened her mouth to speak and I squeezed her hand hard and she didn't say anything. Jay Fisher took out his diary and fixed an appointment, and then he insisted on ordering champagne, whether to celebrate our meeting or to wish us joy wasn't very clear; and Dominic, seeing all this I suppose, went to the microphone and announced that Cass was leaving that night and getting married in the morning, and she was someone they'd all be seeing a lot more of, and it was au revoir and not good-bye, nonsense like that; and he had the spotlight turned on our table, and the people raised their glasses to us. It was rather nice, really. We went home a bit high on the champagne, pleased with ourselves, Cass inclined to giggle.

Indoors, the euphoria left me. It had seemed to me, briefly, that we had won something; but we hadn't won anything, or I hadn't. The Demon King was still with us.

Cass, too, sobered suddenly. "Greg, is it all right?"

"What makes you think it isn't?"

"Something you said to him. We're only going away for ten days. You told him three weeks."

"That was just so as to have you to myself for a little longer. Before the balloon goes up."

She said uneasily, "Is that the way you see it?"

"Cass, listen. At heart I expect I'm as much of a male chauvinist pig as the rest of mankind. I won't pretend I wouldn't rather your heart wasn't set on such a demanding career—or on a career at all. But it's what you want, isn't it?"

She nodded soberly. "I'm afraid so. But I don't want to spoil things—"

"Neither do I. I knew how things were when I asked you to marry me. It's what I settled for. I want you to be happy, Cass. So don't let's say any more about it."

Saying this, basking in her look of love and gratitude, I felt rather noble, wise, and tolerant.

Getting oneself married is so quick and easy, I sometimes think it shouldn't be. At twelve o'clock the following day our wedding guests gathered at the register office: my mother, Russell, Maddy, Hugo, Ben and Liz; and Cass's parents, who had elected to come, after all. In about five minutes flat, it seemed, Cass and I had called them all to witness that we took each other for husband and wife, I put the ring on, we signed the register, and submitted to the usual embraces and congratulations. Cass was very nervous all through. Well, brides are supposed to be nervous, though you could hardly call Cass a bride in the usual sense of the word.

Maybe it was having her parents there, though, strangely enough, it seemed to have more to do with Maddy, the only person in that group whom Cass had not met before. While we were waiting to go into the registrar's room Maddy was being very vivacious in that new sharp way of hers and it seemed to me, when the two girls were introduced, there was a kind of tension there, almost hostility. Well, I knew very well what was eating Maddy, who felt hostile, I daresay, to all the world and would be feeling sad, and envious of Cass and me. Cass was quick to pick up that kind of thing. Anyway, perhaps there is some kind of sister-in-law syndrome, Maddy had never liked Tessa much. I don't know. You never can tell with women.

Not that any of that mattered. Only the wedding lunch to get through and then we could make our escape. Considering what an ill-assorted lot they were, it didn't go too badly.

121

As often happens on these occasions, no social effort is required from the people most concerned. Cass and I could sit back and observe the others, with, on my part at least, a certain ironic amusement. Maddy was getting so much tender attention from Hugo that I began to wonder what he thought he was up to; Mrs. Clayton, shy as ever, relaxed wonderfully with some kindly cherishing from Ben and Liz; Cass had briefed them to do just that, I expect. Russell shed beams of genial authority, and old Clayton, thawed by wine and my mother's charm, became quite affable, and even cracked a joke or two.

Cass recovered and began to show some of the bride's traditional radiance. As we drove away afterwards she was garrulous with relief. It reminded me of the day we met, when she had just turned her car over; she had, as it were, survived.

"Well!" she cried. "It was all right, wasn't it?"

"Of course. Did you think it wouldn't be?"

"I wasn't sure. I was afraid they wouldn't get on with each other, I suppose. Did you see my father? He was positively jolly. How on earth does she do it?" she asked, meaning my mother.

"Talent," I said. "And lots of practice, of course."

She said softly, with that percipience I sometimes found unnerving, "Don't sound so *disapproving*."

"Do I sound disapproving?"

"Darling, you know you do. Well, she's hardly the standard mother figure, is she? But you must admit she's absolutely gorgeous and remarkable. You should be proud of her."

"Oh, I do. And I am. It's just that neither Maddy nor I are very close to her. Pity, but a fact."

"It's sad, though, isn't it?"

"I don't know about sad. We're used to it."

"I didn't mean sad for you," said Cass unexpectedly. "I meant sad for her. Especially if you and Maddy sort of ganged up. And you *are* very close, aren't you?"

"Maddy and I? I suppose we are. Not very usual for a brother and sister, but the circumstances made it like that. How did you make out with her?"

122

"I don't really know. There wasn't much opportunity."
I didn't want the girls to get off on the wrong foot and thought of telling her about Maddy's troubles. I knew that story would engage her ready sympathy. But I'd promised Maddy to keep my mouth shut, so I let it go. It would all sort itself out some time. I really couldn't be bothered with it now.

We fetched up at Ian's cottage in the early evening of the following day, having picked up stores and the key from the village shop, three miles away at least.

When we got out of the car, Cass looked around her and drew a deep breath. "Greg, it's heavenly."

"What did I tell you?" I said.

It was a fine evening; strangely, we had that sort of weather almost all the time we were there. The cottage was small, whitewashed, tucked into the side of the mountain, facing a small loch which this evening reflected a cloudless burnished sky. On either side of us the great hills marched away in the regal splendor of their summer colors—purple and green and gold. There wasn't a sound except for the curlews overhead and the cry of a sheep heard faintly, far away. All the pressures and demands of urban living fell away from us; it was like being alone on the top of the world.

As I've said, the cottage lacked conveniences, but even the chores, so remote from ordinary life, had charm for us. We fetched our water from the well, we cooked with canned gas, and collected kindling for the fire we made each evening when the long northern twilight set in and the temperature fell. We explored on foot or in the car, idled and sunbathed in the heather, and sometimes made love there, with only the curlews to see us and they didn't care. We woke to magnificent dawns after nights of love, and got up to look at them, shivering in the dawn chill, and laughed at ourselves for doing it, surely we must want our heads examined; and scrambled back into bed, staying close to get warm, and slept late after all, wrapped in each other's arms.

Apart from the little scullery where we washed the dishes and ourselves and did the cooking, there was only one room in the cottage. The double bed was there, tucked into an alcove in traditional Scots fashion. The original flagged floor had been boarded over and strewn with bright, coarse-woven rugs. There were a couple of armchairs, Ian's desk, a table and chairs for eating, shelves crammed with books, and that's all. I can see it now, that plain whitewashed room, as it was in the evenings after we had eaten: wood crackling in a cheerful blaze on the hearth, Cass curled up on the hearth rug, cupping a glass of wine in her hands. Quite a lot of the time we sat silent, in peace and communion, listening to music from the transistor radio we'd brought. Sometimes the radio spoke of news in the outside world, of disasters, fires, hijackings and bombs. We turned it off then. That was the real world; selfishly, we didn't want it any nearer. Occasionally I thought about Hunter's, wondered what Hugo and Russell were up to, and once spoke of going down to the village to telephone the office; but I didn't go, I didn't want to break the spell, and neither did she, for all her dreams and ambitions. On our last evening, I remember, Cass sighed and said, "I wish we could stay here forever and ever."

I laughed. "We've probably struck the best fortnight of the year here. We'd be snowbound in the winter, don't forget."

"No problem," she said dreamily. "We'd get in loads of stores and canned gas and logs and wine. And do the weekly shopping on skis, with a sled to carry the things—"

"And trudge out to the frozen loo—and break up ice to get water for a cup of coffee. And you can't even ski. Come off it, my love. Civilization calls. I have to go back to Hunter's and you to a dazzling new career." I could say that easily, far away as we were now, in the mountains.

"I may be kidding myself about that. It may not come to anything."

Yes, I thought, she could be right. And she'd be very disappointed, and I would comfort her. And then she might settle down, to be my wife and the mother of my children, and be content. It could be. In the peace and harmony of that wonderful place, where we had been so happy, it did seem as if anything was possible; that things might, after all, go my way.

That night, the wind changed. It rained, the first rain since

124

we arrived. We woke to hear it hammering on the roof, to a dark morning, the mountaintops wrapped in cloud. As we drove southward it rained all day, sometimes so hard I could hardly see through the windshield.

The honeymoon was over.

Eight

So WE came back from Scotland, as I've said, and settled down to married life. Of course, we had been together before; but it's curious how the ritual, the formality of marriage made a powerful difference. Before, it had been a delight to be together, true, in the little time snatched out of every twenty-four hours, between the demands of my work and hers; but living like that had been hectic, transitory. Now we had an established, permanent base, something to build on. Cass had given up her flat and moved her stuff, such as it was—there wasn't much—into mine. There was this respite I had won from Jay Fisher's attentions, and she had finished with the Silver Rhino, so she was around for me to come home to, and our evenings were our own, to spend peacefully by ourselves or go out somewhere, to entertain or be entertained, unimpeded by Cass having to leave for the club, Cinderella-like, at half-past ten every night.

I think she quite enjoyed being the married lady of leisure for a bit. We had already decided to move if we could find a suitable house, and she went around following up some of the dazzling descriptions the estate agents sent us. She got a lot of fun out of doing the cooking, too; with more money to spend on food she shopped and experimented more adventurously. Apart from the cooking, though, she really wasn't at all domesticated. So far as the routine things went, it didn't matter, as Mrs. Cross continued to come; but I was surprised to find that she was entirely lacking in that feminine desire to change things around, to make a nest, as it were. I urged her to do anything she liked with the flat, but she only looked vague, and said it was lovely as it was. "I'm no good at that sort of thing, Greg. I'm terribly ignorant, really. I should

127

probably buy something ghastly that would jar on you . . ."
Yet she left her mark on the place, just the same. She simply
lived in it; so that my handsome paralyzed living room was
scattered with books and newspapers and music scores and
record sleeves, and came alive at last. I found I liked that. We
were very happy. I would have liked it to go on that way forever, though I knew quite well it wasn't going to.

At Hunter's, it was different. I knew something was up the
moment I returned: there was tension in the air. Carol on
the reception desk had lost her usual bright smile and said
good morning sullenly, avoiding my eye. When I got upstairs
I found Mrs. Ferguson typing at high speed and looking distinctly harassed. She only stopped long enough to say good
morning and that the mail was on my desk and: "Mr. Tarrant's in your office, Mr. Hunter. Waiting for you."

Robin, our designer. He only worked part-time for us and
his hours were flexible; I'd never known him to appear this
early.

"What's the matter with him?" I asked.

"I'm afraid I don't know, Mr. Hunter."

I said mildly, "You know, you're supposed to protect me
from importunate visitors. Especially first thing in the morning."

Mrs. Ferguson looked at me coldly. She said stiffly, "I'm
very sorry, Mr. Hunter. But short of throwing him out bodily, which you will appreciate I am not capable of doing, there
was nothing to do but let him stay."

I had never known her to talk like that before.

Robin was pacing up and down my office like the caged
lion which, in a way, he resembled. He was a massive young
man, extravagantly adorned with golden hair—a curling
mane, lavish beard, and whiskers through which he seemed
to peer with blue eyes usually as mild and innocent as a
child's. However, at the moment the mildness was in abey-
ance: as soon as the door was closed he burst out, without
even a greeting, "Look Greg, if you want me out, just say so.
Don't send your stepfather to give me the treatment."

I sat down at my desk. "Robin, what *are* you talking
about?"

"He seems to think I spend my time here loafing," said Robin bitterly. "I explained that I work half the week here and half in my own studio, and he said didn't that make for divided loyalties, and I said what loyalties, I work for Hunter's for the regular bread and because it interests me, and that's all there is to that. So then he wanted to know—all in the interests of efficiency or productivity or something—how I spent my day here, hour to hour, sort of. Well I tried to explain how I worked and then I thought, sod it, why should I, so I told him the story about the scientist and the time-and-motion expert . . ."

"Which is?"

"You must know it. The scientist didn't know what to say about how he spent his day so he just wrote down, 9 a.m. to 1 p.m., thinking; 1 p.m. to 2 p.m., lunch; 2 p.m. to 5 p.m., thinking."

I burst out laughing. Robin peered at me through his thickets of hair and mumbled, "You don't know a thing about all this, do you? I should have known. Sorry."

When Robin, pacified, had gone, I sat on at my desk staring thoughtfully at the folder of mail placed in the exact center of the blotter. Outside, Mrs. Ferguson's typewriter went on and on. I riffled through the mail, pushed the papers aside and called her in.

"Will you let me into a secret?" I asked. "What's all the panic about out there? It can't be anything you're doing for me."

"Oh!" She colored faintly, as if caught out in some misdemeanor. "That's Mr. Cornforth's work—"

"Oh, yes? And what work is that?"

She glanced at me, her expression reflecting her thought: Mr. Hunter in one of his funny moods.

"It's a confidential memorandum for you. He wanted it to be on your desk first thing, but I'm afraid I couldn't manage that. It's rather long and . . . he didn't start dictating it," she added with an unwonted air of grievance, "until five o'clock on Friday." She hesitated, then went on resolutely: "I thought perhaps, if you approve, I should arrange to engage a secretary for Mr. Cornforth. Or a temporary typist—"

"Temporary," I said. "Yes."

129

"I have to get on to the agency today anyway. About a new receptionist."

"A new what?"

"Receptionist. Carol is leaving."

"Is she now. And what's *that* about?"

"I think," said Mrs. Ferguson, looking past my ear, "you should ask Mr. Cornforth that."

"I see. Where is Mr. Cornforth this morning?"

"He's gone down to the works, I think—"

I said involuntarily, "Oh, Christ." Mrs. Ferguson pretended not to hear; she was plainly embarrassed by the whole thing. "Now look," I said. "Don't worry any more about that memo."

She said uncomfortably, "I did undertake to do it, Mr. Hunter—"

"So you shall. When you have time. But I'm back now, and you work for me, nobody else. Is that understood?"

"But of course. I'm sorry—"

"Don't be sorry. It's not your fault. But if Mr. Cornforth asks you to do anything else for him, refer him to me. Well, we'll get on then, shall we?"

All the same, when I came back from lunch that day Russell's memorandum was on my desk: four foolscap pages, closely typed, copy to Hugo. It was headed: "Some First Thoughts on Management Problems."

Life with Russell had begun.

I didn't see him all day, which was just as well, but I did have a talk with Hugo, who said with an air of patience: "Well, you tell me what I ought to have done about it. I had to find him something to do for the time being—till we could sort things out—so I suggested that he should look around, and come up with some ideas."

"The fresh eye, like you said? A sort of one-man management consultancy?"

"Something like that . . . actually, that's what he thinks we need. You've read the report?"

"Enough of it to see he's going to become a God-awful nuisance if we're not careful."

Hugo exclaimed, "Look, Greg, it's no good taking up that attitude. There's a lot of good sense in that report. I think Russell can be an asset to us. I don't know why you resent him so much—"

"And I don't know why you're so much in love with him all of a sudden. He's a meddler. He upsets the staff. And we need management consultants like we need a hole in the head."

Hugo sighed. "I'd better warn you. He'll show up at the next Board meeting, with the proposals in that memo. I suppose it's too much to expect that you won't shoot them down, but you have to recognize Russell has a sizable interest in the company, he's a full member of the Board through nobody's fault but our own. And there's the family connection as well. We've got to live with him, so we might as well make the best of it—"

"All right," I said. "All of which is no reason why we should sit back and let him wreck the joint. And you, my dear Hugo, had better be sure which side you're on."

Hugo looked offended. "That's childish. I don't take sides."

"You may have to," I said.

Cass, finding her way uncertainly over unfamiliar ground, said, "Darling, I can see it's difficult. But we can't not have them here. I mean, there's your mother and . . . well, they kind of expect it. Anyway, mightn't it be a good idea?"

She was sitting on the floor, a habit of hers, gazing at me with big-eyed, solemn concern about my problems, absorbed in them and in me. I'm not going to pretend I didn't delight in that. I was lying with the back of my neck on the sofa, we were having drinks before dinner, a promising aroma came from the kitchen. This was surely one of the best moments of the day, with all its past irritations soothed away just by being with her.

"I just thought," she went on eagerly, "we wouldn't ask anyone else, just the two of them, and give them a nice meal in a relaxed atmosphere, with some music and that . . . and after dinner you and Russell could have a friendly chat over

131

a brandy and sort things out, while your mother and I retired from the scene—"

She broke off, seeing the grin spreading over my face.

"My dear love, my mother never retires from any scene while there's anything still going on in it. Besides, where would you go? The bedroom? The kitchen, doing the washing up? And Russell and I have had our chat. Not all that friendly either."

Cass's face fell. "You think I'm being silly—"

"No, I don't. You're very wise and wonderful and diplomatic and absolutely right. We'll ask them. Only you're not to get steamed up about it, and do your nut over the dinner. Don't let them intimidate you."

She looked surprised. "They don't intimidate me," she said.

So Mother and Russell came to dinner—Russell, I think, faintly surprised at being asked. The meal was simple but good, and served without fuss. I carried dishes in, dispensed drinks beforehand, poured the wine, casting myself in the role of supporting player and letting Cass run the show her way. I watched with pride and amusement as she handled both of them beautifully, her manner just touched with a gentle deference—deference, one felt, to age, not to money or status. They weren't easily pleased as a rule, but they purred, they loved it, delighted with her and pleasantly surprised to find me so genial with them. I could imagine Mother saying to Russell afterward how much more relaxed Greg is these days, that girl has done wonders with him.

After dinner Mother asked Cass to sing for us. I knew that like most professional performers, Cass really rather disliked doing this, but she made no fuss, went directly to the piano, drew a few soft minor chords from the keys, and began to sing a song I hadn't heard before.

I can see that scene now: the dusk of a summer evening, one lamp lit above the piano, the glimmer of Cass's white dress and her lovely voice singing about loneliness and a love turned sour. There were tears in my mother's eyes. When Cass had finished, Mother, always given to extravagant gestures, got up in a flurry and embraced her.

132

"My dear child, that was beautiful, quite beautiful. But what a very sad song that is."

"Most of my songs are sad," Cass said. "I don't know why. They just come out that way. But I'm glad you like it."

"You write them yourself?" Russell asked.

"Mostly. Not all."

Russell began at once to say that a talent like that, quite remarkable, mustn't be wasted. "What about it, Greg? She could make a fortune for you, my boy." This remark irritated me exceedingly.

"What you need," Russell went on, "is a boost up—"

"Yes," Cass said. "Well, there is somebody interested. But I don't know yet whether anything will come of it."

Then, of course, he had to know who this somebody was, and of course, he had heard of Jay Fisher, but he wasn't the only fish in that pond, ha ha, no pun intended, and if it didn't come to anything, perhaps he, Russell could help; he had a lot of contacts in the entertainment business. I daresay it was true, Russell had a lot of contacts everywhere.

"Yes," said Cass. "It's very kind of you. We shall just have to see."

She managed to convey, with the utmost delicacy, the message that it was none of Russell's business. Typically, he took no notice, and went on booming away, until my mother, looking from one to the other of us, said, "Russell, I think it's time we went home. A wonderful evening, my dears. Bless you both . . ."

When they had gone and the door shut behind them, I went to get myself another drink. Cass came up behind me, put her arms around my waist and leaned her head against me. "Darling . . ."

"What?"

"Don't mind him."

"No," I said. "All right."

"He is irritating. I can see that. I'm afraid the evening didn't achieve quite what I hoped—"

"Don't worry about that. It went over great. Only it would take more than that to make Russell and me see eye to eye. It's that way he has of muscling in on everything—"

133

"My mother?" Cass said. "My business? My wife?"

I swung around to look at her. "What do you mean? That I'm morbidly possessive, is that it?"

"Not *morbidly*—"

"Look," I said, "Russell is a pest. He gets on my nerves. It's natural enough. Why do you have to start looking for some peculiarity in me to explain it?"

"I'm not. Darling, I'm on your side. I just want to understand—"

"There's nothing to understand. And not everybody wants to be understood, anyway."

"I do," said Cass simply.

"Well, we're not all the bloody same, are we?"

Cass went rather pale. She said quietly, "I suppose not. I'm sorry." She gathered the coffee cups on to a tray and went off with them into the kitchen. Remorseful, because she had tried so hard over that evening, been so beautiful and good, I went out there after her and we made it up. If there was anything to make up. It was just a little spat, a common enough occurrence in the early days of marriage. I don't exactly know why I've remembered it; because, perhaps, it represents a link in some sort of chain.

Cass kept her appointment with Jay Fisher, but nothing very startling happened for a bit. She was still around in the evening and what she did during the day naturally didn't impinge on my life much. She spent a lot of time with a voice coach: "Jay says I've got what he calls a touch of the operatics; it's my early training. He's quite right, I can hear it myself." I had a feeling that everything that Jay said was going to be right, from now on. She worked at home quite a lot, too, with the new piano I had given her for a wedding present, recording herself and playing the tapes back, listening critically to the disembodied voice as if it belonged to someone else. She was sent off to a Mayfair hairdresser who wanted to give her one of those "twenties" hairdos, all over frizzy curls, but fortunately for my feelings she resisted that. Photographs were taken, and although she hadn't done anything since she left the Silver Rhino, pictures of her, and little

134

pieces about her, began to appear, as if by magic, in the show-biz columns of the national press.

She saw less of Jay Fisher than I expected. Jay had many other interests beside his stable of young talent, and was often away somewhere. So Cass had more to do with a sidekick of his, a young woman called Emma Gilmore. She brought Emma back with her one evening; or, I suspect, Emma invited herself. Anyway, there she was when I got home, perched on the sofa with a drink in her hand, and the two girls talking away. Emma was very pretty and excessively self-assured; when we were introduced she fluttered her long eyelashes at me, not really in a come-on way, but, it seemed, as a sort of routine flattery. She had come, she said presently, to invite us to what she called Jay's Summer Party—she said it like that, in capital letters—at his house in the country near Maidenhead. "Cass wasn't sure you'd care for it, so I came along to help persuade you."

I couldn't think why she thought she could persuade me if Cass couldn't or why Jay couldn't do his inviting himself. It's always seemed faintly offensive to me, the way some people have of relaying invitations through secretaries and assistants. It makes me react in a sort of blunt, crass way and I said, "What's it all about, then?"

"Oh, it's quite informal, Sunday brunch . . . bring swim things, there's a nice pool . . . you must come, there'll be all sorts of interesting people there . . ."

"Those who get their names in print and their faces on the box?"

Emma's face stiffened; she knew I was making fun of her.

"I suppose you could say that."

"What happens if it rains?"

"It never does rain," Emma announced, "the day of Jay's party."

When she'd gone, Cass and I looked at each other and laughed.

"Whew!" I said. "Does she think he's got a hot line to the Almighty?"

Cass shrugged and said placidly, "She's in love with him."

"With Jay Fisher?"

"Why not? Jay's little and ugly and running to seed a bit, but he's very attractive to women. There's a sort of magnetism about him. Even I can see that. Quite objectively, of course," she added hastily, with a twinkle at me.

"Yes. Well, mind it stays that way. Are they having an affair?" I asked idly.

"That, I wouldn't know. I just know she's quite besotted about him, but it isn't mutual . . . well, he's run through two wives already, perhaps he's just being cautious. Anyway, are we going to this thing?"

"I don't see why not," I said. "It might be fun."

Nine

RATHER annoyingly, Emma's weather prophecy turned out
to be exact: the day of Jay's party there was not a cloud in the
sky. The house was both old and beautiful, surrounded by
velvet lawns, shady walks, a profusion of roses. There were
the expected well-known faces, a great many pretty girls, a
vast buffet and a seemingly inexhaustible supply of drink.
Emma, looking very elegant, was flying importantly about,
supervising waiters, making herself agreeable, playing a role
halfway between a hostess and some sort of female butler.
There were also two large men who did their best to mingle
unobtrusively among the guests—a sign of the times.

In the midst of all this was Jay himself, playing the squire
with two Afghan hounds at his heels. Tubby and benign in a
loudly patterned shirt, espadrilles on bare feet, and his flabby gut spilling from the top of his pants, he should have
looked absurd. But he didn't look absurd: he had presence.
This is what Cass had meant, speaking of him to me.

Some time in the afternoon I found him beside me, my
turn, I suppose, to be chatted up by the genial host.

"Lovely place you have here," I said, and he kindled at
once.

"Isn't it? Saved by the bell, you might say, from the devel-
opers; I just got here in time. Have you seen around the inside? Come on then, I'll show you. Don't disturb your little
one, she can see it some other time." Cass was stretched out
in the sun by the pool; already brown from our trip to Scotland, she was now toasting herself to a deeper shade of cin-
namon. She opened one eye, grinned sleepily and waved us
away.

Jay and I went off together. He led me from room to room, all exquisitely restored, decorated and furnished by some firm of experts, I guessed. Some good original paintings hung on the walls. Jay gestured toward them. "Pretty, aren't they? Good investment, they say, but I don't buy 'em just for that. I mean, I've got to like them. Won't have some art expert telling me something's good when it gives me a pain to look at it." He went on talking knowledgeably about the house, its history, the problems he had had with modernization. At a long window on the upper floor he paused, his hand on my arm. "Take a look at that, now. You won't find a finer view than that anywhere in the south of England."

I looked out on long lawns falling away gently to the water meadows, the river gleaming in the afternoon sun, trees heavy with summer leaf, a blue untrammeled distance.

"Far cry from Whitechapel," said Jay. "Eh? That's where I come from. Evacuated here—a village over that way—when war broke out. Nine years old I was, scared out of my wits, wanting me mum, and inclined to wet the bed. But I got to like it, the country. Some time or other I saw this house, and I thought then—I was still just a nipper, eleven years old—I'll have a house like it one day. Never thought it would be *this* house. But it came on the market just at the right time, I had to have it. So there it is. A dream come true." His voice deepened and softened and the cockney sibilants, usually ironed out in his classless, mid-Atlantic tones, were hissing away.

Faintly embarrassed, I said, "That must give you a lot of satisfaction."

"Oh, it does," said Jay. "It does. There's luck in it, of course, there has to be some luck. Being in the right place at the right time—in my case, with the groups. I was in right at the beginning of that boom. The money rolled in and we all had a good time and some people saw it lasting forever. But I thought to myself, nothing lasts forever, so I diversified. Groups came and went, some of them sank without trace, some made a fortune. But one day they'll all go, altogether—like vaudeville, and the big bands—musical comedy too—all

138

that twinkle toes, top-hat-and-tails stuff, remember? Ah, you're too young."

"So are you," I put in dryly.

He gave a crow of laughter, caught out in affectation. "Got me there, haven't you? Well, anyway, there it is. The passing show. Carrying with it the dreams and the hopes and fears of everyone involved, and most of them lost and forgotten in ten years."

"Yes," I said. "And so?"

I had met with this ploy before: the sudden expansiveness, innocent and confiding. They told you the story of their lives, these boys, they sent themselves up, they were rueful and self-critical. I can tell *you*, they seemed to say, what I'm really like behind the mask of power and success, I can trust *you*. A subtle form of flattery, designed to make you relax, open up, become vulnerable.

"Where was I?" said Jay. "Oh, yes . . . there's one exception to that rule. The individual performer with star quality and wide personal appeal. They have to be of their time, of course. *And* move with the times. Given all that, they can stay at the top all their working lives. They're rare birds. But, you know, Cass will be one of them. Other things being equal."

Ah, now we were coming to it.

"The other things," I asked carefully, "being what?"

"Well," said Jay, "it's a matter of temperament. You know Cass much better than I do. I find her a bit of a puzzle. She's serious and professional. She has a lot of pride in herself and what she can do. Yet at the same time, in a way she lacks self-confidence."

"Oh, yes." I smiled. "That's Cass."

"Ah. You know what I mean. She relies on you a lot, you know. Naturally. Perhaps only you can give her the kind of support she needs—"

"You think I hold her back," I said. "Is that it?"

"Oh, come," said Jay, "I didn't say that. But there was just this thing about the northern clubs—you know we've got this little tour lined up for her for the autumn. She was very excited about it at first, then she started to panic a bit. I wanted

139

to know why and eventually she admitted that you'd said you thought they were too tough and she'd get slaughtered up there."

I didn't say anything.

"It isn't true, you know," said Jay. "She's got all the warmth and sincerity that goes down well there. We have to take care with the program, that's all, none of that way-out material, good though it is. It will be all right, but she needs to be sure it will be. In fact she needs to believe absolutely that she can have everything she wants if she wants it *enough*. It works, you know." He glanced at me keenly and added, "So it's up to us. We're all in this together, aren't we?"

I said stiffly, "I think I can assure you, Jay, that I shall do what is best for Cass, always."

Emma came into the room. She said, "Jay, your call's come through."

"Ah," he said, "no peace for the wicked, even on Sunday. Excuse me."

He went away. Emma lingered politely.

"Don't you ever stop working?" I asked. "Even on Sunday?"

"I don't call this working," she said. "It's fun. And I love it here."

Yes, I thought, you do, don't you? You'd like to be mistress of this house, which is something you'll never be. I knew the signs too well. Emma was one of those women who devote themselves to a man in a work situation, fall for him, make themselves indispensable, and end up being taken entirely for granted. Poor Emma, all that grace and intelligence running to waste in that deadest of dead ends.

"Has Jay been showing you the house?" she asked. "Telling you about his dream come true?"

"Something like that," I said.

"He's never here, of course," she said dryly. "He wanted the place, but now he's got it, he hasn't the time to enjoy it. Too busy making more dreams come true. It really does work for him, you know."

"What works for him?"

"What he was saying when I came in. You can get anything

- 140

you want if you want it enough. And if it seems unattainable, he's bound to want it . . . a challenge, you see. I've sometimes wondered what happens if whatever it is belongs to somebody else."

There was something faintly chilling about this. What was it supposed to be, some sort of warning? But she would not bother to warn me unless she was, in some way, fighting for her own hand. I didn't say anything. She smiled, and looked at me with her large shining eyes, which the smile didn't reach. There really was something chilling about Emma altogether, in spite of her surface prettiness.

I said lightly, at last: "As you work for him, Emma, perhaps that's the sort of thing you shouldn't wonder."

I went back, rather thoughtfully, to the swimming pool and Cass, who had now woken up and was talking animatedly to a young woman I hadn't noticed before. She was dressed in one of those voluminous long dresses all the girls wear now, which did little to hide her advanced pregnancy. Like so many people there her face looked vaguely familiar: from the box, of course—a minor actress, whose face is recognized by millions who can never remember her name, which was Bridget Marlow, or rather, Smith, as she was now married, and busy, it seemed, bringing up a family. Of either husband or family, however, there was no sign. We chatted for a bit and then Bridget got up. "I think tea is in the offing," she said, "and I'm dying for some. Look, here's the photograph . . . you talk it over with your husband, and if you'd care to come back for drinks and have a look, you'd be very welcome."

"What was that about?" I asked when she'd moved away.

"They're selling their house." Cass handed me a color snap of a small Georgian house in mellow brick, a fig tree against the wall, an ornamental fanlight over the front door. "Doesn't it look lovely? Too small for them now, with another baby coming. I'd love to go and look at it, Greg. I kind of took to her, anyway. Don't you think she's charming?"

"Charming," I agreed. "But we'd be buying the house, love, not the lady. Did she say what they want for it?"

Cass mentioned a price of mind-blowing proportions. "Well, I know," she added quickly, seeing my expression, "but I might be making quite a lot of money soon. And we could make them an offer, couldn't we?"

"Perhaps. It seems to be my day for looking over houses. But we may as well go, I suppose."

We gave Bridget a lift, and she telephoned her husband before we left to say that he was saved the bother of collecting her. He did not like her to drive in her condition, she explained, so he had brought her to Jay's in the morning and was taking care of the children for the day. "He doesn't mind. He sees so little of them. And it was such a wonderful chance for me to get out and see people, I get so browned off in the last stages, you know how it is . . . but of course you don't know how it is, do you?" She laughed merrily; a little chattermag, she kept the conversation going all the way back, doing most of it herself. I thought the husband sounded a mild fellow, tame and devoted; she had him on a string all right, poor chap.

I am a bit skeptical as a rule about alluring photographs of houses for sale, but this time the camera had not lied. Cass stared at it as we drew up and exclaimed, "Oh, Greg! It's lovely!" and I squeezed her arm warningly; Cass had no business sense at all.

Bridget got out of the car nimbly, considering her size, and led us up a flagged path into the house. We passed through a hall paneled in pale green into a sitting room suffused with sunset light. Long windows, lavishly curtained, gave on to a wrought-iron balcony. Bridget waved us into enormous velvety chairs and buzzed out again, calling as she went: "Auden! Auden, where are you?"

And I froze where I sat, because while there are many men called Smith, there could, surely, be only one Auden Smith. I heard, as in a rather unpleasant dream, his voice answering her: loving, reproving, with a hint of laughter: "Shush. The kids are in bed. I've given them the run-around all day and they're tired out . . ." He had a beautiful voice, like an actor's; he was, in fact, a stockbroker.

Bridget was bubbling on: "Darling, I met these nice people at Jay's and I've brought them back to see the house . . ."

They came in. I think he froze, too, when he saw me. His wife started to introduce us, and he moved in, fast and neatly, to cover up for us both. Obviously she didn't know anything about it and he didn't want her to. He said easily, "We've met before, haven't we? Rather a long time ago now?"

I played along. "So we have. Of course. But just where escapes me at the moment—"

"I know," he said with a convincing air of discovery. "You're a sailing man, aren't you?" He mentioned the name of the club I belonged to at that time and I said, yes, of course, that was it, and the women exclaimed over us and somebody, I forget who, had to say it was a small world, wasn't it? We put up a good show, or, at least, I felt I did; it was probably no effort for him at all.

"Well," he said, "drinks first, or the house?"

"Oh, please," said Cass, "the house. I'm dying to see it all . . ." She was putting a couple of thousand pounds on the price every time she opened her mouth, but, of course, that didn't matter now.

Bridget excused herself from coming round with us, saying with a grin: "You don't want to have to circumnavigate my bulk every time you want to get out of a doorway." I thought: she was happy, contented with this man; she radiated fulfillment. Well, why wouldn't she? Fantastic, he was. Fantastic: the in-word of the nineteen-sixties. It rang in my head.

We went downstairs to the kitchen: fashionable farmhouse style, stripped pine paneling, chunky scrubbed wooden table, strings of onions hanging up, brightly colored, heavy iron casseroles from France. Next to it, with a door leading to the garden, the children's playroom, the walls blackboarded for crayon scribbles at child's height, toys scattered on the floor. Upstairs, main bedroom all femininity and grace, brass bedstead, Victorian drapes. The children's room; no, no, quite all right, they never wake. Twins, two little mounds,

143

yellow hair like chick's down, small faces rosy in sleep. Cass began to make the soft clucking noises women make at such times, lovely, aren't they lovely? He was grinning, being casual and deprecating, without meaning it, of course. There it all was, the textbook image: devoted father, loving husband. The lovely fruitful wife downstairs. The lovely kids upstairs. All highly recommended by the Marriage Guidance Council.

Downstairs again, he proposed a look around the garden. "I expect you'd like a look at the outside, wouldn't you? The garage and that?" Cass, with Bridget, hung back and let us go on ahead, I think she had some hazy idea that there was some sort of protocol involved, including, at some stage, a private chat between him and me.

The garden was delightful. Espaliered fruit trees spread their arms against walls of old, rose brick; the recently mown lawn was like striped velvet. There was the woody, slightly bitter scent of early chrysanthemums.

He showed me the two-car garage, pointed out guttering recently replaced, the built-on annex at the back which housed a second bathroom. I nodded at everything and said nothing.

When we were well away from the house and the girls, he spoke suddenly.

"No deal?"

"No deal," I said. "I don't suppose you'd want to sell it to me anyway."

He shrugged. "Don't see why not. Your money's the same color as anybody else's." He looked sidelong at me: a merry, matey look. "Your wife likes it."

"Yes."

"Charming girl," he said amiably. "Things have worked out all right for you, then?"

"One could say that. If it were any of your business."

He laughed. "Oh, come, Hunter, let's not go on like this, it's childish. It's all a long time ago—"

"And we're both men of the world," I said. "Is that what you were going to say? Let's have the whole bit, shall we? 'No woman is worth it'? Especially when she's dead."

144

"Well," he said softly, "that, at least, is something you can't blame me for."

On the way home, I said, "Well, that was rather a waste of time, I'm afraid."

"We won't get it?"

"He's had a better offer already. I hope you're not too disappointed."

Cass said cheerfully, "Darling, a few months ago I'd have just as soon thought of living on the moon as in a place like that so why would I be disappointed? I enjoyed going there, though. Weren't they nice?"

"Very nice," I said.

"Wasn't it odd, you and he having met before?"

"Not all that odd, I suppose."

I caught the flash of one of her unexpectedly shrewd, bright glances.

"You don't like him, do you?"

"I don't know about that. I hardly know him."

"Perhaps he *is* a bit supercilious. Thinks rather a lot of himself. Perhaps he's one of those men who get on better with women than other men . . ."

"I've really no idea. Does it matter?" I was trying to keep the edge out of my voice and didn't succeed. I stared at the road, feeling the prickle of sweat on my forehead. God, it was ridiculous.

There was a pause. Then she said gently, "Of course it doesn't matter, darling." She was rather quiet after that; she didn't have much to say all the evening. And neither did I.

The thing was like a mousetrap except that it was not for mice but for men, a large mousetrap, as it were. The whole contraption towered above me. If you didn't know about the spring it might have been the skeleton of a building under construction, all steel girders and scaffolding. But I knew about the spring. It was right above my head, a great coil of steel, automated: one set it by a time device. I had set it my-

145

self for six o'clock and at six o'clock the great guillotine arm would come sweeping down.

I stood there under the spring and waited. One was quite safe, of course, under the spring, inside the trap. Everything was in reverse: nobody could spring the trap coming in, only going out.

She appeared beside me quite suddenly and said crossly, "I'm fed up with hanging about here, I'm going." "Don't be a fool," I cried, "the trap's been set, you won't get through," and she said petulantly, "Oh, you're always saying that and not meaning it. I'm going." I tried to stop her, but she fended me off, quite easily; I held her, and she slipped through my fingers, and walked toward the opening, where there was a sign which said, in huge letters: "EXIT AT YOUR OWN RISK. DANGER. YOU HAVE BEEN WARNED."

I couldn't follow her. That was part of the pattern, that I couldn't follow her. I shouted, I begged her to stop, I kept on shouting don't go, don't go, even after the siren began its wailing warning and the trap was sprung and I heard her screams; it seemed, though I was not sure, that she screamed my name.

"Greg! *Greg!*"

The bedside light was on and she was leaning over me, holding my shoulders, shaking me. "Greg, wake up." She looked frightened. But she was real, thank God, real and alive.

"What's the matter?"

"You were shouting," she said.

"Was I? I was dreaming, I suppose," I mumbled. "Sorry to wake you, love. Go back to sleep." My mouth was dry; I muttered something about getting a glass of water, heaved myself out of bed and stumbled like a zombie into the bathroom. I ran the tap, filled the glass, and drank it down, the whole glassful. When I came back, Cass was lying back on her pillow, watching me. I wished she wouldn't. I said irritably, "Why don't you go back to sleep? I'm all right."

"No," she said. "I'm not going back to sleep. And you're not all right, Greg. I want to know what's the matter."

146

I didn't say anything.

"This isn't the first time. Last time, you woke up by yourself, and got up and walked up and down the room for ages . . ."

"I thought you were asleep."

"Yes, well . . . I pretended to be, that time. I wasn't sure what to do. Then you came back to bed, remember, and woke me—only I was awake already—and we made love. It wasn't like it usually is." Her voice wavered. "It was . . . well, a bit frightening, really."

"Oh, Lord," I said. "I remember. I'm sorry, darling. But why didn't you say something then?"

"I don't know. I felt sort of confused and . . . you went off to sleep again, quite peacefully, so I let it go. But it has worried me. It's *not knowing* that frightens me. Tell me. Let me help."

I said, "You won't like it, you know."

I reached out to the bedside table for cigarettes and lighter; I was supposed to be giving up smoking, but this didn't seem to be quite the time. Across the room I could see myself in a mirror: a sour, ill-used face, dark with yesterday's beard, already marked by life. It's always disconcerting to be suddenly faced, off-guard, by your own reflection: this is how you really are, it seems to say, with the mask off. Beside me, Cass looked young and untouched and gentle, and in that dark hour before dawn, the hour for dying, I wondered why she loved me, for I felt unlovable, and, in a way, unloving too.

I lit the cigarette. I could see that my hand, holding the lighter, was shaking. I knew that Cass, watching me, could see it too. Christ, you see too bloody much, my darling. Leave me alone.

But she wasn't going to do that, pursuing me relentlessly with her love and concern.

"I don't expect to like it. But you can't shock me. I love you. You could have killed somebody. It makes no difference."

I didn't answer. Overhead came the jet-whine of an airliner, losing altitude on the home run to Heathrow. It passed

147

and died away; it seemed as if we were both listening to it, holding our breath.

Then I said loudly, "That's what I did. I killed somebody. Tessa. My wife."

"But that was an accident—"

"No accident. I meant it to happen. I meant us both to go, of course. That didn't come off. But I did it. So now you know."

She didn't speak: the silence of horror, of repulsion? I added roughly, "I told you. You wouldn't like it." I turned around to look at her. I had to know how she was taking it, however badly that might be.

She was curled up on the bed in the tangle of bedclothes. Her expression hadn't changed: it was extraordinary. She said thoughtfully, "So that's why you never want to talk about her—" and then added quickly, "Darling, it's all right. Honest. I find it a bit difficult to believe, though."

"I don't see why. I'm as violent as the next man, when it comes to it. And I had come to it—the end of the line. It's a long story. I've never told anyone before—"

After all, it was easy.

"I loved her so much. At least, that's what I called it at the time. I was out of my mind about her, anyway. The competition was steep and I'd won out, and it was all going to be wonderful. Only it wasn't wonderful. We couldn't make it, in bed I mean. I couldn't give her any pleasure—"

"What?" said Cass. "You? It's not possible. Why, Greg, you're a *magician* . . ."

"For you perhaps. You and I . . . we got it together the very first time, simple as breathing. It isn't like that for everyone, you must know that. She wasn't frigid; she was a violent, passionate sort of girl. Only it was as if it was all locked up, and I hadn't got the key. Incompatibility—nobody knows much about it, do they? We might have worked it out, perhaps, with enough love and patience on both sides, but both were in short supply. It wasn't long before we were both embittered and frustrated; we blamed each other; things went from bad to worse—tears, quarrels, accusations, we went through the lot. We didn't split up; I didn't want to; I still

148

hoped, I suppose, that things would come right, and Tessa . . . Tessa wouldn't go until she had someone to go to. So it went on, stretching into months and years. We had no life together at home, we went out a lot, meeting people, going to parties. I don't think anyone guessed just how wrong everything was. Then she began to play the field, looking for someone who had got the key I was talking about. You can imagine what that did to me, and that meant more fights, more scenes. It was one of the last things she ever said to me, that she was sick of my jealousy and possessiveness—Well, there we were in the car that night, quarreling; the last of our many quarrels. About him. Auden Smith."

"That man we met last night—"

"That's the one."

Cass said slowly, "Oh, Greg, darling. I'm so so *sorry*. I must have driven you crazy, chattering on—"

"You weren't to know, were you? Well, anyway, she said it all that night. That she was leaving me. That she'd never been happy with me, never. That they'd been lovers for months. I don't remember what I said, it was as if I had a bomb inside me about to explode. I didn't do anything except drive faster. And then she said the last, the final thing. She was laughing; she knew just what would hurt me most, and she said, 'Do you know, it's all right with him! It's *fantastic* with him!' And she went on telling me just how fantastic it was, in every last detail, and I pulled the wheel right over and she screamed . . .'"

I heard Cass let her breath out slowly. She reached for my hand and clutched it.

"I don't remember anything else. I came to in the ambulance. She was dead, killed outright, they said. I escaped with a couple of cracked ribs and concussion. We'd gone right off the road, down a steep incline and hit a tree. The car was a complete write-off. The irony of the whole thing was, I wasn't even blamed. The coroner at the inquest offered me his condolences. The other driver carried the can."

Cass stirred. "What . . . what other driver?"

"Well, it was just an extraordinary coincidence. There was this bend, you see, and the other bloke took it wide, just

149

missed me, skidded and turned his car over, or so they say; I don't remember seeing him at all. When the police examined the tire marks, the final score was that I'd taken avoiding action. He got done for dangerous driving; he had a bad record, and lost his license. I didn't feel too good about that either . . . what are you looking like that for?"

Incredibly, she was radiant. "So you didn't do it."

"Cass . . ."

"Of course you didn't! Of course you didn't kill her!" She threw herself into my arms and said eagerly, "You don't remember exactly what happened, do you? You were knocked out. Nobody ever does remember that little bit of time just before a crash. You remember what Tessa said and how you felt. Then the accident happened and she died. You wanted to kill her so you believe you did it. And you weren't punished for it, so the debt's never been paid and so you have all this guilt and these nightmares. Darling, I can remember, when I was a child, hating my father. I used to lie in bed in the dark telling myself I wished he'd die. Supposing my wish had come true and he *had* died? I'd have gone on feeling guilty forever and ever. I would have done a bad magic, don't you see . . ."

I said, "But I'm not a child, Cass." I spoke coldly, without meaning to; after all, it was not her fault, she meant well. But in some obscure way I felt exposed, humiliated. My instinct had been the right one, after all: never, never let anyone, even someone you love, in on something like this. And then I added, God knows why, I could have spared her that: "And I don't think that bits of half-baked psychology, picked up from women's magazines, are going to be much help, you know."

She took that between the eyes, you might say, and as always when snubbed, fell silent. At once I thought how loving and good she had been to me and what an ungrateful brute I was, and I said quickly, "I didn't mean that like it sounds, Cass."

She sighed. "No. All right."

"I don't mean to shut you out. But I'm stuck with this

150

thing, and I have to cope with it my own way. I can't stand being analyzed. Having *me* explained to *me*."

She said quietly, "Okay. I wanted to help but if I can't . . . if this is the way you want it . . ."

"Of course you help, just by being you. You're the best thing that ever happened to me. You don't have to do anything else, just love me. *Love me*," I said..

So she did. But afterward, when we were ready for sleep, and I at peace, knowing I would sleep well with no bad dreams, she lay there on her pillow with her eyes wide open, looking up at the ceiling.

I had no idea at all what she was thinking.

151

Ten

WE DIDN'T talk about it anymore. I was released, it was over. I loved Cass more than ever for her faith in me. But I'd made it clear that I now wanted her to let me be, and she did that, though it wasn't natural to her. So long as she did, it seemed to me, all would go well.

Anyway, we had a lot of other things on our minds along then. My business problems increased, and Cass, shortly due to make her first recording, became more and more worried as the day approached. "Will you come with me?" she said at last.

I laughed. "Darling, whatever for?"

"Moral support. I don't feel confident enough to cope on my own. This producer, Phil Carson . . . everybody says he's great, but a bit formidable. I'm not sure I'll have the nerve to speak up if I don't like what's being done. I'm *new*, you see. He doesn't know much about me. I simply don't know how it will work out. Emma's got summer flu and anyhow she'd be no good; she'd just want to keep things sweet and want me to go along with him about everything. You'd help just by being there. Being on my side."

"I don't know a thing about it," I warned; but she could see I was weakening and she threw her arms around me. "Please come, Greg! Please!"

Well. It was a whole afternoon taken out of an already busy week. But I said I'd go.

I don't know that it comforted her all that much. The night before she was as restless and jumpy as a cat. In the morning I said as I left, "See you at two o'clock at the studio, then"; but about half-past ten she telephoned me.

153

"Greg, it's about this afternoon—"

I was dictating; Mrs. Ferguson was sitting opposite me, her face instantly assuming the special polite mask reserved for my private telephone conversations.

I said irritably, "Look, I've said I'll be there and I will be. There's no need to remind me."

"That's just it." Cass sounded uncertain, breathless. "I was only going to say, if you've got a lot to do—"

"I've always got a lot to do."

"Well . . . that's what I mean. I've just rung to say I'll be all right. I mean if you'd rather not come . . . I know you're busy . . ."

I said, "What's all this? I've rearranged my appointments so I'll be free this afternoon, till four anyway. Now you say you don't want me to come."

"I don't mean that . . . I just thought . . . well, it doesn't matter. You will come, then?"

"This is a ridiculous conversation. Do you want me to come or don't you?"

"Of course I do. I was only thinking of you . . ."

She seemed to be near to tears.

I said firmly, "Look, darling, *it's all right.* I'll be there. Now just relax. Go and get dressed, have a large drink and something to eat, and I'll be at the studio to meet you. Got that? Now I must get on or I *won't* get there. All right now? Sure? See you later, then." I put the phone down and said to Mrs. Ferguson, "Where were we?"

As she read out, expressionlessly, the phrase I had just dictated, I wondered what she thought of us. Mrs. Ferguson lived a life weighted with worry: the mortgage, the rates, the children. She did a full-time job, ran a home, was father and mother in one. To her it must all seem very trivial, the boss making reassuring noises to his silly little wife about something that didn't matter much anyway. However, whether it did or not was something I'd never know.

I skipped lunch, had some sandwiches sent up and worked straight through until I left at half past one to drive up to Hampstead.

The studio looked as if it had once been a warehouse, in a

154

side street that was a jumble of little shops: a dry cleaner's, a delicatessen, a kosher butcher's. A lot of young men were extricating themselves and various musical instruments from a mini-van; this done, they propped the instruments against the railings, lit cigarettes and stood about gossiping as if waiting for somebody. I went in the main door and told the commissionaire my business. He gestured toward some stairs where a notice read "Studio Two." I went down the stairs into the basement and looked around for somebody to ask where to go next. It all seemed very bare, in need of a coat of paint, and somewhat depressing. I heard voices and laughter coming from a door on my left, and pushed it open to find myself in what was evidently the canteen. There were two women there, one behind the counter and another girl, who was leaning against it talking to her. The girl had a little snub face, and a fringe flopping into her eyes; she wore one of those long, rather bedraggled garments which made her look like an orphan out of Dickens. She grinned cheerfully at me and said, "You look a bit lost. Can I help?"

"I was to meet my wife here," I said. She looked blank and I added, "Cass. Cass Clayton."

"Oh, yes, of course. I think she's already arrived, she'll be around somewhere. Perhaps you'd like to go through to the control room, Mr. Clayton."

"Hunter," I said.

"Pardon?"

"My name's Hunter. Not Clayton."

"Oh, I see. Sorry. Awful to be called Mister-whatever-your-wife's-name-is, isn't it? Men hate that, don't they?" She led me down the corridor, opened another door. "Well, this is the studio, as you see, and that's the control room through there. The boys are all around somewhere; they'll be in soon. Make yourself at home," she said, and vanished.

The studio was neon-lighted, walled and ceilinged with soundproofing. The floor was a tangle of cables, microphones, stools and music stands. Along one wall ran a large glass window which looked only into the control room; there were no other windows. The effect was slightly claustrophobic. A piano on a raised dais stood at one end, and a small,

155

melancholy-looking youth was improvising on it. He leaned over the keyboard sadly, listening to the notes. An elderly man in a bow tie was taking the cover off his cello. After a bit they both nodded at me incuriously. I nodded back. I went into the control room, full of panels and dials and a large object which, I learned later, was the console mixer. A typewritten notice pasted on the corner of the window announced tersely, on behalf of the management, that it was FORBIDDEN to place Coca-Cola bottles or glasses on the control room instruments.

It was extremely cold in there, somebody having left the air-conditioning on full blast. I looked around for the switch, couldn't find it and gave it up, sat down in a polar draft, and waited.

Outside in the studio the musicians were beginning to gather, jokes and gossip were bandied to and fro, and then, gradually, came the mingling of tones, high and sweet, deep and mellow, the sound, nerve-tightening as always, of the instruments being tuned.

Presently a young man in a sweater came in, looked me over, unsurprised, said "hallo" with a vague friendliness and, taking no further notice of me, went over to the console mixer and began to do things to it. After a moment I said to his back, "I don't suppose you know who I am."

He turned, grinned and hazarded: "A friend of Cass's?"

"Cass is my wife," I said. There was something irritating about this anonymity I found myself in. I added, "She asked me to come along. I suppose that's all right."

"Surely," he said. "Why not? I'm Ken Jones, by the way— recording engineer."

"Gregory Hunter."

"Glad to know you," he said. We shook hands. He went back to what he was doing.

Cass came in, accompanied by two men, to whom she was talking very quickly and gaily, with her a sure sign of tension. She had all her armor on, I could see that. She brightened when she saw me, came over and put her hand through my arm, hugging my arm to her while she introduced me to the

156

others. One of them was the producer, Phil Carson. He was less affable than the others, glanced briefly at me with what was, I realized, an extremely shrewd and authoritative eye, and went off to have a long mumbling conversation with Ken Jones. At last he jabbed a button which made a red light appear in the studio, after which all sounds immediately ceased. He said gently, not making an issue of it: "All right, fellers? Let's have the woodwinds on A." The long, warm, single note filled the room.

Cass said to me, "Let's sit down. There'll be a lot of this." She put her hand into mine and squeezed it; hers was very cold.

I said, "Don't be scared, love. You'll be all right."

"Oh, yes. I know that, really . . . when I get out there. It's the hanging about I don't like, while he rehearses the orchestra."

I said doubtfully, "Haven't they rehearsed it before?"

"Heavens, no. They'll get all the rehearsal they need today. They'll have played this umpteen times before they do a final take."

"It seems a funny way to go about things. You'll be telling me next they haven't seen the music before."

"Nor have they." She laughed. "Darling, they're musicians. They read music like you read a book . . ."

Phil Carson said in his inexpressive voice, "Right, we'll take it right through this time . . . give them the beat, Jock."

Jock was the drummer. He waved his right-hand stick in the air, said loudly, "One, two three, *one.*" The stick made a decisive arc downward and the music began. After a moment the theme took shape for me, a song called "The Stone Desert." To my untutored ear the whole thing sounded rather . . . well, overcooked was the only word I could think of. I looked at Cass, whose head was bent; after a moment she shook it. But she did not attempt to catch Carson's eye. He sat with his feet up on the edge of the console; he moved and shrugged in time to the music, his sharp, dark face quite blank. Once or twice he called the whole thing to a halt, jumped up, went out into the studio, picked up somebody's

157

score and scribbled on it; or he called out incomprehensible instructions—incomprehensible, that is, to me—and after much tedious repetition said, "Thanks, fellers, that's not bad so far, now we'll take it through with the voice." He looked at Cass and smiled; that made him seem more human. "You set to go, Cass? Okay?"

"Okay." Her voice came out in a nervous croak and she coughed. "If I could just have a glass of water."

"Mike! Get the lady a glass of water." The assistant producer, a pale lad who up to then didn't seem to have much to do, went off for it. Cass sipped at the water and smiled and went away and there was a bit of fuss while they got her settled at the piano, the mike positioned, a couple of baffle boards screening her so that I couldn't see her at all. Then they began all over again, until Carson once again called a halt, told Cass to take a rest and said they'd play back the last take. The musicians put their instruments down and relaxed. Cass came back into the control room. As she did so, the outer door of the studio opened and someone wove his way between the players toward us.

I didn't register who it was at first. After all, I had seen him only once, and then only to throw him bodily from Cass's flat. He opened the control room door and came in.

Phil Carson looked up and said, "Hi, Nick."

Then I understood why Cass had telephoned me that morning. Why she hadn't, after all, wanted me to come.

Nick looked at her and grinned. "Hi, Cass. How are you doing?"

Cass said nervously, "I'm not sure, really." She didn't look at me or at him. Nick stared at me over her head, nodded, said "Hi" again, still grinning, perfectly at ease.

There were other people present, there was nothing to do or say. I nodded back and turned away. Successive bursts of anger, immediately suppressed, exploded and died in me like gun shots. Cass had known he would be there. She was in touch with him. Perhaps she always had been. There he was, anyway, with as much right to be there as I; more, probably. The assistant producer, who acted as tape jockey, set the spools spinning and Cass's voice came back to us, disembodied and strange, somehow not quite Cass's voice, wrapped around with the heavy, oversweet orchestration.

Nick sat down on Cass's other side, listening attentively. After a bit he said softly, "Soup, eh?" She gave a sort of rueful grimace and nodded. Then he added, "*Treacle* soup," and she giggled nervously, her eyes on Phil Carson's back.

As the tape spun to its end, Carson turned around, looked quizzically at Nick and Cass. He said, "What are you two looking so glum about?"

"Well . . ." Cass murmured.

"Well, what?"

She bit her lip, and said bravely, "I feel a bit overwhelmed by the backing."

"Oh, you do. Nick?"

"It's a nice sound," Nick said. His tone was placatory, tactful. "And so far as the voice goes, the way she's feeling it, it's just great—or it could be. But . . . well, look, Phil . . . this is a song about loneliness, the real thing, not boo-hoo, I'm lonely for you-hoo. This is a girl alone in a big city where there's nobody to give a damn about her, where she could die and no one would even know. So she's crying out in a concrete wilderness, right? 'Where will I find the gentle faces,'" he sang suddenly in a passable tenor. "'Where will I find the ones who care? Where, tell me where, tell me where . . .' It's a cry of despair, man, it's got to come out like that. Stark. *Plangent.*"

I was astonished by this outburst, mostly, I think, because he was less of a lightweight than I thought. Phil Carson seemed quite unruffled, which is more than I would have been in his shoes. He said gently, "Yeah . . . well, maybe you've got something. Cass? You go along with that?"

"I'm afraid it is . . . I mean, Nick's put it very well, really." As she said this she once more put her hand through my arm, as if apologizing, placating me. I didn't respond.

From then on, the discussion became technical, out of my field. Cass joined in it vigorously, she'd got her confidence back, and it was not I, but Nick, who had done that for her.

159

They might argue the toss, these people, but they were all, Cass included, in a charmed circle in which I didn't belong. I began to look at my watch. Cass saw this and whispered, "Oh, don't go yet, darling. Wait till we've had another run-through; I want to see what you think."

"It doesn't matter what I think—"

"It does to me," she said.

To get up and go just then would have looked odd, and anyway I left it too late. Cass went back to her piano and the whole business began again, over and over. A transformation had taken place, even I could hear that. At last at the end of a take Nick was nodding his head and Carson threw his arms up and said that was great, just great, and announced a break for tea. The musicians stowed their instruments and began to make a move into the corridor which led to the canteen.

I went out into the studio where Cass was sitting at her piano behind the screens. She looked pale and filled with apprehension.

"I must go," I said.

"Yes," she said. "All right. Thank you for coming, darling."

I said carefully, "It seems to be going all right now, doesn't it?"

"Yes . . . Greg, I'm sorry. About Nick turning up . . ."

"Yes . . . well, we can't talk about that now. I *must* go. See you."

I gave her a peck on the cheek and left. Outside the place, I stood on the steps of the building for a moment, trying to remember where I had left the car. Then I heard my name called. I turned around: it was Nick Edwards, smiling broadly, as if we were the best of friends.

"What do you want?" I said.

"Nothing much. Little chat."

"You'll have to excuse me. I have an appointment." I started down the street. He fell into step beside me, refusing to be shaken off. He looked innocent, eager to please.

"Now we've got the trouble ironed out," he said cheerfully, "that's going to be a great disc. She's on her way."

160

I didn't answer. I went on walking.

"I hear you got married," he said. "Congratulations."

"I'm sure," I said, "you didn't hare after me just to say that."

"Not exactly. My apologies as well."

"Your what?"

"Apologies, I said. I was a bit out of line, last time we met. I wouln't like you to hold it against me."

This weird air of humility couldn't be real. What did he want? I stopped and looked him in the face; there was nothing there except that deprecating grin. His eyes were like glass.

"Look," I said, "I don't know what you're after, but there's nothing to be gained by trying to ingratiate yourself with me. And I'm in a hurry."

The street was hilly, drafty with a chilly breeze coming down from the Heath. A piece of newspaper blew by us into the gutter. An elderly woman dragging a shopping basket on wheels passed us. I caught her intent, almost frightened look: something about us, I suppose, a suggestion of squaring up, of trouble to come. She hastened away from us, dragging the basket, the wheels squeaking. Cars slowed for the lights at the top of the hill, waited for them to change, drivers looking out, bored, impatient. Quite a lot of people about. Too many.

Nick sighed. He made a mournful face, a clown's face of sadness, his mouth pulled down.

"Nothing to gain," he repeated. "Ingratiate. Depressing language you use. Of course I've nothing to gain. You can't do anything for me or against me. I'm just part of the scene, where Cass is concerned. You've just seen that for yourself back there. We speak the same language, Cass and I."

"Professionally, perhaps," I said. "Otherwise, she's no time for you at all."

"Did she say that?" He laughed. "Yes, I suppose she might. She doesn't mean it, you know. Oh, she married you and you've got a big thing going, I daresay. But I'll always have a share in her. I was round at your place yesterday, didn't she tell you? I spent the afternoon there and we had ourselves a ball. One way and another."

161

So that was it. All the rest was chatter, to soften me up while he planted the knife neatly between my ribs.

Rage spurted out of me like blood. I was going to hit him, but he was ready for me, recoiling lithely out of reach; I became aware of people pausing, staring.

"Now, now," he said, reproving, grinning. "Violent fellow, aren't you? A bit public here, isn't it? I wouldn't hit you back, you know. All these old bags doing their shopping would run screaming for the fuzz and I'd have you for assault. Lovely publicity it would make, wouldn't it?"

I said, "Keep away from my wife or it will be the worse for you. You've got away with it this time. Next time I'll see there are no witnesses."

I turned my back on him and walked away, around the corner to the side street where I had left the car. I got into the car and sat there for a while. This was one of the penalties of civilized life; one does not brawl in the street, so that the rush of adrenalin to the blood, the primitive aggression, had no outlet except feeble, unimpressive threats. I felt the unexpressed violence almost like an illness. Not for the first time. In childhood and adolescence, I can remember thinking, terrified by my own rage, one day I shall kill somebody. As I had, of course. As I had.

At last I made myself start the car and drive away. Having to drive, to concentrate, helped a bit. But with the ebbing away of physical rage came the reaction that was almost worse: the sour taste of betrayal.

Cass. Cass. She had lied to me.

I kept my appointment. I went back to the office. The usual folder of beautifully typed letters lay on the desk. I started to look at the letters but couldn't concentrate on them. I signed them without reading them and buzzed. Mrs. Ferguson came in for the letters, took them away, and was back again within a minute. She came in quietly and I didn't see she was there.

"Mr. Hunter," she said and I started. "Yes? What is it?"

"You haven't signed some of these. Is something wrong?"

"Something wrong?" I repeated.

162

"With the letters," she said patiently. Then she looked at me rather hard and added: "Are you feeling all right?"

"Yes," I said. "Of course. I'm fine. Sorry." I took the folder and signed the letters I had overlooked. As I handed them back to her the telephone rang. Mrs. Ferguson picked it up.

"It's Miss Quayle," she said. "For you."

I tried not to let my astonishment show; or my pleasure. Sarah. She had come, as it were, to cue.

Eleven

"SARAH!" I said. "How nice to hear from you—" Mrs. Ferguson melted away.

"Greg," said Sarah. She sounded brisk, businesslike. "This will have to be quick. I'm in a call-box and I haven't much change. I've got to talk to you. I don't want to come to the office, and I don't want to discuss it over the telephone. It's a . . . business matter."

"I see. Well, what about lunch tomorrow?"

"I'd rather not do that. It's rather confidential—"

"Well . . . you're on your way home?"

"Yes . . ."

"Shall I come round presently?"

"Perhaps that would be best. Come and have a drink," Sarah said.

Mrs. Ferguson was still there when I left the office. I stopped by her desk. "I wonder if you would mind telephoning my wife before you go, and telling her I've an unexpected appointment, and not to wait dinner?"

I daresay she was putting two and two together madly, but her expression did not change.

"Certainly, Mr. Hunter. Shall I say what time to expect you?"

"No," I said.

From some girls, this unexpected approach might have seemed like a trick, a come-on. But Sarah being Sarah, I never even thought of that. All the same, it felt strange, nostalgic, going back to that flat, a place of pleasant memories, of candlelit dinners, music and wine. And love, of course. Only it hadn't been love; like the dinners and the wine and the music, just a delightful way of passing the time.

165

As always, the place looked gracious and orderly, beautifully arranged fresh flowers reflected in shining wood surfaces, not a trace of dust or untidiness anywhere. It was, like everything else in Sarah's life, well under control. I thought, not for the first time, that this was above all why I had never been in love with her.

She greeted me coolly and pleasantly, the past a closed book, not to be reopened; except that she remembered what I liked to drink and how to fix it. I sat back in one of the comfortable chairs and relaxed, and the afternoon and everything connected with it receded. We chatted for a bit, like old friends whose friendship is uncolored by emotion.

"Well," I said at last, "why the cloak and dagger stuff? Phoning from a call-box. Confidential, you said. What's up?"

"I'm not exactly sure," said Sarah. "It may all be nothing, really. But I thought you'd better know, anyway. You know the setup at Pargiter's, don't you?"

"My dear, I worked there myself for a bit, very early on."

"So you did. I don't think it's changed much. It's still a family concern, they've never gone public, and the old man still rules the roost. The two sons are both directors of course, Mr. Robert and Mr. Edward—"

"Do you call them that?" I asked.

Sarah laughed. "Not if I can help it, it makes me feel like a nineteenth-century millhand. I call them all Mr. Pargiter, when I can. I mostly only have dealings with Robert so it's not that difficult. Anyway . . . there they both are, running the business but not in control. Old Mr. P. has a heart condition and he's pushing eighty. I wouldn't like to say they're longing for him to die, but the way things are is very frustrating for them; and I can't tell whether this idea that's come up comes from them or from the old man . . ."

"My dear Sarah, I'm on tenterhooks. *What* idea?"

"As I say, I'm not sure. But the other evening just as I was leaving the office, Robert called me in. He's a chilly sort of character, as you know, and doesn't unbend much with the staff, so I was a bit surprised when he got the drinks out and seemed all set for a cozy chat. Then he started pumping me about Hunter's." She looked at me doubtfully. "Perhaps you know all about this already."

166

"Not a thing," I said. "Go on."

"I played as dumb as I dared. I can't afford to seem too dumb. After a bit I said I'd just worked for you and wasn't in your confidence and he said, 'Oh, I thought you were.' So I pretended I hadn't heard that, and he waffled on for a bit and I finished my drink and said I had a date, and he said I'd been very helpful—which I hadn't been—and hasn't mentioned it since. If that was all there was, I daresay I wouldn't have thought any more about it. Only, the other day I was lunching with a friend—at the Miraflora—and who should come in together but Robert and your stepfather."

"*Russell*—"

"Russell. They didn't see me—we were sitting in one of those alcoves tucked away at the back, and anyway they were absorbed in conversation. It looked like a working lunch, couldn't be anything else, really. Unless he has a business engagement, Robert has sandwiches and coffee at his desk. Well, perhaps it doesn't mean anything—"

"But you think it does?"

"I suppose I have a sort of instinct about it. I thought you should know. I know Russell is living permanently in England now, and he's more involved with Hunter's than he used to be. I see Hugo from time to time—"

She glanced quickly at me, and added defensively, "He rings up now and then, and we have a drink together."

"Why not?" I said. "It's a free country."

She let that pass. "I've got the impression there's some sort of . . . disputation going on . . ."

"You can say that again," I said.

"Hugo feels he's pig in the middle and isn't enjoying it too much. But I think he sides with Russell, really . . . I thought I'd better put you in the picture, anyway. I suppose you'll know what to make of it."

"I'm not sure. Perhaps Russell is putting out feelers for a deal. Could be that he and Hugo both want out. I don't know."

"You mean they really want to sell out? But you wouldn't, would you?"

I laughed. "No way. And whatever skulduggery Russell and Hugo get up to behind my back, they know they can't move without me. Perhaps they think they can put some pressure on. We'll see. But it was very nice of you to warn me, Sarah. Thank you."

"You don't have to thank me," Sarah said. "I did it for myself. I mean . . . if anything comes of this, I wouldn't like you to think I'd been involved. That I'd worked against you . . ."

I said gently, "I'd never think that of you, Sarah."

She looked me in the eye. "You might. You might think I'd done it . . . you know, out of spite. The hell-hath-no-fury bit. So it's just a matter of personal pride with me. Just to make sure you wouldn't think it. Well . . ." She rose, the polite gesture of dismissal, and I rose with her. I knew what it had cost her to say those words, and I had never admired her more. Admiration is not love and I wished it were.

I wanted to do something for her, make some gesture, so I said, "Come and have dinner with me, Sarah."

She smiled faintly and shook her head. "Greg, thank you, but that's not necessary—"

"Who said anything about it being necessary? I'd just like to take you out to dinner."

"I'm sure," Sarah said, "that you have . . . dinner . . . waiting for you at home." She could not, I could see, bring herself to mention Cass by name.

"Cass is working this evening," I lied. "I would have eaten out anyway."

"Oh! I see." She changed suddenly, became cheerful and animated. "Well, if you're really at a loose end, you could take me to a party. If you feel you could bear it. It'll be one of those parties where there's a buffet and nowhere much to sit down, so it's best to have a quick bite beforehand. Look, we could have something here, if you like . . ."

"Well," I said. We looked at each other, smiling.

"There's some iced soup in the fridge," Sarah said. "I could make omelets. There's cheese and fruit. How's that?"

"Perfect. There's just one snag. If this is a smarty party, I could have done with a clean shirt—"

"Even that," Sarah said, "can be arranged."

"What?"

She said rapidly, "You left a shirt here once. I don't remember when. It was laundered and . . . I meant to give it back to you but somehow we didn't get round to it. It's still here."

For some reason I was deeply touched by this. I said, "Oh, my dear Sarah."

In another moment, I think, I would have taken her in my arms, but she moved away, saying in that rapid bright tone, "Well, there it is, it's yours, after all, and . . . you could have a shower and change the shirt while I get the meal ready."

Well. I had the shower, and changed my shirt in Sarah's bathroom, fresh and elegant as always, ornamented with pretty bits of women's gear, vials of bath oil and perfume and cosmetics all in exquisite order; not a bit like our bathroom at home, usually left by Cass in what the Scots call a stir—damp towels in a swatch on the side of the bath, jars with the tops left off and the toothpaste squeezed in the middle. We had the excellent simple meal, and I would have settled for not going to the party, but I didn't quite have the nerve to say to Sarah as I had done once before, don't let's go, let's just stay here. I remembered that evening, remembered that if she had said yes then, all my present troubles would never have been. I was taken by nostalgia for the tranquillity of that past time. Of course there had been something missing. But there is always something missing. It depends what you want most.

We went to the party, where, perhaps fortunately, there was nobody I knew. It was like all other parties of its kind: a long, light room, opening on a balcony, the leafy bowers of a London square outside; the atmosphere of money, prosperity, the soft surfaces and the shiny surfaces of furniture, carpets, mirrors; elegant girls, men with the solid look of success; the rise and fall of a dozen different conversations, getting progressively noisier the more people drank; the occasional outburst of merriment where somebody was being very witty, showing off in the center of a group. Sarah had been right though, there were far too many people there, and there's a short limit to the amount of time I'm prepared to stand about with a glass in my hand, no matter how often

169

it's filled; and I was driving, anyway. After a bit, none of it seemed quite real to me, and I began to wonder what I was doing there. At my insistence, we were the first to leave.

Sarah was quiet going back in the car. At her door, I said, "Aren't you going to ask me in?"

I couldn't see her expression. She said gravely, "No. I've been thinking . . . about this evening. It was a mistake. My mistake, not yours. Go home, Greg. You're married now. You've made your choice. Stick to it." I didn't say anything, and after a moment she added, "I'm sorry."

"I'm sorry too," I said. "You're right, of course. Good night, love. Take care."

"Good night."

Now there was really nothing to do but go home.

I thought Cass might have gone to bed but the moment I entered the flat she came rushing out into the hall.

"What happened?" she cried. "Where have you been?"

I walked past her into the living room; I didn't touch her or kiss her, and she must have got the message about that pretty fast. I threw the papers I was carrying on the sofa and said, "I asked Mrs. Ferguson to phone you. Didn't she do that?"

"I haven't heard anything—"

"Then you must have been out when she phoned."

"You could have phoned yourself," Cass cried. "I couldn't think what had happened, I've been frantic—"

"Have you, now?" I said, and she stared at me and gasped: "What is it? What's the matter?" And then, before I could answer: "It's Nick, isn't it? He told you some story—"

"Some story," I said. "Yes. He said he spent the day here. Is that true?"

Cass hesitated. Then she said, and my heart sank: "He wasn't here all day."

"But he was here. Why did you lie about it?"

"I didn't lie. I just didn't tell you, that's different. It wasn't important—"

"Not important? So unimportant that you did your damndest to prevent me from coming today and seeing him there?"

"I didn't know that till the last minute. I thought it would upset you, that's all. Phil Carson invited him, not me. Anyway, Nick and I wrote that song together, ages ago, he has as much stake in it as I have. I didn't ask him to come round, he just turned up. Look, Nick's mixed up and he's malicious but he isn't all bad and he does know about music. We rehearsed the song and talked it over and I gave him some lunch and that's all that happened. But I'm sure he told you we went to bed together. He did, didn't he? He would have enjoyed baiting you, it's one of the ways he gets his kicks. He thinks you're a stuffed shirt." She stared at me scornfully. "And that's just what you are."

The way these things go has an awful inevitability about it. From then on we were embroiled in a violent quarrel, wild, irrational and absurd, both of us reaching out for any weapon, seeking to strike at the most vulnerable spot. She soon found one of mine, crying, "If this is the way you went on with Tessa, I'm not surprised she got tired of you."

And I shouted, "You shut up about Tessa!"

God knows what else we said to each other, I don't remember most of it. But I do remember Cass saying bitterly, "You don't trust me at all, do you? You just fell for all that rubbish Nick was talking before you'd even asked me what happened. You went off somewhere, nursing your grievance, while I've been nearly out of my mind with worry. Anyway, where *have* you been all this time?"

It was intolerable, this insolent turning of the tables, demanding that I should account for myself. It was an opportunity too, though. She had laid herself wide open to the most cunning blow of all.

I said coolly, "I spent the evening with Sarah."

"You . . . what? You did what?"

"We had some business to discuss. She gave me a meal. Then I took her to a party."

"You went to *her*? You've been with her all the evening, while I've been sitting here waiting and worrying?"

"My dear Cass," I said, "two can play at that game."

Cass said in a strange high voice, "You make me sick," and the next instant she had slapped my face, quite hard, and

171

that's something that nobody, but nobody, does to me and gets away with it. So I slapped her back, a good deal harder. She stood there rocking from the blow, her mouth working. Then she snatched up a porcelain ornament from the shelf near her and flung it at me; it glanced off my shoulder and shattered against the wall. Then she burst into loud sobbing and ran out of the room and out of the flat.

For the first minute or so after she'd gone I didn't do anything. Then I went over to where the remains of the broken figurine lay on the floor. I began to pick up the pieces. All my movements were heavy and slow. In the silent room our angry voices, the blows, the crash of the broken porcelain, the slammed front door, still seemed to reverberate. I stood there with the only two sizable bits of porcelain in my hands. It was a Meissen piece, quite valuable, a pretty thing, now broken beyond repair. Somewhere, a clock chimed the hour. It was one o'clock in the morning and on my way home it had begun to rain. Cass had rushed out into the rain, without money, without her keys, without a coat; and she was hysterical.

I threw the pieces of porcelain back on the carpet and went out to find her.

By the time I got out into the street of course there was no sign of her. If I had had any sense, I suppose, I would have gone back for the car, but she couldn't be far, after all. For the moment the street, glassy-black with rain, was empty. I started off down the street, around the block. I looked down the next side street I came to and saw a small, dark figure walking briskly. I sprinted after it; I think I shouted. The brisk footsteps faltered. As I drew level with her I saw a glimpse of a pale face and large frightened eyes under a dark rain hat with a brim. It was not, of course, Cass. The girl said breathlessly, "What do you want?"

"I beg your pardon," I said. "I thought you were somebody else." I went past her, walking fast to put a reassuring distance between us. At the house on the corner they were speeding the parting guest. A blond girl in a long pale dress was caught in a stream of golden light from the open door. "Lovely party, darlings," she cried, in a high, affected voice.

172

Another party, like the one where I had, so pointlessly and cruelly, spent the evening. I went on, rounded another corner. In the part of London where we lived the dividing line between the prosperous areas and the shabby ones is very narrow. I had soon crossed it into bed-sitter land, rows of tall houses, each with a dozen bells beside the front door. It was late; the pubs and the betting shops and the little corner stores all in darkness, only the coin laundry still open and people, mostly young, sitting, half asleep, watching their washing go round. The gutters were littered with paper and trodden cabbage stalks, relics of the market stalls that stood there during the day. There was a sadness and weight about the atmosphere here, the land of the lonely and insecure. Where shall I find the gentle faces? She wouldn't find them here and I'd never find her, this way, either.

A car turned the corner and drew up at the curb just behind me. The driver switched his headlights on. I was caught in the dazzle like an insect impaled on a pin. I turned, and saw the blue light on top of the car: a police patrol. It was ridiculous, they were not looking for me, but I felt, momentarily, exactly as if they were.

One of the policemen got out of the car. He made as if to go to check one of the shop doors, seemed to change his mind, and came up to me. I suppose if you do that work, you get a sixth sense about people's demeanor: urgency, distress or guilt is somehow conveyed to the practiced eye.

So he came up, looked me over, and said civilly enough, "Anything wrong, sir?"

I said idiotically, "I'm looking for my dog." Improvising, I added, "A Bedlington."

"Pardon?"

"A Bedlington terrier. It looks rather like a lamb."

He stared at me woodenly and I wondered if he thought I was drunk.

"He's got a woolly coat. Curly. Sort of grayish color."

The situation seemed to be degenerating into farce.

"He's rather valuable," I said. "Pedigree. Only a puppy really. You know how they run out, go wild."

"Yes . . . well, we could keep an eye out for him, sir, if

173

you like. If you'll give me your telephone number, we can let you know if we pick him up."

"That would be very good of you." I gave him the number and he wrote it down and I said, "Well, thanks very much" and was moving away when he said, "Just a minute, sir."

What could he want now?

"What does he answer to?"

"Answer to?"

"His name," he said patiently.

"Rosy," I said, improvising again.

"Rosy? That's an unusual name for a dog. You did say it was a he, sir?"

"Just a family joke," I said.

"Oh, I see," he said, not seeing. We said good night and I walked away. Once around the corner, out of his sight, I broke into a run, now as anxious to get back to the flat as I had been to leave it. Anything wrong, he'd said. I wondered what he would have said if I'd told him. Everything's wrong, officer. It's my wife I'm looking for—five foot, six inches—long dark hair and the beginnings of a fine black eye.

I could see the lights of our windows from the street but that didn't mean anything, I'd left them all on. Cass couldn't get in, not unless she got the porter and I didn't think she'd do that. I hurried into the entrance hall; one of the lifts was just disappearing upward and I was too impatient to wait for the other. I started up the stairs.

As I came out onto our landing I saw her. She was leaning against the wall outside our door, with her back to me.

"Cass," I said.

She didn't look at me. She said in a dragging voice, "I've been ringing the bell. I thought you weren't going to answer it."

"I've been out looking for you. Here, let's get this door open."

She went in front of me into the hall and waited while I took the key out of the lock and closed the door, as if she didn't know what to do next. She looked a mess, poor Cass, with her hair in rat's tails and her face pale and pinched. The mark was still on her cheek and I saw it with pain.

174

"Oh, my dear love," I said. "I'm so bloody sorry."

Her face crumpled and she stumbled blindly into my arms. I picked her up and carried her through to the sitting room and sat down with her on my lap. We clung together and kissed and murmured the broken phrases so many have said before us: I'm sorry darling, I'm sorry too, it was all my fault, no, it was mine, I didn't mean it, I didn't mean it either, I love you, I love you too.

So we were reconciled and in an exhausted way we were happy. All the same, we both knew that damage had been done.

Twelve

"WE'RE going to have a blow," Tom Munro said. He squinted out of the clubhouse window at the estuary. It was blue and brilliant still under a sunny sky, but clouds were crowding up from the horizon and the first flecks appearing on the water. It looked all right though, a good sailing day, with the promise of a fast race and the test of skill, judgment and speed which is what dinghy sailing is all about. It also meant the rescue boat would be busy, and a lot of wet cold people pulled out of the drink.

Behind us, the main room of the clubhouse was filling up. It was as chaotic as usual, duffel bags and sailbags and lunch-baskets everywhere, an ever-louder babble of greetings and conversation; children ran about squealing and getting underfoot; resigned-looking, non-sailing wives prepared to while away the day knitting, gossiping, admonishing their kids, with the occasional obligatory peer through binoculars to see how their husbands were doing. Cass was in the changing room; I was taking her sailing for the first time.

"Think she'll be right?" Tom asked. I didn't mind his fatherly tone. Old Tom, as we sometimes called him (though not in his hearing), and his stringy weatherbeaten little wife were very much the elder members of the club. They didn't race anymore these days, but sailing was their life, so they were always at the club at weekends. Tom ran the rescue boat, and Molly was the undisputed queen of the Ladies' Committee.

"I don't see why not," I said. "She doesn't get seasick, and she's keen to have a go. If it gets too hairy we'll have to retire, that's all."

177

"Yes," Tom said. "Well . . ." He made a hrr-umping sound, indicative, perhaps, of doubt.

"I feel," said Cass behind me, "exactly like a trussed chicken." Mrs. Munro was with her, having, I gathered, helped her to get the gear on. Cass did indeed look uncomfortable, strapped into both life jacket and trapeze harness. Her expression was compounded of apprehension, valor, and determined cheerfulness.

Mrs. Munro said in her loud decisive voice, "I hope you know what you're doing, Greg, taking this child out for the first time on a day like this. There's going to be a blow, you know—"

Tom's bushy eyebrows twitched. He muttered, "Yes, dear, he does know." But Mrs. Munro was not to be stopped.

"Now, if you have a capsize," she admonished Cass, "there's nothing to worry about. The boat's buoyant, she can't sink, so you just hang on; never let go of the boat. And if she turns turtle, the best place is underneath her."

Cass said faintly, "Underneath . . . ?"

I said quickly, "Molly means that the hull is above the water and there's air in there and the water's calmer. But it doesn't have to happen. Let's get going, shall we? There's a lot to show you before we get started."

On the way down to the boat we were hailed by a couple just getting out of their car: Mike Summers and his wife, Valerie. They were by way of being friends of Maddy and Paul—friends, that is to say, who met at the sailing club and went to each other's parties. Mike was all right, but Valerie, I felt, would one day be another Mrs. Munro. Perhaps most of the sailing girls would. The non-sailing ones were not much better. Maddy, with whom we were spending the weekend, had refused to come with us that morning. "Can't stand those women," she said. "Not en masse, anyway."

Still, there the Summerses were, and we stopped to greet them, and they said it was a long time since I was last down, and I said we'd been busy and they said yes, of course—there was a faint smirk of amusement and envy on Mike's face—and I introduced them to Cass and explained it was her first day out.

178

Valerie, looking at Cass with a cool, inspecting eye, said, "Brave, aren't you? There's going to be a—"

"A blow," I said. "Yes. All right, Valerie."

Cass smiled. "Greg won't let me drown," she said.

They walked with us down to the boats. The girls dropped back a little, and through Mike's rather tedious story of a race the previous Sunday, I heard Cass say, "I don't think so. You could have seen me, perhaps. I'm a singer—"

Valerie said really? and, how super, and what kind, and I head Cass rather resignedly explaining.

"What was she on about?" I asked, Mike and Valerie having left us.

"I don't know. Something about us having met before. I can't think why people have to say this, it can't possibly matter."

"It's because you're so memorable," I said, stripping the covers off the dinghy.

Cass stared at it with dismay. "Greg, it's like a *machine*. I'll never get the hang of all those ropes and things—"

"Yes, you will. Come on, we've got work to do. And I want you to have a dry run on that trapeze."

I won't pretend that I wouldn't rather have had someone with me who knew what he, or she, was about; but our decision to come at all had been a last-minute affair and I couldn't get a crew. So I had to settle for Cass, the novice volunteer, anxious, eager to please, and not knowing a thing about it.

All in all, she didn't do too badly. I took her through the trapeze drill while still on dry land and then, on the water, tried her out on it on both tacks. I know perfectly well that to a novice the trapeze on a racing dinghy can seem a fearsome thing: there you are, feet on the gunwale, leaning out backwards with nothing behind you except air and water, and only the hook on the harness holding you on. But I found she was both fearless and trusting—trusting, that is, of me; that helped. Anyway, it was good just to be out on the water again, with the dinghy moving under my hand like a living thing, raring to go, the sense of joy and freedom I always felt when sailing. The sense of escape, too. My working life be-

179

came more stressful and ulcer-forming with every day that passed. Cass was going up north to start her club tour the following week. I didn't want to think about any of it. It was going to be a good day. All boats of the fleet were out that morning, the last of the season. With their multi-colored sails moving and dipping they looked like a cloud of oversized butterflies.

I did all the routine checks and then we were up at the line, jockeying for position. When the starting gun went we got clean away.

"All right?" I shouted.

Cass turned a rapt face toward me and screamed, "It's wonderful, Greg, it's terrific, it's like flying . . ." She glanced back at the fleet, plowing along several lengths in our wake. "We're *miles* in front, we're winning, aren't we?"

I laughed, as we hadn't yet rounded the first marker buoy.

"Some way to go yet, love. Now, when we round the buoy, we'll be off on the other tack, so get ready to move when I say the word and mind you don't hit your head on the boom— right, ready about, now, *now*, get the jib sheet in your other hand, that's it, good girl—" And indeed she got it right first time, more by luck than judgment of course, and we were off on the other tack, increasing our lead and going like a bomb. It looked for a while as if she might be right, we might be first at the finish, though winning on handicap is another story. We were both exhilarated, at one with the boat and the wind and the sea. However, the wind, the treacherous wind, had other ideas, and the sudden gust hit us hard.

"Free off!" I yelled, but Cass didn't understand, or she had forgotten what the command meant. In the split second before the capsize I saw her bewildered face and the jib sheet still clutched in her fist. Then the dinghy went over, the mainsail hit the water with a slap, and the next moment she was sitting in the middle of the sail; she had a look of rather comical astonishment. Then another gust came, the dinghy turned completely over, and down into the dark salt sea went the sail and Cass with it.

I knew it was all right really, though it was a scary moment. She had a life jacket on, she had to come up, and she did

180

come up, coughing and spluttering, under the hull. I was hanging onto the stern and I could see her through the transom, her white face and her wet hair all over it; she seemed to be tangled up in the mainsheet.

"Are you okay?" I shouted, when I saw she'd got her breath back, and she answered with a deceptive calm, "Almost. Greg . . . there's a rope . . . it's round my neck, I can't get it off. *It's getting tighter.*"

"Hold on. I'm coming in with you." I ducked and came up beside her, found the slack of the mainsheet and released her. The wet nylon rope had made a mark on her throat.

She clutched me, laughing with relief. "Oh, *God,* I nearly panicked. I thought I was going to be strangled." She was shivering uncontrollably—the water was very cold. All we had to do now was wait for the rescue boat, and there was no danger, but I knew she had had a shock. She wasn't letting on about that, reproaching herself for ineptitude. "I should have let that rope go, the one on the little sail—"

"The jib sheet."

"The jib sheet—I got muddled. Sorry—"

"Don't be. We wouldn't have weathered that second gust anyway." I smoothed the wet hair out of her eyes and kissed her and we clung together in the cold water, in the dim light under the hull; and then, at last, we heard voices hailing us from above.

Tom Munro had his son Peter in the launch with him. Tom took Cass straight back to shore, while Peter, ready for anything in a wet suit, obligingly came over the side to help me with the dinghy. It was hard work and took quite a while to right her and take her limping back to her moorings. Mike Summers was there, dismally contemplating a broken mast. I looked disgustedly at the muddle inside the dinghy and decided to leave it all until later, while I went to see how Cass was and get a hot shower and a change of clothes.

On the steps of the clubhouse I met Valerie.

"I see you came to grief as well," she greeted me. "What a day! The water's littered with casualties out there . . ." She looked at me quizzically. "How's your wife?"

"I'm just going to find out," I said.

181

I found Cass lying back in a chair with a drink in her hand. She had changed into dry clothes and somebody had thoughtfully wrapped a car rug around her. She was being made rather a fuss of, but she didn't seem to be enjoying it much. She looked up as I came in and said with dismay, "Greg, you look frozen, do go and change . . ."

"I'm going. Just wanted to make sure you were okay."

"Oh, I'm fine now. Only I'm so sorry I made a mess of it—"

"Nonsense. You didn't make a mess of it."

"It can happen to anybody," somebody said. "Just take a look out there."

"But I got terribly panicky, I shouldn't have done—"

"Very natural," said somebody else. There seemed to be a faint air of disapproval about, disapproval, that is, of me, for taking her out in that weather.

Valerie sat down beside Cass. "I think we should change the subject," she said brightly. "Do you know it's just come to me, in a great white light?" Valerie was inclined to talk in this exaggerated fashion; Cass looked at her in bewilderment.

"I've *remembered*," Valerie said triumphantly, "exactly where we've met before. It was at the Carpenter's Arms at Fatcham, and you were with Maddy and Paul."

Cass frowned. "I don't see how that could be. I didn't meet Maddy until Greg and I were married and I don't . . ."

"Well, now I come to think of it, I don't remember Maddy being there that night, but I suppose she must have been. But I do remember Paul was . . ."

Cass said, "I was just going to say, I don't know Paul. And I've never been to the . . . what did you say it was called? . . . the Carpenter's Arms . . . in my life."

Valerie said disbelievingly, "But I could have sworn . . . I mean, you were just going out of the door as we came in—"

"I'm sorry. You're mixing me up with somebody else," Cass said. She had a fraught and hunted expression. Valerie made one feel like that sometimes.

I said shortly, "Valerie, do you mind? Cass isn't feeling well, and what does it matter anyway?"

"It doesn't," said Valerie. "Of course." She got up and walked away, offended.

There was no more sailing for us that day. When we got back to Stallington, Maddy, who hadn't expected us back for hours, greeted us with some concern, and Cass came in for some of her warmhearted and hospitable cosseting. The two girls seemed to get on all right after all, which was a relief.

All the same, things had changed in that house; its peculiarly serene and welcoming quality had gone. Perhaps it was simply to do with the absence of Paul, the family unit broken up. But it hadn't broken up . . . or had it? Helga, too, had gone. She had acquired a man friend who worked in London, and wanted to get a job there to be near him. So Maddy was now alone with the children, and it wasn't doing her any good. The children, too, seemed disturbed and out of hand, and Maddy's temper with them uncertain. While we were having dinner that evening, we heard one of them crying.

Maddy put down her knife and fork with a sigh. "Oh, dear, here we go again. None of the children used to wake in the night, and now they do it all the time, I don't know why it is—"

I nearly said, "Don't you?" but refrained, seeing her expression. "Look," I said, "I'll go, shall I?"

Maddy's face cleared. "Oh, Greg, would you? Thanks a million . . ." She turned to Cass and added more cheerfully, "You know, Greg's wonderful with the kids, when you think how impatient he can be, it's extraordinary . . ."

"Well, thanks for that too," I said dryly. I went off upstairs.

It wasn't one of the little ones. Jane and Jeremy slumbered peacefully in their bunk beds; Lucy, the eight-year-old, lay sobbing in hers in a tangle of bedclothes.

I switched on the lamp and addressed her in the cheerfully tough, mock-hectoring tone I always adopted with Maddy's children; they adored it, I don't know why.

"Hallo, mate. What's up with you, then?"

Lucy stared at me suspiciously, with tear-filled eyes.

"Where's Mummy?"

"Mummy's awfully tired, love, and we're just finishing dinner. Won't I do?"

"Don't know," she muttered.

I sat down on the edge of the bed and gathered her into

183

my arms; it seemed to be my day for comforting frightened girls and wiping their tears away. "Come on, sweetheart, what's the matter? Had a bad dream?"

"No. I haven't been to sleep . . ."

"What then?"

She gulped and whispered, "I've been having horrible thoughts."

I recalled all the times I had lain awake having horrible thoughts; and I was not eight years old.

"What sort of thoughts?" I asked gently.

"Mummy and Daddy are old, aren't they?"

I suppressed a grin. "Not very old really, you know."

"Older than me," she insisted. "Years and years older. Old people *die*, don't they? One day they'll die, and leave us alone."

So that was it. I said carefully, "Look, Lucy. You're eight years old. That's all the time you've been in this world. It seems like forever, doesn't it? Now you think of fifty years. It's a long, long time. So long you can't imagine it, can you? All right. Now, Mummy and Daddy are going to be around all that long time . . ."

She stared at me, and I thought I'd got through to her.

Then she said, "But they might be killed."

"Killed? Why should they be killed?"

"They might be. With bombs," she muttered. She was only eight. Talking about bombs. Jesus.

". . . Or a lion. Or a crocodile . . ."

"Lovey, what *are* you talking about?"

"One of the big girls at school . . . she said there are lions in Africa, and crocodiles . . . and they eat people and they might eat Daddy and then he'd be dead and he'd never come back, never." She wailed and buried her head in my shoulder.

Well. I'd certainly got myself into something. I thought of calling Maddy and decided she would probably do no better than I, especially in her present mood. Anyway, it was a challenge, something I can never resist. So I talked my way out of it. Now listen, Daddy's not stupid, he'd have more sense than go anywhere near a lion or a crocodile . . . or a bomb, I

184

added with less conviction, seeing that bombs do not announce their presence, and are no respecters of persons. Somehow Lucy had picked up a sense of insecurity and change from the atmosphere that Maddy had created; yet, in a way, her nightmare images were a reflection of a real and violent world.

I managed to reassure her at last; tears were mopped, she blew her nose on my handkerchief and consented to lie down while I sorted out the muddle she had made of the bedclothes and tucked her in. In the sudden and enviable way of children, she fell asleep almost immediately. I left the light shining on the landing and crept off downstairs.

The dinner debris had been cleared from the table, there was a smell of coffee being brewed, I heard the girls' voices from the kitchen.

"What a super thing that is," Cass said, referring, I gathered, to Maddy's dishwasher. "I've never seen one working before."

"A gift of conscience," Maddy said. There was that edge to her voice which always seemed to be there nowadays.

"What do you mean?"

"Well, you know the old joke about unfaithful husbands coming home with bunches of flowers. I suppose Paul felt a bunch of flowers wasn't enough, so I got a dishwasher."

So she had evidently decided to confide in Cass. I was glad about that, at least.

Cass said in a bewildered way, "But, Maddy, you don't really know, do you? I mean, you've no evidence . . ."

"Evidence," Maddy said, "evidence is for lawyers. I don't need evidence. It's what I see. What I feel. That's what matters. I mean, like, you know, Paul writes to me. It's not in what he says. It's what he doesn't say."

"But it could be that it's all over and he's just feeling depressed and not knowing how to get back to you—"

"I wish I could believe you," Maddy said with a sigh. She looked up as I walked in. "It was Lucy, wasn't it? Is she all right?"

"She's okay now, she's asleep. She's missing her father," I said pointedly.

"Yes, I know. We've had a lot of that lately. I don't know what to do about it."

"You could reassure her," I said.

"Oh, yes? Like how? Tell her Daddy will soon be back from Africa and we're all going to live happily ever after?"

"If you'd only make up your mind that's how it's going to be," I said, "you could do just that."

Cass looked uncertainly from one to the other of us, sensing conflict in the air. "Shall I pour out the coffee?" she asked, diffidently.

"Please. Would you? You see how it is," Maddy went on, addressing Cass. "Greg thinks I should put up with whatever comes, for the sake of the children. He won't even let me get my hands on my own money in case I use it to do something he disapproves of."

I said quietly, "That's grossly unfair, Maddy, and you know it."

"Well, *is* it? Not that it matters. Hugo will oblige, even if you won't."

"*Hugo?* You've asked Hugo to buy your shares in Hunter's?"

"Yes. And he's going to."

I said stupidly, "You can't do that. I'd lose control of the company."

"I don't see that's so terrible. You've only had control because you controlled *me*. You've never told me anything, never consulted me—"

"You've never been interested—"

"I've never had a chance to be."

Cass, murmuring something, put coffee cups in front of us. We both ignored her.

"Anyway," I said, "you can't do it. You have to have the agreement of the board before you can transfer—"

"A *majority* of the board," Maddy said. "That's what it says. I can read, Greg. I've read the Articles of Association. You've had your chance to help me and you wouldn't take it. Now I wouldn't sell you the shares if you asked me. I'm absolutely sick and tired," she said loudly, "of being told what to do and manipulated by everybody and lectured about the children.

186

They're my children and it's my marriage and my money and I'll do what I think best for once."

I said, "You won't, you know. Because if you do, I shall write to Paul."

"You wouldn't," Maddy cried. "You wouldn't dare—"

"Yes, I would. I shall tell him exactly what's going on here. I shall tell him he'd better get back here and sort things out—sort *you* out, before you break up the home and take his children away from him."

I spoke brutally and meant to. A paralyzed silence followed this remark. Cass kept her face turned away from me.

At last Maddy said incredulously, "You *can't* do that. You can't. If you did, I'd never know—"

"Never know what?" I said. "I shan't do anything if you're sensible."

There was another long pause. Then Maddy said in a small cold voice, "All right. You win."

I don't like being on bad terms with Maddy. I put my arm around her shoulders and gave them a squeeze. "That's a good girl. I knew you'd see it my way."

Maddy moved out of my encircling arm. "Don't be patronizing, Greg. I didn't say I saw it your way. I said, you win. And now I'd rather not talk about it anymore. If you don't mind."

We left soon afterward, our leave-taking, at least Maddy's and mine, distinctly on the cool side. Driving home, Cass was rather quiet. I thought she might still not be feeling too good. To divert her I gave her an account of my conversation with Lucy.

Cass listened gravely. "Poor little poppet. But she was all right afterwards?"

"Oh, Lord yes, for the time being anyway. Reassuring noises, a cuddle, a joke or two . . . it didn't take much to cheer her up, really."

"With you to cheer her up, I don't suppose it did." I felt her warm glance on my face, like a caress. *"I love you,"* she said, with a sort of soft vehemence.

"Well, that's nice," I said cheerfully. "I love you too. But why the solemn declaration? Because I was nice to Lucy? Not

187

much to that, love. I'm fond of Lucy. I'm fond of all Maddy's kids. Which is more than I can say for their mother at the moment. I could gladly wring her neck. She's behaving like a lunatic."

"She's very unhappy—"

"I know that. I'm sorry you had to be in on that dust-up. You didn't like it much, did you? You thought I was hard on her?"

"Well . . ."

"It was necessary, you know. What she threatened to do could be quite serious."

"Yes. I'm sure you're right. It's just . . ." Cass looked down into her lap and added quietly, "I'm afraid of anger. My own, anybody's. It's like a car crash—noise and shouting and people crashing into each other and getting hurt; it makes me feel really sick. It's feeble of me. I know that."

It was the only reference, if it was a reference, she had made to our own shattering fight about Nick. I said gently, "I know what you mean. But you can't avoid it altogether, you know. Anger and conflict are a part of life, after all."

"Yes. I know that too. Why are you stopping?"

"This is rather a nice old pub. We've just time for a quick one before they close."

We found a corner for Cass to squeeze into and I went off to the bar. I had just given my order when a voice behind me exclaimed, "Mike!" Naturally, I paid no attention.

"Mike! I say, Mike!" cried the voice; it was so persistent that I turned around. A red-faced man of about my own age was standing there with his hand out; he had, I thought, had a few.

"Sorry?" I said.

He stared at me, the look of delighted recognition fading rather comically from his face. He said uncertainly, "It is Mike, isn't it? Mike Burton? You remember me?"

"I'm sorry," I said again. "You're confusing me with somebody else." I picked up my change and the drinks and began to move away.

"But you're the dead image of him. You're not having me on, are you? Are you sure you're not Mike Burton?"

188

I stopped and looked at him. "Absolutely sure. My name is Gregory Hunter. And I've never heard of Mike Burton. Excuse me."

When I got back to Cass I glanced back at the bar where the red-faced man was still staring at me with a look of dashed bewilderment.

"What was that about?" Cass asked. "Did you meet a friend?"

"No. Gentleman's convinced that I'm a friend of his. He's somewhat sloshed."

"Oh!" said Cass, and laughed. "Poor thing, he looks quite upset."

"I'm the one who should be upset. It doesn't do one's ego any good, to know you have a double around somewhere. Now I think of it, perhaps you have too."

"Perhaps I have what?"

"A double. Valerie Summers was so convinced she'd seen you in the—Carpenter's Arms, was it—with Paul, of all people, whom you've never even met. I find it a bit difficult to believe, though."

"What's difficult to believe?"

"That you have a double. You seem to me to be absolutely unique. Oh, well. Perhaps Valerie was a bit sloshed at the time, like the gent over there."

"Yes," said Cass. "She must have been, mustn't she?"

Thirteen

MADDY didn't forgive me for winning that argument. There was no open breach, but we didn't go to Stallington for Christmas as I had done in previous years. Cass was working on Boxing Day, but we weren't invited, anyway. I sent gifts for the children via my mother, who was going; with Russell, of course. Paul was still away, not expected back until some time in January. Christmas would not be much fun for Maddy, with her private obsession gnawing at her, while she put a good face on it for both the older and younger generations. The parents would arrive loaded with lavish gifts, spoil the children abominably and leave Maddy to cope with the results. When I had time to think of it, which wasn't often, I felt bad about Maddy and the possibly permanent loss of a relationship which had always been close and mutually supporting; but during that autumn and winter I had too much else on my mind.

Cass's career had taken off, in the sudden way this often happens. Her first record came out, the sales climbing far beyond our expectations. There were cabaret engagements, television shows planned for the spring. She was getting a lot of publicity now, the genuine kind, critics who mattered were beginning to notice her. There was talk of her being signed for a film.

Inevitably, this wrought a change in her. Her confidence grew, she was surrounded with the glow, the aureole of success. The personal magnetism which I had thought of as something for me alone was now recognized by other people: Cass was having a love affair with the public, and it felt like she was cheating me. It shouldn't have done, I suppose, but it did.

Perhaps it wouldn't have seemed so bad if things had been

going well in other ways, but they weren't. The cold wind of economic change, mostly in the shape of astronomically rising costs, was beginning to blow. If it blew into a storm, it could be that we wouldn't weather it. I might lose Hunter's altogether. To me that meant much more than financial loss, for my whole life was bound up in that enterprise, which bore my name, and where beautiful things were made.

But these were the days of caution and calculation, of hard-headed men who got their sums right. Russell and Hugo were in their element at such a time. I liked Russell no more than I ever did, which didn't make it easier to admit that his commercial judgment was often better than my own. I didn't admit it. I just said yes, where formerly I might have said no. So, gradually, the two of them, Russell and Hugo, began to govern me.

As I lay awake at night, thinking about the problems of the company, it seemed to me that Cass was on her way up, while I might well be on my way down. If that happened, if her victory coincided with my defeat, she would not continue to love me; not, at least, in the way I wished to be loved.

So, the world laid its soiling, spoiling hands on us. My temper was really filthy along then. As people often do, I took my frustrations out on the only person I really cared about. It might have been better if Cass had responded in kind, but she didn't. She reacted to my most evil moods with a guilty and diffident concern for me which contrasted strangely with her public radiance. It should have worked but it didn't. It only provoked me more.

Still, our lives weren't yet a disaster area. We did have our good moments. We were still in love. Or thought we were.

Until one day, in the middle of January, when I walked out of my office after a stormy meeting, brushing aside Mrs. Ferguson with her messages and letters to be signed, saying I wouldn't be back that day. It was neither wise nor sensible to do this. It looked too much like retreating after a defeat. But it was a defeat, and I didn't care what it looked like. I needed to get away from the place, to think. What had happened still seemed to me not quite believable.

They faced me, Hugo and Russell, with a united front,

192

masked by a persuasive amiability. They would win me, if they could. They thought they could. I had yielded over many things in the past months. Why not this?

"It's not a bad offer," Hugo said. He smiled. "As a basis for negotiation. The least we can do is take it seriously."

"Seriously," I said. "Pargiter's? You're actually suggesting that we should sell out to Pargiter's? I suppose you realize what that means? The end of the firm, of everything you and I have worked for and built up?"

"*Greg*," said Russell. He had a slightly weary and tolerant air. "Don't be so *emotional*. It means the end of Hunter's as a separate financial entity, that's all. We should continue as we do now, as a separate operation, only with much greater resources—"

I said rudely, "If you're naïve enough to believe that, you'll believe anything. What I'd like to know is how long you've been cooking this up behind my back." But I knew, of course. Sarah had told me.

Russell sighed. "Nothing's been cooked up, dear boy. It came about quite naturally because George Pargiter is an old friend—"

"Which is why, I suppose, you were having lunch in the Miraflora with Robert Pargiter. Back in the summer, wasn't it?" If I'd felt like laughing, I would have laughed at the expression on their faces. "My spies," I said, "are everywhere. It's a pity I didn't take it more seriously then. Anyway, you can forget it. You must know I'd never buy a proposition like that. I won't even consider it—"

But they wouldn't take that, and a long inconclusive wrangle ensued which got more heated and bitter every minute. Eventually I said, "All right. This isn't a formal meeting and the whole thing has been sprung on me. A matter like that has to be a decision of the shareholders."

Then Hugo said gently, putting the boot in: "I think I'd better tell you now, Greg, that I have Madeleine's proxy vote in my pocket."

So I left the office and went home, at four o'clock in the afternoon. I didn't know whether Cass would be there or not. I

193

hoped she would be, and she was, not expecting me of course, and startled by the sound of the key in the door. She came running out into the hall. "Why are you home? What's the matter?"

I said irritably, "I suppose I can come back to my own home what time I like." My sense of frustration and betrayal made me sensitive to the faint intimation of impatience, of something interrupted, though there was nothing to interrupt, she was alone in the flat. I had wanted to talk to her. Now, suddenly, I didn't want to talk to her.

She said, "Greg, aren't you well? Is something wrong?"

And there, in her voice, was that note again, the tone in which people say, "What is it *now?*"

And then the front doorbell rang.

All through my life I've been much aware of the web of circumstance. It works unseen, the product of many different wills, each working to a separate end, meshing together to entangle you in its center. In this way one disaster is brought about by another. If Russell and Hugo had not worked against me. If Maddy had not let me down. If I had not gone home that day at that hour, so much that happened later would never have happened. If, if. But it did happen, all of it.

So the doorbell rang and I said, "I'll get it," and I went to the door and opened it.

Paul was standing there.

He looked different, very tanned, wearing a lightweight tropical suit in the middle of January, somehow faintly foreign as people do when they've been in the tropics for a while. I was surprised to see him. But what really struck me was his utter astonishment and dismay at seeing me.

Well. Civilized manners take care of such moments, which is, after all, what they're for. I didn't say to Paul, what the hell are you doing here in the middle of the afternoon, obviously not expecting to see me? Why, when you've just got back from Africa, you have come to see my wife, whom you're not supposed to know, when you should be on your way home to your own. No, I would not say anything like that to Paul. Whatever explanation there was, if there was any but the obvious one, was strictly a matter between Cass and me. So appearances were kept up, affable greetings were exchanged, I made the usual inquiries about his flight and what time did he get in. He had come up to Victoria on the airport coach he said, thought he'd drop in and see us.

"You should have phoned," I said. "It's only by chance that I'm home at this time of day." He had nothing to say to that, and I let it go. "Cass," I called, for when we got back into the living room, she was nowhere to be seen. Well, women do that, belt off into the bedroom when a visitor arrives, to fix their hair or their faces, though this behavior was not at all typical of Cass. She appeared at last, reluctantly it seemed; she had a fixed social smile on her face and looked pale and nervous. As well, I thought grimly, she might.

I said, "Cass, this is Paul, Maddy's husband; he's just flown in from Africa. Paul, my wife, Cass."

Cass said "Hallo" and he said "Hallo" too, and their hands just touched.

"Would you like some tea?" Cass said, and Paul said he would, thus letting her off the hook, as she could now go away and make it. I asked Paul about the trip, and he relaxed a little, and we chatted quite amiably, and I looked at him and thought, this is Paul who was my friend and whatever he is now, God knows; and he thought his own thoughts, whatever they were; and Cass came in with the tea and we drank it and didn't let too many silences fall. I asked if he had phoned Maddy and did he want to do it now, and he said he had already done that, thanks. And at last he went away, without ever having spelled out what he came for. He was very, very uncomfortable, I could see that, he didn't know how to handle the situation, he didn't know what would come of it, and that suited me fine: let him sweat. Anyway, for the moment my quarrel was not with him.

I shut the door behind him and went back into the room. Cass was standing in the middle of it; our eyes met.

"All right," I said. "Let's have it. It was you, wasn't it?"

Cass gasped. "What are you talking about?"

"You know perfectly well what I'm talking about, you deceitful bitch. You were Paul's girl—"

"No! No!"

195

But I wasn't listening and went straight on, driven by a sense of outrage, of being made a fool of; not only by her either.

"What happened? Did he ditch you before he went, or did you ditch him? Did you take up with me on the rebound, or just decide you fancied me more? Or are you both planning to start again where you left off?"

She didn't answer, she seemed as if struck dumb, and this infuriated me further. I stood over her; I had not yet struck or shaken her, but any moment I might and she knew it, but I had forgotten one thing; if you tried to terrorize Cass, she would defy you. Her face slowly crimsoned and she said thickly, "I won't be bullied, I won't. It's just the same as last time. When in doubt, think the worst, that's you, isn't it? Don't even ask for an explanation. Start right in grilling me like a detective."

"What the hell do you expect?" I shouted. "When you've always pretended you didn't know the bloke, you'd never met him? When he turns up today obviously expecting to find you alone? Valerie Summers said she'd seen you together and you denied it—"

"Of course I denied it! It wasn't any of her business—"

"Or mine either?"

Cass said, "Oh, *God*." She began to pace about the room as if she couldn't bear to stay still; she put her fists up to the side of her head in a frantic gesture. "Look, can't we just talk about this, without shouting at each other? I would have told you about it that day. But you know what it was like. I'd just been pulled out of the sea, I was cold and sick and all to pieces. Later on you had that fight with Maddy, it just wasn't the time—"

"So you went on deceiving me."

She cried, "Oh, stop talking like that! I didn't *deceive* you. There was nothing to deceive you about. I kept quiet, that's all. I didn't want to make trouble. It wasn't my affair and I didn't know how much you knew, or if you knew anything. About Paul and Julie."

For a moment, this threw me. I said stupidly, "Julie? Julie who?"

"Julie Herriot. My friend Julie. The one in the Barn Theatre Company. I told you about her, the night we met I'd been down to Stallington to see her—"

"Oh, yes. A friend, you said. You didn't say what the friend's name was. So she and Paul were having an affair. Is that it?"

"Yes. It's all over now. He broke with her before he went to Africa—"

I didn't believe any of it. The capacity for belief was not in me that evening: Maddy, Paul, Hugo, Russell, liars and conspirators all it seemed; and why should Cass be any different? No matter what she said, in my heated imagination I still saw her—Cass, my wife, my love—in Paul's arms; in the arms of my friend, in the arms of Maddy's husband. This tormenting image was superimposed on other images: Maddy and Paul by my bedside in the hospital the night Tessa was killed, their steady concern and affection holding me up. It seemed as if everything were lost, tarnished or destroyed. Yet I couldn't quite give up hope. So I had to go on probing and prodding.

"So? Where do you come in?"

"I don't. I just knew about it. I met Paul just that once, when Valerie Thing saw us. I was working with the Barn for a fortnight, staying with Julie. Paul came one Sunday night and they took me out for a drink. The bar was crowded. I didn't see Valerie there, but I do remember somebody saying hallo to Paul just as we left and that he was a bit put out about it. But that's all there is to that, I haven't seen him since, until today. He rang up from the airport, said he wanted to talk to me. We never did get to do that, so I don't know what he wanted. My guess is, he's not sure what he's going home to, and wanted to know if I'd said anything. About Julie."

"Oh, yes," I said. "Julie. We keep coming back to her. A bit of a mystery lady, Julie, isn't she? I thought I'd met all your friends. Where have you been hiding her all this time?"

"She had a breakdown. She's been away, staying with her parents . . ." Cass's voice trailed away. She stared at me. "You don't believe me," she said slowly. "You don't believe a word I've said, do you?"

I didn't say anything. I looked at her; and we stood there.

The bright blush faded from Cass's face, leaving it very white. She said softly and deliberately, "I see. Have it your own way, then. There isn't any Julie, it was me, and I was having an affair with Paul. Now are you satisfied?" And then, without warning, she burst out: "That's really got to you, hasn't it? You don't know what to believe now, do you? You don't know what to believe!" And she began to laugh, peal after peal of hysterical laughter, and I slapped her, not so much in anger but because I couldn't stand the sound and had to stop it, and the force of the blow made her stumble into the table with the tea things on it and they all went flying, tea cups and tea leaves, and milk and sugar spilled on the carpet; as she'd said, it was all the same as it had been before, the atmosphere thick with hate and accusation, blows and shouting and the broken shards on the floor. This sort of crisis sometimes has a way of reaching a peak in which it becomes ridiculous, the people involved feel like fools, start laughing, fall into each other's arms. But, of course, we had gone too far for that. Cass stopped laughing when I hit her, she was crying now, though not in a soft, defeated way, the tears glittered in her blazing eyes, and she screamed, "That's right, go on, beat me up, you did it before . . . why don't you, you hate me enough, you hate everybody, I wonder you've got a friend in the world. Now let me tell you something, I hate you, I hate you—"

She was beside herself, goading me to violence, but I didn't touch her again, I was too afraid of what might happen to us both if I did. The only thing to do was to walk out, and I did.

I went downstairs and got the car out again. I drove out of town and on to the motorway and put my foot down.

I've never been able to stand all the talk about psychology that some people go in for, quoting Freud and Jung and talking about their repressions and canalizing aggression and all the rest of it. Yet, I suppose, this idea about the motorcar being an instrument of aggression has something in it. There was I, at the wheel of a powerful machine, and there was something assuaging in its forward thrust, the handling of it at speed. The motorway too suited my mood, inhuman, nightmarish, lit by the yellow sodium glare, loud with the

198

sound of engines and tires on tarmac and the rumble of the container lorries, the sense of a race in which I was going to be the winner as I passed them all exceeding the speed limit by miles—and why I wasn't gonged I'll never know. It was as if we were all rushing toward destruction, although the rest were just doing the permitted maximum or a bit more. I was the only really hell-bent lunatic about.

After a bit I calmed down and recalled that I had done this sort of thing once before and had no intention this time of killing myself or anybody else. I took my foot off the accelerator and got into the slow lane and off the motorway at the next turn-off, moving immediately into a different world: a stretch of suburb, the outer edge of commuterland, and then the country.

I hadn't much idea where I was and didn't care. The road was dark, hemmed in by trees. I came to a rise where the trees thinned and the ground fell away beside the road, opening out to what would have been, in daylight, a view. I pulled up, and sat there. The evening was clear and cold. Darkness all around, except for lights twinkling in the valley, and above, the high stars. There was little traffic on this road, so it was quite quiet except for the muted thunder of the motorway, a few miles behind me. I sat there for a long time.

The reaction from violent anger is often very like a hangover. One feels depressed, slightly ill, and extremely fatigued, with no initiative left at all. I thought about Hunter's, and I thought about Cass, and had no very clear idea what to do about either, or even, in Cass's case, what I felt. Perhaps when I saw her again, I'd know.

I turned the car around and went back the way I'd come.

The flat was in darkness. I thought for a moment she'd gone to bed, but of course, it was still quite early in the evening. I went around switching lights on. She wasn't anywhere in the flat. In the living room the tray and the crockery had been removed, there was a faint, damp mark on the carpet where she must have scrubbed it. I stood and stared at this for a moment, thinking stupidly: spilt milk. Don't cry over spilt milk. Then I swung around and went to look in the bedroom, in the wardrobe.

All her clothes had gone. The drawers of the dressing table were empty too, the tabletop cleared of cosmetics; but right in the center of it, beneath the mirror, were a few, small, glittering objects: the sapphire ring and the other bits of jewelry I had given her. I went back into the living room. The music score paper usually left on top of the piano was no longer there. The tape recorder wasn't there either.

There was no note. But I didn't need one. Cass had not only gone. She had gone for good.

There's only one thing to be done when you have two crises on your hands at once—that is to take firm hold of the one that can be acted upon and lock the other one away. So far as Cass was concerned I'd locked her away anyhow; seeing her, in some way, from a distance, as someone not quite real. I knew quite well that there was something wrong with this, that emotionally I was not, as we say, myself. At Hunter's, I was myself all right and a bit more so as there was a challenge to be met, the familiar atmosphere charged now with a feeling of conspiracy. I don't know how the rumors got around but get around they did, making everybody jumpy, and when I asked Robin, our designer, to come down and see me, he came in looking at me warily out of his cloud of golden whiskers, like an animal scenting danger.

I said pleasantly, "Sit down, Robin, and stop looking as if I was going to put a bomb under you. Your contract comes up for renewal quite soon, doesn't it? Has Hugo had a word with you about it?"

Robin said stiffly, "It's been mentioned. We haven't discussed the terms yet—"

"Then don't."

Robin said, "Greg, if you mean what I think you mean, I find that—"

"Don't jump to conclusions. How would you like to work for Pargiter's?"

Nothing much along then made me feel like laughing, but I had to laugh at Robin's look of horror.

"Pargiter's? Then it's true."

"Not yet. Anyway, I take it you wouldn't want to work for Pargiter's. '

"God, no. Have you ever looked at the sort of stuff they turn out? It's rubbish anyway, and all they'd want a designer for is to put a few new trimmings on the same old thing they've done for years. Greg, they'd kill us stone dead—"

"You don't have to convince me, you know. Still, what would you do if it happened?"

"I'd rather get out of the industry altogether. I enjoy working here, Greg, you let me have my head and I think I've done a few good things, but I'm beginning to feel I'd like to do something quite different for a bit. You know. Get around. Travel."

"Take the golden road to Nepal?" I asked. "Get a party together and drive an old ambulance through the African bush or the Gobi Desert or wherever? Shack up in a tent in Nairobi city park? Everybody under twenty-five does it these days. Wish I'd done it myself. Too late now."

"Yes, well . . . I wouldn't mind doing something like that. Before one gets, you know, kind of settled. In a groove . . ."

I, I supposed, must be in a groove already, at the moment a most uncomfortable one.

Robin's forehead was creased. He looked doubtfully at me. "Are you trying to get rid of me, Greg?"

"Not in the least," I said.

I explained.

After Cass left me I went back to an old habit, of dropping in at a local pub at the end of the day, thus postponing the moment when I had to go back to the empty flat in which all traces of her presence had disappeared except the piano. On one such evening, as I walked to my door from the lift, I could hear the telephone ringing.

It could have been any one of a hundred people but I didn't think of that, I couldn't get into the place fast enough, fumbling with my key and cursing; clumsily I got the door open at last, burst into the hall, while the telephone obliging-

201

ly went on ringing. I grabbed it, repeating the number in a kind of croak. I was out of breath as if I had been running.

A woman's voice: "Greg? Is that you?"

It was my sister Maddy.

The letdown was immediate and immense; for a moment I didn't answer. When I did I sounded peculiar, even to myself.

"Are you all right?" she asked.

"Of course I'm all right. I've just this minute come in. What is it?"

She said sadly, "I was afraid you'd bark at me like that. This isn't easy, so just listen a minute, will you? I just want to say . . . to say . . . " She paused, and then added in a rush, "Look, I know I've been a stupid unreasonable bitch and I've let you down and I'm very very sorry. That's all."

I was taken aback. I had almost forgotten that I had parted with Maddy, also, on bad terms; just now there seemed almost nobody with whom I had not quarreled. Maddy had a lot to answer for, but I didn't want to fight with her anymore, so I said gently, "All right, love, all right."

"Oh! That's such a relief, I can't tell you . . . I've been scared to death of ringing you, but Paul said—"

"Paul? What did Paul say?"

"He said I'd never have any peace of mind until I did." She went on eagerly. "We've told each other everything, Greg. We've talked and *talked,* all night, the first night he came home . . . and it's *absolutely all right.*"

I said mechanically, "Well, that's fine. I'm very glad."

"We both agreed that we'd got dull, into a groove, with the kids and that and Paul's work . . . and he met this girl and sort of broke out, that's all it was, and I expect part of what *I* felt was resentment that I couldn't break out too, perhaps I would have done if I'd had the opportunity. Anyway, it's all over, it was over before he went away. If only we'd talked about it then! But neither of us could, somehow, it was a sort of failure in communication—"

"That's the thing with most marriages that go wrong, I expect." I spoke carefully. "What about Celia Ross?"

"Who? Oh, her. She met some man and got engaged while

202

she was in Africa. It was nothing to do with her anyway, I'd got that all wrong. No. It was a girl in the Barn Theatre Company, their stage manager I think she was. Julie somebody . . . Julie Herriot, that's it. She's not there anymore. I think she took it all rather hard, Paul feels badly about that. But I expect she made most of the running, you know," Maddy added, a little smug in her role of the forgiving wife, blaming it all on the other woman.

Julie Somebody, Julie Herriot. About this, Paul would not lie. If the truth had been what I had believed, he might have prevaricated, but he would not have lied. He would have said to Maddy: It doesn't matter who she was, it's over. But he had no reason for concealment, so he was remedying that failure in communication which had bedeviled them for so long. While Maddy chattered on, I stood there silently holding the telephone, astounded at the extent of my own folly.

"Greg," Maddy said, "are you still there?"

"Yes. I'm here."

"I must ask you this. Has the deal gone through?"

"Not yet. It's in process."

"Oh, dear, I do feel awful. Isn't there anything I can do?"

"Not a thing now, I'm afraid, you're out of the picture. Never mind. These things take time, fortunately, and I still have a few tricks in the bag. Don't worry."

"Well, I do. I can't help it. I can't think now how I could have been so crazy, stupid . . ."

"Oh, well," I said, "we all do crazy things sometimes, under pressure," and as far as I was concerned that was the understatement of all time. "Forget it, now," I said to her. "Be happy." I knew she would be. As I spoke I remembered the night she'd cried on my shoulder and told me her troubles, I hardly able to concentrate on them, absorbed as I was by my ruthless private joy. Now the tables were turned. Conscience-stricken though she was, Maddy couldn't help being happy, now she'd made her peace with me. If she had known Cass had left me, she'd have been sorry and concerned and gone right on being happy. We made a good pair, she and I; both, in our way, egotists.

I didn't tell her anything. She asked about Cass and I said

she was fine, out this evening, she had an engagement. Maddy said we must come down for a weekend soon and I said yes, we'd love that; wanting only to put the phone down, to get rid of her.

That was done, at last. Now I had to find Cass. And I had no idea where she was.

Fourteen

THERE was Jay, of course, Emma, the Fisher organization. I was not going to them. Not yet.

The Morgans were the most likely. If Cass had confided in them, they might not be feeling friendly toward me. But surely they'd know something.

It was painful to go back there, to that house. I parked the car around the corner, where I'd parked it that very first time, beside the red door in the wall that led to Cass's old flat, the little yard with the geraniums. I went around to the front of the house and rang the bell.

Liz opened the door. She stared at me in astonishment. Perhaps I looked a bit odd.

"Greg! Is anything wrong?"

"Liz," I said, "Cass isn't here, is she?"

"No," she said, bewildered. "Should she be? I mean, what's happened?"

"I don't know where she is," I said.

Liz said gently, "Here, come on in."

I followed her upstairs. The Morgans' living room was as untidy as ever. Ben sat at the table, eating spaghetti with one hand and nursing his daughter with the other. The child, rosy from a recent bath, stared solemnly at me out of round brown eyes like her mother's. Ben greeted me cheerfully. Liz said, rather too dramatically: "Ben, Greg's come about Cass. She's disappeared."

"Steady on," I said. "She hasn't disappeared, not like that. We had a row and she cleared out and I've got to find her."

Ben said seriously, "Oh, I see. Well, she hasn't been here,

Greg. Look, have you eaten? There's plenty more of this on the go."

"No, really, thanks all the same. I don't want anything just now."

"A drink, then. We've got some of our Christmas booze left."

They fussed over me hospitably. I sat in a chair turning a large Scotch—all that was left in the bottle I suspect—around and around in my hand while the Morgans gazed at me, their gentle twin-like faces solemn with concern.

"I don't suppose you want to tell us what happened," Liz said.

"Not really, if you don't mind. Not just now, anyway."

There was a tap on the door, a girl's voice said, "Liz, sorry to bother you—I wonder if you've any milk you can spare? I forgot to order any—"

"Yes, of course. Come in, Julie."

The girl came into the room. I recognized her at once: the peaky little face, the long fall of mousy hair. Our eyes met; I knew that she remembered me, too; as part, I suppose, of the worst evening in her life.

"Julie," I said.

She put her hand up to her mouth in the age-old woman's gesture of distress; Liz was saying, "Julie, this is Gregory Hunter, Cass's husband . . ." She looked from one to the other of us. "But . . . you know each other?"

"Not to speak to," I said. "We've seen each other before." I turned to the girl. "At Gatwick, wasn't it? Last June? You were sitting next to a fat woman who was eating sweets."

"Yes." A look of pain crossed her face, like a shadow. "And you were one of the people seeing him off."

"And, of course, you were seeing him off too, in your own way, without a chance to say good-bye? That must have been tough."

Her face began to break up into tears. She said, her voice trembling, "What's that to you? What right have you to talk to me like this?"

"None at all," I said. "I'm sorry."

206

"Of course, you . . . you're her brother, aren't you? His wife's? If you've come here to reproach me, you're wasting your time. It's over—"

Ben said loudly, "Will somebody for Pete's sake tell me what's going on?"

"Ben," I said, "be a good chap and keep out of this, just for a minute." I turned back to the girl and said gently, "Look, I know it's over, and of course I didn't come here to reproach you. I didn't know you'd be here. I'm sorry I upset you. I'm not hostile, believe me; I'm only too glad to have it confirmed that you exist. I'd just like to ask you one thing. Has Cass been in touch with you?"

"No. I haven't heard from Cass for weeks. Excuse me," she said, and fled.

Liz called after her, "I'll come up with the milk in a minute, Julie."

Nobody said anything. Ben went off, carrying his now drowsy child, to put her to bed. Liz fetched the milk from the kitchen and went upstairs with it; she was away some minutes, returning just as Ben emerged from the bedroom. They both looked at me reproachfully.

Liz said mildly, "Greg, why on earth did you do that?"

I took a large gulp of the whisky, and said heavily, "I suppose I'd better tell you."

After I left the Morgans I went back home again and telephoned Jay. No reply from his London flat; I tried the Maidenhead number. A foreign voice answered, presumably the male half of the Spanish couple Jay employed; he didn't seem to understand me very well. He repeated several times that Mr. Fisher was not there, and gave me the office number which of course I knew already.

I considered and rejected the possibility of telephoning other people; I couldn't and wouldn't spread the news around that Cass and I had parted. There was nothing to do now except wait for the morning, settle for a period of forced inaction. I wandered restlessly around the flat, foraged in the refrigerator for food I didn't really want, had a

207

drink, two drinks, grabbed the telephone with futile hope every time it rang. Then I remembered that there was a transmission of a television show that evening on which Cass had a guest spot. I switched on the set and waited impatiently through the finale of an ancient film, through the following commercials. Then the show began: dancers, the smooth young star of the show in his groovy suit, making jokes, wailing away in a fake American accent, the whole thing punctuated with well-regulated laughter and applause from the studio audience. He did a gushing lead-in to Cass's appearance, and there she was at last, without her piano, wandering about in that absurd way singers do on television, in and around a series of silvery arches, up and down steps. The camera rested lovingly on her in close-up, sometimes on two Casses at once, the pictures melting from one lovely angle to the next.

Then we were back to the star again, applauding, on the two of them while he kissed her and told her she was wonderful and there was a joky bit of dialogue—rehearsed or spontaneous, I wouldn't know; then they sang a song together, perched on two stools side by side, gazing into each other's eyes. Cass seemed perfectly at ease, as if she had been doing this sort of thing for years. Halfway through I'd had enough and switched off.

Of course, she wasn't there. There was nothing there but disembodied voices and images; the show had been recorded some weeks ago. I tried Jay's London number again. No reply. I made up my mind to ring him first thing in the morning; and I did that, after a restless night.

The telephone rang a long time, but eventually I heard Jay's voice, furry with sleep, repeating the number.

"Jay, this is Gregory Hunter."

"What? Who?"

I said my name again.

"Jesus, do you have to wake me in the middle of the night? What's the time?"

"Half-past seven, actually."

Jay groaned. "Oh, well. It feels like the middle of the night. I didn't get to bed until four. What do you want?"

I said rapidly, "Look, Jay, I'm sorry about this, but I couldn't risk trying to get hold of you later in the day and failing. I've got to find my wife. I don't know where she is but perhaps you do. Just tell me and I won't bother you fur ther."

There was a pause. Then he said, "Sorry. I can't help you."

"Or won't, is that it?"

There was a click, the whirring of the dialing tone. He'd hung up on me.

I got the car out and drove around there. He'd been too sleepy to have got up and gone out; if he wouldn't see me, I was fully prepared to wait on the doorstep until he emerged. I leaned on the doorbell and waited.

After not too long an interval he opened the door. He wore a purple silk dressing gown and yesterday's beard and looked rather less than benign. He said resignedly, "All right, all right, you'd better come in. Had breakfast yet? I thought not. I'm just making some. Come in the kitchen."

Jay's London flat was a machine for living in; we walked through a living room, inhumanly tidy, which looked as if nothing had ever happened in it but a business conference, to a kitchen gleaming with gadgetry which I'm sure was hardly ever used. Coffee, percolating on the stove, smelled delicious; as we entered the room the toaster, working as it were on cue, delivered its two pieces of toast. Everywhere I went, I thought vaguely, people kept offering me food I didn't want.

"Where is she?" I said.

Jay had evidently decided to humor me. "Gregory, sit down, there's a good chap, and don't get excited. Have some coffee. Black? White? Sugar?"

"Black. No sugar. And no soft soap either, please."

Jay sighed, and busied himself with the coffee. "Now, there's one very nervous upset little girl, Gregory, and we've got problems, I'm afraid . . ."

"So you've seen her," I said. "And she's confided in you." Saying this gave me the most acute pain.

"Up to a point. Anyway, I've packed her off for a complete rest. I think she shouldn't be disturbed for a bit."

"*You'd* rather she wasn't disturbed? Jay, this *is* my wife you're talking about."

"Well, she did say that she'd left you, and that it was final. Now, I know women say things like that sometimes without meaning them. But I think she meant it, all right."

"It was a misunderstanding. It can be put right in five minutes."

"That's not the way I read it," Jay said. "She said that if you got in touch with me about her—she said *if*, she seemed to think it unlikely—I wasn't to tell you where she was. Sorry."

"I don't believe you," I said.

Jay gave me a hard stare with those opaque brown eyes of his, set shallowly on his doughy face like bits of dark pebble. I looked back at him, angry and afraid of my anger. He was years older than I, he was out of condition, we were alone in the flat. I thought of shaking him like a terrier shaking a rat and saying over and over, where is she, till he told me. Only he wouldn't tell me, unless he chose to; that long, fearless stare meant he knew exactly what was in my mind and didn't give a damn. He was both powerful and menacing, this flabby middle-aged man who played far too large a part in our lives, Cass's and mine. He stood calmly between her and me and might succeed in staying that way. He would comfort and console her; the warm liking she had for him might develop; when he had succeeded in finally parting us, he might even marry her one day . . . he might. It was up to me to see it never got to that stage. One thing was plain, trying to bully Jay was totally counterproductive. I stopped trying.

"Look, Jay, it's not like you think. I don't want to see Cass to make a scene. I got the wrong idea about . . . well, about things, it doesn't matter what they were. I just want to tell her I'm sorry for what happened. That I love her and want her back."

Jay said gently, "That 's better." He seemed to make up his mind. "She's at my place in the country. There's nobody else there except the staff." He added with a faint grin, reading my mind as usual: "And I'm here in London. As you see."

I couldn't get away during the morning. When I returned to the office from an appointment, just before lunch, Mrs.

210

Ferguson said: "Mr. Hunter, Mr. Pargiter's secretary telephoned. Old Mr. Pargiter. The chairman."

"Ah," I said, half to myself, "I thought that might happen."

"I beg your pardon?"

"Nothing. It doesn't matter. What does he want?"

"To invite you to lunch."

"You haven't committed me? Good. Well, look, don't be in an overwhelming hurry to ring back. Say I'm tied up for the next few days. Suggest one day next week. And, Mrs. Ferguson—keep that appointment to yourself, eh?"

She said with a puzzled air, "Yes, of course, Mr. Hunter—"

"And stall everybody else for the rest of the day. I shan't be back till the morning."

I drove down to Maidenhead, stopping briefly for a beer and a sandwich at a pub on the way. I had extracted a promise from Jay not to telephone a warning of my coming. He said Paolo had his instructions—which probably accounted for that frustrating telephone call—and might try to keep me out. "Let him try," I said. "You're not holding her incommunicado, are you?"

It was a fine, mild day for January, and other times I would have enjoyed getting out into the country, plowland and stubble and the naked woodlands switching by, all bathed in the milky winter sunshine. As it was I didn't pay much attention, concentrating solely on getting where I was going as quickly as possible. But I felt a lot better. I was on my way, I was taking action. I only had to see her, and everything would be all right again.

I didn't have to deal with Paolo. As I came up the drive of Jay's house I saw Cass in the garden, returning, I suppose, from a walk, Jay's two Afghans bounding about her. I slammed on the brakes and leaped out of the car, making my way along a path through the trees. The two great, graceful dogs, feathery fringes of hair in their eyes, came leaping toward me, barking.

"Cass," I called, and she turned reluctantly, to face me, callng the dogs off. She was wearing pants and a polonecked sweater under an anorak, and her hair was tied up in a ponytail, scraped off her face. She looked pale, but otherwise all right. With the mellow old house behind her and the dogs fanning round, she might have been posing for a picture in *Country Life.*

"What do you want?" she said.

"To talk to you. Can't we go indoors?"

"I suppose so . . . I ought to take the dogs round to the kitchen first, their paws are muddy—"

"Leave them. They'll be all right for a bit, won't they?"

I had a feeling that if she took the dogs to the kitchen, she might not come back.

"All right." She led the way through a French window into a little sitting room which she was evidently using. A bright log fire burned in the grate, there were books and newspapers about, and, of all things, some knitting. It didn't look as if she'd got very far with it, and that told me a lot. She was just passing the time there, waiting. Waiting for me?

All the same, she had gone a long way away. She pulled off the anorak and threw it on a chair, but she didn't sit down and didn't ask me to, either. The dogs, shut out, nosed at the glass of the French window and whined disconsolately.

I said, "I've come to take you home, Cass."

She didn't say anything to that, just looked at me and shook her head.

"Darling, don't be like that. I'm sorry. I'm so very sorry. It was all my fault, every bit of it. I love you, Cass. Come home, darling, please."

Well, I could hardly have groveled more, or so it seemed to me, and it did seem to work. She flushed, and her eyes came alive again, and it looked as if she might start crying any minute, and that was enough for me. The next moment we were in a tight embrace, rocking to and fro with the pain and delight of being together again, and I knew everything would be all right.

Or it might have been, if I'd kept my mouth shut. But in between stroking her hair and kissing and comforting I said, "Darling, don't cry. It's all over, and it won't ever happen again. I know it now, the whole story. I just don't know how I could ever—"

"The whole story?" Her head came up, and she stared at me. "What whole story?"

I told her: Maddy's phone call, the visit to the Morgans, my meeting with Julie. "That settled it. Of course, the moment I saw her, I remembered seeing her at the airport, the night Paul left, and everything fell into place—"

"I'm sure it did," said Cass loudly. "Now you've checked up and sifted the evidence and cross-examined the witnesses. Let me go, Greg. It's no use."

Dumbfounded, I said, "What do you mean? What's no use?"

She moved away, putting a space between us, the width of the world. She said, "You'd believe Maddy, Paul, Julie . . . anybody. Anybody, but me. You wouldn't believe me. You wouldn't even listen to me."

"For God's sake, Cass! I was upset, jealous. I acted like that because I love you—"

"Is that what you call it? You don't love me, Greg. You just want to own me—"

"Rubbish. You've always done exactly as you liked. I let you go on with your career—"

"Yes, you did, didn't you? You *let* me. That's what I mean. And there's been trouble ever since it looked like coming to something—"

I wasn't going to argue about that. I said, "You told me once you wanted to belong to somebody."

"Belong *with*," said Cass. "Not belong *to*. There's a world of difference. That sort of thing has to be two-sided anyway. You've always wanted me to account for everything, my thoughts, my life before I knew you, everything. But you . . . you keep your secret self locked away. You never want to tell me things. Just that one time, about Tessa . . . when you couldn't avoid it. Do you think I don't know how much you hated that? And I hated your hating it and . . . it just means we're not right for each other."

"But you love me," I said, and she answered with her head down: "You can love somebody and not be able to live with them. It happens all the time—"

"*And you want me.* You always have. You always will—" and

213

she flinched and cried, "Don't, don't," and I followed up my advantage, taking hold of her again and caressing her and jeering at her, "What are you going to do nights, Cass, in your little cold narrow bed? Thinking about me, remembering me? The magician, that's what you used to say, remember? How are you going to try and find what you found with me with some other bloke, knowing all the time it's a dead loss? This is stupid, love, come on, don't fight me . . ."

But she did, and broke away at last. She took out a clean, folded handkerchief, and wiped her eyes carefully. I found this gesture in Cass, who would normally have let her tears run, or rubbed them from her eyes with her knuckles, more alarming than anything she had done so far. I stood there, not knowing what to do with her. Of course, I could have used my strength. I could have forced myself on her. I could have taken her there and then on the floor of that room. A lot of good that would have done.

As if echoing my thought, she said, "Greg, that's blackmail, and you know it. Of course what you say is true. We could make love, here, now, and everything would be wonderful for a little while. But we'd soon be back to square one again and . . . I've been *miserable*, Greg, these past months, and now this last thing . . . I've been so miserable. I can't take anymore. I mean it."

She did mean it. She faced me, tear-stained and inexorable. There are times when you have to recognize when you're beaten. When that happens to me, a deathly chill sets in.

"All right," I said. "So you mean it. Only don't talk about love. It's you who doesn't know the meaning of the word. What are you going to do now?"

"I don't know. Find a flat, I suppose . . ."

"Well, when you're settled, let me know and I'll have the piano sent."

"I don't want you to do that—"

"Why not? It's yours. And these are yours, too." I took out the jewelry she had left behind and put it on the table. "Keep them to remember me by. Good-bye, Cass."

She didn't answer. I opened the French window and the

dogs, muddy paws and all, scrambled past me into the room. They rushed up to Cass, nuzzling and pushing her. She threw her arms round them, and my last sight of her was just her bowed dark head, buried in their feathery fur.

Outside, the early winter twilight was closing in. There was just enough light for me to find my way back across the garden to the car. A damp chill rose out of the ground and there was a heavy mist, too, after the unseasonable brightness of the day. I turned the car back toward London, though it didn't seem to matter much which way I went.

I came to a junction, a road sign, right to London. Left to Polney. The name leaped at me. "A village near Maidenhead," my mother had said sulkily, "I expect he's in the book."

Neville, my former stepfather, lived at Polney. We hadn't met for twenty years. At this particular moment the thought of that long-lost paternal affection and kindness was irresistible.

Neville. Like Sarah on another occasion, he had come to cue.

It was rather a pretty village, what there was of it. There was an old church, an ivy-covered vicarage, a village shop and post office, a row of neat Georgian cottages abutting almost directly onto the roadway, only two feet or so of cobbled path between. The cottages had been tarted up with the usual wrought-iron lanterns and window boxes and fanciful door knockers. I stopped at the post office and went in to look up Neville's address in the telephone book. There it was, 4 Challenor's Row, the cottages I had just passed.

I left the car where it was and walked back, found Number 4.

The bell-push evoked melodious chimes. I waited.

The door was opened by a young man in his twenties. He wore an expensive purple sweater, trousers in raspberry-colored velvet, and a gold chain around his neck. He had long yellow hair, and was staggeringly beautiful.

I was so taken aback that I almost forgot what I had come for. He was clearly used to this reaction and welcomed it. One well-kept hand went up to pat the golden hair; he swiveled a little at the hips and gave me a slow-burn smile. He said in a fluty voice, "Yes? What can I do for you?"

I found my voice at last. "Does Mr. Grant live here, please?"

"That's right. What name shall I say?"

"I'm his stepson. Gregory."

"Oh, of *course!* I've heard of *you!* Come in. I'm Stephen, by the way."

"How do you do," I said blankly.

I entered the small hall: white paint, a Bokhara rug, a spindly antique table, delicate prints on the walls. Stephen opened another door and cried brightly, "Visitor for you, Neville! Surprise, surprise!"

I thought, oh, my *God.* I entered a room furnished with chintz armchairs, white bookshelves, a lot of china ornaments. It was suffocatingly cozy, with central heating radiators combined with a sizable fire on this mild afternoon. Neville sat in one of the chintz armchairs by the fire, a Siamese cat lying across his knees. As my mother had said, he had got much fatter, pink-cheeked, chubby and serene. His hair was quite white. Well, as she had also said, twenty years had passed.

The cat seemed to resent my presence. It glared at me with its azure eyes, leaped down from Neville's knee and dashed past me through the open door with an indignant yowl.

Neville got up, with some difficulty, and said with emotion, "My dear boy! My dear old chap!" His voice was heavy and old. "This is an unexpected pleasure!" He shook my hand, and embraced me clumsily with the other arm. "But how did you find us?'

"Mother told me you were living here. I was passing so I—"

"I'm very glad you did. You'll have some tea, won't you? Stephen, put the kettle on, there's a dear. Come and sit down, Gregory."

216

We sat down on either side of the fire. Stephen went off, presumably to get the tea.

"Well," Neville said. "This *is* nice."

I said with an effort, "Are you well, Neville?"

He spread reddened hands, swollen at the joints, in a deprecating gesture. "As well as I can be, dear boy. Arthritis, you know. Painful of course. Can't do what I used to do. Stephen looks after me. He's a dear child. Most devoted."

I didn't say anything.

Neville said gently, "You've had a shock, Gregory."

"Well . . ."

"Don't pretend. No need for that, not anymore. Of course, you didn't know. You were only fourteen when I left. She never told you?"

"Mother? No."

"That was good of her," Neville said.

I burst out suddenly, "Why, for God's sake? Why did you do it? Why did you marry her?"

Neville sighed. "People don't always come to terms with their own nature. I thought we could make a go of it. Lydia had had a bad time; first your father was killed, then later she had a disastrous love affair. I was around when that came to an end. That's all, really. As I say, I thought we could make a go of it, but of course in time it became clear that we couldn't, or rather, I couldn't. Once she realized the situation, her one thought was for you."

"For me?"

"Who else? She thought I would corrupt you. She knew I loved you," Neville added with simplicity. "But I am not a pederast, Gregory. It was a father's love. You must believe that. But she didn't understand, and she was frightened. For us to separate, divorce, wasn't enough for her. I was never to see you again. She threw the book at me, as they say. She was like a tigress defending her young. You can't blame her, really."

"I did," I muttered, "I blamed her for the breakup, for everything, I thought it was because of Russell—"

"Oh, no. He came later. He's not responsible. So, all this time, you've never understood?"

"No. I must have been a dumb unobservant kid—"

"Youngsters were less knowing then, I suppose. Well, anyway—" He looked across at me and smiled, and for a moment he was the old Neville, full of fun and kindliness. "I'm glad you came today. Very glad."

"I'm glad too," I said.

The tea-trolley rattled outside, Stephen making a great business of opening the door. "Well," he cried merrily, "if you two old buddies have finished your heart-to-heart—"

We had tea, Stephen pouring it from a silver teapot into old porcelain cups. There was a plum cake, and delicate little sandwiches. Neville talked about the old days, reminiscing comfortably. He asked after Maddy, and I was glad to be able to tell him that Maddy was fine. "She's married, very happily. Three lovely kids."

"Well, what do you know," said Neville. "Little Maddy, grown up and married with a family . . . it's hard to believe. Give her my best love when you see her."

"Yes. Yes, of course."

About me, he seemed to know everything already. He had watched my career from afar, he said. He spoke, with gentle sympathy, about Tessa's death. He knew about my marriage to Cass. "Lovely girl. Beautiful voice. You must be proud of her." I said yes to that, and let it go.

Stephen began to grow bored with a conversation in which he had no part. He interrupted, made jokes, clowned about like the spoiled child he was, displaying like a peacock. I saw Neville's eyes following him, warm with indulgent love, and felt the sadness of it: knowing that Neville knew, none better, that one day his golden boy would leave him for a more attractive, more powerful protector. I felt no scorn for Neville's feelings. In the house of love, one might say, there are many mansions.

I was there for more than an hour, but when Neville and I said good-bye, we both knew that I would not come again. I drove away from Polney in a confusion of feelings: comforted in a strange way; trying to sort out what Neville had told me about my mother. I had thought of her for years as a vain, ruthless and egotistical woman, putting her own satisfaction first and her children last. But she was not quite as I supposed, and for the first time I began, dimly, to understand how a long buried resentment against her had colored my relationships with other people. With women, particularly. Above all, with Cass.

But it was too late now to do anything about that.

Fifteen

"I ASSUME," said old Pargiter in that measured and majestic manner of his, "you know why I have invited you here, Mr. Hunter."

I said nicely, "Well, that has been puzzling me somewhat, I must confess." His style of talking was catching.

Up to then, the atmosphere had been quite genial. We had lunched alone in his flat on the top floor of the Pargiter building ("over the shop" as he liked to say), waited on by a glum elderly woman with a slight moustache, dressed in an old-fashioned maid's dress with apron and cap. We ate grilled sole and drank water, and beforehand I had been offered, rather reluctantly, a very small Scotch. Robert, the elder of the two Pargiter sons, would join us, he said, for coffee. Typical touch, that was: Robert, pushing fifty and Managing Director, admitted at the end of the meal like a child parading for dessert after a Victorian dinner party. The old man had been a long time coming to the point, whatever that might be, and I saw no reason to help him.

He stared at me rather coldly now with his small blue eyes sunk in a·mass of wrinkles. He looked pink, and very clean, rather like an elderly baby.

"As you know," he began, "my son Robert"—and I recalled the enmity between them, which had probably not softened with the years—"my son Robert has been engaged in some negotiations with your company. I was not aware until the other day that you had taken no part whatever in these negotiations. Why is that?"

"Why didn't he tell you, or why didn't I take part?"

"Please don't let us bandy words. I mean, of course, why

221

have you held aloof in this way? I find that curious and unsatisfactory. I don't like mysteries—"

"No mystery," I said cheerfully. "I don't want to sell. If it were up to me, I'd see you in hell first. No offense meant, of course. But it's not up to me. My codirectors, if they wish, can sell the company, its name, the stock, the capital equipment, the existing designs . . . all the assets, in fact, except one. Me. I'm not for sale, I'm afraid."

About then, Robert appeared. I had first known Robert when I joined Pargiter's fresh from college, and he had then been in charge of the manufacturing end of their business. He hadn't liked me, and I don't blame him, really. I was a cocky kid, and I think Robert always knew I was there to pick their brains and learn the trade and would get out to start on my own as soon as I could raise the capital. In latter years Robert and I ran into each other from time to time, at trade shows and such, and had fallen into the superficial bonhomie of business acquaintances; so we were Robert and Greg to each other, and even had a drink together now and then.

But there was not much bonhomie about Robert today. I felt a bit sorry for him. I would have taken a large bet that he hadn't known till the last minute that his father had asked me to lunch. He greeted me dourly, sat down and poured himself some coffee. The old man ignored him, saying sharply, "I have been misled." He made it sound like lèse majesté at least, and that Russell and Hugo, and perhaps Robert too, should be taken out and shot at dawn.

I murmured something about being sorry if there had been a misunderstanding. Old Pargiter was not mollified.

"May I say I find your attitude most extraordinary. You really mean that you would abandon this firm, which you have created and built up, which bears your name—"

"That's right."

"But why? Surely you understand that there will be great advantages in this new arrangement? Opportunities for development and expansion? Doesn't any of that weigh with you?"

"Of course. But freedom of action weighs with me more. I'm sorry."

Robert stirred. He said in his grating, unattractive voice,

222

"Leave the man alone, Father. If he doesn't want to know, that's his affair. It doesn't change anything." Looking at me, he added, "After all, you don't even do the designing now, do you?"

"Ah," I said, "you're thinking of Robin Tarrant. His contract with us won't be renewed, I'm afraid. Robin is going abroad. Well . . . if you're happy with what you're getting, gentlemen, there's not much more to be said." It may seem strange, but I was rather enjoying myself. I had nothing to lose, after all. I looked from one to the other of them: the old man's face frosty and remote, Robert's with an expression of dawning affront and suspicion. I added, with an air of mild speculation, "I wonder what you'll do with it."

Robert said, "I beg your pardon?" He sounded outraged.

I said gently, "I'm just interested, Robert. There's the trade name, of course. It has a reputation for quality and originality—at the top end of the market. You could produce a cheaper version of the existing designs, and sell them under the Hunter label. Only we're not all that widely known in the mass market, in which case you might just as well call the stuff New Sheraton or anything else that takes your fancy. If that idea doesn't seem viable you could always strip the assets and wind the whole thing up. In that case, on the present showing, you're being rather overgenerous, I'd say."

I started to get up. "I have been running on a bit, haven't I? It really is not my concern. Do forgive me. Thank you for lunch, Mr. Pargiter. It's been very nice meeting you again."

The old man said, "Just a moment. If the deal were to go through, what would you do?"

"Me? Start again, of course."

Robert looked disbelieving. His father suddenly came out with one of those old men's chuckles, like the sound of dry leaves. He said in his cold old voice, tinged now with unwilling admiration, "You are a headstrong young man, Mr. Hunter, and I'm sorry for your colleagues. But, in a way, you are a man after my own heart."

"Sheer duplicity," said Hugo. He looked furious. "I suppose you know what you've done is most improper? Acting behind our backs, without our knowledge?"

223

I laughed. "Come off it, Hugo. You know I don't give a toss how improper it is. And the least said about duplicity the better."

He didn't know how to answer that one, and I went on more gently, "Look, don't let's have a fight over this. Your scheme's come unstuck because you saw it only as a business deal and ignored the human element. So you couldn't see the whole affair revolved round the personality of the old man. Old men are like children, Hugo; they like toys. If they've been in business for fifty-odd years, the only thing that's going to amuse them is another business. Of course, it's got to be viable, he's not quite senile yet. But a prestige outfit like ours, something different from what he's used to—would be just the job. He'd have done a lot for us, I don't doubt, *and* been on our backs the whole time. But the moment he saw he was only getting a de-gutted version of the original thing, he went off the idea. And, of course, Robert never wanted it anyway; he only went along with Pa because he had to. Supposing the old man died? That would be our lot, you must know that."

"All very plausible," Hugo said sullenly, "but they may still want to go ahead."

"I don't think so. They're either going to retreat altogether, as they still can, or come up with another, less favorable proposition. In that case, we shall have to reconsider the whole thing." I let a little silence fall, and added, "Maddy rang me the other day. We've made up our differences. I don't think you can count on her support anymore, Hugo. I really don't."

At the end of the afternoon, Mrs. Ferguson came in for my letters, and lingered.

"Mr. Hunter, I've been wanting to ask you. What is going to happen? To the firm?"

It came to me that behind that reserved and correct exterior, she had been eating her heart out with anxiety for weeks. I hadn't told her anything, I hadn't even thought about her, or the many others worrying about their jobs. I would have to go down to the factory tomorrow, where blunt questions were already being asked.

I said gently, "I'm sorry. You've been worrying, haven't you?"

"A bit," she admitted.

"Well, you needn't. Nothing's going to happen, with any luck. Not that you'd have any problem anyway, you know. You could command a good salary anywhere."

She smiled. "Well, thank you. But I enjoy working here and . . . not everybody wants to employ somebody my age as a secretary. Most of them want the dolly birds."

"More fools them."

"It's nice of you to say so, but there it is. And for me the next five years are crucial. Till the children are off my hands."

"Yes, I know. Don't worry, my dear. I think we can be fairly sure Hunter's will still be here in five years' time. And so, I hope, will you and I."

"I hope so too. Good night, Mr. Hunter."

"Good night."

I went on sitting there after she'd gone and thought about the next five years and what I'd be doing at the end of them. I'd be pushing forty, still beavering away and not much idea what I'd be doing it for. Some time or other, Cass would want a divorce, and that would be done, and perhaps I'd marry again. Third time lucky. Perhaps.

A cold rain, turning to sleet, was coming down as I left. Tom Abbott, our porter and handyman, was pottering about in the hall.

"You want an umbrella to get you to the car, Mr. Hunter? It's a nasty night."

"But isn't it yours?"

"No, no, just one I keep on the premises."

"Good idea. Thanks, Tom, I'll bring it back tomorrow. Good night."

Walking down to the parked car in the rain, I felt faintly warmed by the exchange with Tom Abbott. This is what I'd come to, it seemed, to feel warmed by some such small display of concern by someone who worked for me, because there wasn't much else. I joined the crawling crush of home-

225

going traffic, the rain beating down on us all. At the next red traffic light I saw, between one sweep of the windshield wipers and the next, a girl on the pavement, vainly trying to signal a taxi. The man ignored her, reaching out to slam his flag down—going home, I suppose, to his tea.

Fortunately I was next to the curb. I leaned across, threw open the nearside door.

"Sarah," I shouted.

She turned her head, stared, recognized me and leaped into the car just as the lights changed; the door slammed and we shot away. Sarah turned to me and laughed, pulling off a scarf and letting her hair shake free. "Heavens," she exclaimed, "am I glad to see you!"

"You ought to know better than to try to get a taxi on a night like this," I said. "Where's your car?"

"I've stopped driving to work. I'm so fed up with the parking, it gets worse and worse . . . how are you, Greg?"

"Well. How are you?"

"Oh, I'm *fine*," she said. She sounded warmly happy; I was enormously, absurdly pleased to see her, to have her in my car, leaning back in the passenger seat in the graceful relaxed way which was one of the many pleasing things about her. There didn't seem to be any constraint between us. She said cheerfully, "Well, this is nice."

"Isn't it? Come back and have a drink with me," I said. "I'll drive you home afterwards."

She looked faintly doubtful. "I'd like to, but . . ."

"But what?"

"Well . . . your wife . . ."

"Cass is away. Oh, come on, Sarah, we're old friends, aren't we?"

"Of course. Well, just one quick drink then . . ."

In the flat, she looked at home as she had always done; it was as if she had never been away. I didn't ask her what she wanted to drink because I knew, and I knew how to make it just the way she liked it. Doing this in some way restored our former intimacy and I felt the gray fog of depression lifting just because she was there. She had changed in some subtle way, there was some sort of new warmth about her, she was

226

gayer, more spontaneous. It crossed my mind that I should never have let her go.

I said, meaning it, "It's good to see you, Sarah."

She smiled. "It's good to see *you*." Then she looked at me, not smiling, and asked gently, "How are things with you, Greg?"

I said, blankly, "Does it show that much?"

I saw the flash of puzzlement, of embarrassed reserve, in her face; I had misunderstood her. She said quickly, "I meant Hunter's. All the fuss about . . ."

"Oh, that. Yes. It's all settled, back to square one." I told her the story, making her laugh. She exclaimed, giggling, "They really should fight someone their own weight, shouldn't they? You really are a *wicked* man. But I'm terribly glad you've won out, Pargiter's is too awful, I've realized that after six months . . ."

"Sarah," I said.

She stopped in midsentence. "What is it?"

"You were right the first time."

"I'm afraid I don't . . ."

"Things aren't all right. Not at all. Cass has left me."

"Oh, Greg, I'm sorry. What happened?" Immediately she exclaimed, "No, I take that back, I don't want to know what happened, I know you hate being asked questions . . ."

"Yes. That's part of the trouble, I think. Oh, well. We married in haste and we didn't understand each other. Her career didn't help. Things got as bad as they could be and now the worst has happened and there it is."

Sarah sat there looking concerned and compassionate and gentle. She said gravely, "Is there—somebody else?"

"No. For neither of us. That makes it worse, in a way. She won't come back, though. Oh, well. It was a mistake. There's nothing to do with mistakes except write them off. It takes a bit of getting used to, but I'll live, I expect." I added after a moment: "I should have married you, Sarah. Another of my mistakes."

I expect she got the message, all the things I didn't actually say. Don't go away, Sarah. Stay here. You've always loved me, I know that. So stay. Help me. Comfort me.

227

Yes, she knew all right. And didn't know how to deal with it. I was being unfair to her and I knew it, I had always been unfair to Sarah. I had used and rejected her and whistled her up again and would even now have taken her love to cushion my self-pity; only it wasn't there to take. Her love, I mean. She was nervous; her left hand fidgeted with the clasp of her handbag, which was on the sofa beside her; a slender, well-kept hand with a large, square-cut emerald on the third finger.

I reached over and picked up the hand and looked at it, and she let me, not saying anything.

"Nice ring," I said. She caught my eye and smiled, a little ruefully, faintly apologetic, with the irrepressible radiance breaking through. Warmer, gayer, more spontaneous, of course she was. Her whole personality had flowered. She had loved me, and got little out of it. Now she loved and was loved, she breathed the bright airs on the top of the mountain; I didn't matter at all and I was, thank God, honestly glad of it.

"So you're engaged to be married," I said. "Well, well. Do I know him?"

"I don't think so . . ." She mentioned a name I'd never heard. "He's in the Navy," she added.

"And it's really good? The real thing?"

"Couldn't be better."

"I am glad, darling. Really. I hope you'll be very very happy."

"Thank you."

There didn't seem much more to say. She looked at her watch and exclaimed at the time and said she must go. I didn't try to detain her.

"Let me know what you'd like for a wedding present," I said.

"Yes . . . thank you. And Greg . . . I do hope that things will come right for you. Take care of yourself . . ."

We had parted before, this a more final good-bye than the other had been, yet we looked at each other now with a more genuine affection.

"We had some good times, didn't we?" I said.

"Yes, we did . . ."

228

"You'll have better ones now. Good-bye, love."

We moved into each other's arms quite naturally; the last kind embrace of old lovers who were now good friends. But I suppose the old attraction between us was still there. Sarah kissed me back and the embrace was a bit longer and warmer than either of us had expected.

Neither of us heard the key in the front door or the sound of footsteps, only the door of the living room opening.

Cass was standing in the doorway.

For a single instant I saw on her face the same timid and questioning look it had worn the day she came to meet me at the airport. Then her expression changed, became frozen as she looked at us. Sarah and I sprang apart; but it was too late.

Cass put a hand against her mouth. Then she said, "Oh . . . oh, I'm sorry," and turned and ran; the front door banged behind her.

Sarah cried distressfully, "I'll let myself out, Greg, go after her!"

I didn't need telling. I was out of the door, along the corridor, hoping that Cass would have to wait for the lift. But the lift was there, I saw her vanish into it, the door clanged, it sank out of sight. No use waiting for the other lift. I took the stairs, leaping down them two and three at a time. As I came out of the building I caught sight of Cass between the parked cars in the forecourt, a corner of the bright scarf she was wearing fluttering like a flag. Somewhere among those serried ranks of cars hers must be standing; she would have to find her key, unlock the door, turn on the ignition, start the engine . . .

But she didn't stop anywhere among the parked cars. She emerged beyond the forecourt, on the pavement, about to cross the road. I realized now that the car couldn't be parked there; she must have left it in the cul-de-sac opposite.

The road was thick with homegoing traffic, not a jam, just a steady procession of cars all going faster than they should. It seemed imperative that I should catch up with her before she crossed over; the traffic might delay me in my turn long enough for her to get away. But there was still time to catch her up; she stood there on the curb as if waiting for me.

"Cass!" I shouted. She looked very small standing there. I

couldn't be sure she'd heard me above the noise of the traffic. She took a step forward, off the pavement.

"Cass!" I shouted again, and I saw her head turn, she hesitated. If I hadn't shouted, if she hadn't hesitated, if even then she had stood still . . . But she didn't. She faltered, and then she ran.

The shriek of tires on the road. People running, shouts, curses, somewhere a woman who had seen it all screaming in hysteria. A white-faced driver stammering: she ran right in front of me . . . I couldn't avoid her . . . and after, it seemed a long time after, the clanging of the ambulance bell.

"She's breathing," the ambulance man said.

They let me go with her to the hospital. As I turned to get in to the ambulance, I saw Sarah standing on the pavement; she stood there like a nonswimmer on a river bank, helplessly watching us drown. Then we went away, the sirens screaming over our heads.

At the hospital the machinery of succor and emergency went instantly into action and there was nothing for me to do but wait, in a small room empty but for a table with some tattered magazines on it, and tubular chairs with canvas seats. The window overlooked the main entrance to the hospital through which hundreds of people were now hurrying; it was visiting hour. They streamed in, carrying baskets and carrier bags and bunches of flowers and magazines. They mostly looked cheerful enough, turning right and left purposefully, knowing their way through the grounds, where to find the person they had come to see. In all that vast conglomeration of buildings, I had no idea where Cass was now or what they were doing to her or whether, even, she was still alive.

After what seemed like hours, a young doctor came to find me. Ominously gentle, he spoke of an emergency operation. It would take a long time, he said. He said she had quite a good chance, she was young, her heart was strong, that made a difference. Then he asked, "Is there anyone else who should be notified?"

I said mechanically, "Her parents live in the Midlands. They're not on the phone. She's going to die, isn't she?"

That blank professional kindness: you couldn't get through it.

He said carefully, "She's in a dangerous condition. But we have a lot of bad accident cases here and I've seen many worse who have come through. We're doing everything we can."

"Yes," I said. "Yes, of course. Thank you."

He glanced at me sharply. "Look, I could get the office to deal with that for you. If you'd just write down the address."

"Address?" I couldn't think what he was talking about.

He said patiently, "Your wife's parents. It's just as you like, of course. But we could put a call through from here to the local police. If you want that."

"Yes. I see. All right."

I wrote the address down, gave it to him. He lingered, still looking at me rather hard, and said gently, "It's not hopeless, you know. Don't lose heart."

"No," I said, not believing him. "Thank you."

I went on sitting there for a while after he'd gone. Then I went down the corridor to the men's room and vomited and leaned against the cold tiled wall, disgusted with my weakness. Then I splashed water on my face and dried it ineffectually with a paper towel and walked out, straight into Jay Fisher.

"How did you know?" I asked.

"News like that gets round fast. A chap I know on the *Standard* rang me. How is she?"

"Alive. They're operating. Not committing themselves much."

"Oh, Christ," said Jay. His face looked like gray putty, the same color, I daresay, as my own. He stared at me. "Are you all right?"

"As you see," I said.

Jay nodded sadly, hesitated and fidgeted, said at last, "If it's any help, Greg, I'll stick around."

"Thanks," I said. I kept on thanking people, it seemed like the only word I knew. We went back to the waiting room and sat there silently side by side. Jay produced a hip flask. "Have some of this, you look as if you need it," and I said thanks yet again and took a swig of neat brandy which descended like

231

liquid fire on my emptied stomach. I had always felt hostile to Jay but it was comforting to have him there and I said so. "This is very good of you. I'm afraid I'm not very good company. But I'm grateful for yours. And I'm sorry I was so bloody-minded the other day."

"Forget it," said Jay. He looked at me sidelong and added in a friendly tone, "You've never liked me much, have you?"

"No. I was afraid of you. That you'd take her away from me. Jealous, I suppose."

"Of me?" He seemed astonished. "Look, Greg, in my business there are always a lot of lovely talented girls around. But I don't make time with any of them. Creates too many problems." He smiled, adding, "Besides, I wouldn't reckon I rated with Cass at all. She's very strictly a one-man girl. You should know that."

"Yes," I said. "I should, shouldn't I?"

After a while the door opened, and we both became stiffly alert, but it was not one of the hospital staff who came in, but my mother.

All the customary images I had of people were being knocked about that day. Mother seemed different, the usual patina of grooming and beauty care dimmed and roughened. Her age was showing and she looked kind of determined and frightened at the same time. Frightened: for Cass, of course; but frightened of me too, of how I would react to her coming. Perhaps ever since I had been old enough to make judgments, she had been frightened of me.

I got up and put my arms around her, answering her unspoken question with the words I had used to Jay, adding, "There's no more news yet. We're just waiting. But I'm glad you've come."

I introduced Jay to her. She sat down between us and held my hand as if I were a child going to the dentist. I wondered vaguely how she knew: Sarah had phoned Maddy, perhaps; not that it mattered. We didn't talk much, for there was nothing much to be said. Jay went out to rustle up some coffee for us; while he was gone, I said suddenly, "At least, this time I wasn't driving." I remember my mother's horrified face; she said something like, I mustn't say that, I mustn't think it; I don't know what it was she thought I mustn't think. As I'd never told her anything, she didn't know the half of it.

The long night wore on, punctuated by bulletins: she's holding her own. We had no idea how much or how little this meant. Her parents arrived, Mrs. Clayton white and rigid with terror, bursting into tears on my shoulder when told there was still hope. I patted her, not knowing what to say. Her husband seemed stolid and unmoved as always. I heard him say loudly to Jay: "How did it happen, then?" as if looking around for someone to blame. I couldn't speak to him, because what I wanted to say was, you old bastard, what are you here for, you don't care, you never loved her, you took her childhood away with your grievance and your bloody rejection, get the hell out. But after a bit I looked at him and saw he was the same gray color as everybody else; perhaps, then, he did care, after all, full of fear and guilt as I was.

Morning came, and Cass was still alive.

A new nurse appeared, one we hadn't seen before.

She led Mrs. Clayton and me upstairs, dressed us up in sterile smocks and caps and masks, and took us into the intensive care unit where Cass lay, hardly recognizable amid the mass of tubes and apparatus that was keeping her alive. It was a frightening, almost inhuman sight, and Mrs. Clayton was knocked sideways by it. I should have tried to comfort her, but I was concentrated, with everything I had, on the small mound in the high narrow bed, the helpless center of all that medical hardware. Somewhere in there was my girl.

Somehow, out of anxiety and despair, was growing an angry hope, a rebellious will: she was not going to die. I would not let her die.

Well. I don't really know if that sort of thing really makes any difference.

The hospital staff urged us to go home: get some rest, they said—as if we could—have something to eat, we'll be in touch the moment there's any change. I daresay the ghoulish group we made, with our fears and our silences, was becoming a nuisance. Jay went back to his own place and I took Mother and the Claytons back to mine. Cass's parents and I sat and looked at the telephone, while Mother made tea and prepared breakfast and tried to coax us to eat. It seemed strange to see her there, in our kitchen, busying herself with food and drink, and being, as they say, a tower of strength. As I believe I've said before somewhere, Mother was great at rising to an occasion. On this one, I don't really know what I would have done without her.

The phone rang at last, and I fell on it. The voice said: "She's conscious."

So back we went, and went through the caps-and-masks routine again, and stood by the narrow bed, and Cass opened her eyes and she was Cass again, and knew us. I wanted to say forgive me, for so much folly, for my lack of faith and love. But that was only self-indulgence. All any of us could do for Cass now was to love her, and hold on.

Sixteen

AGAINST the odds, Cass got better.

It was a long job, of course. But for all she seemed so frail, she had a resilience, an inner toughness I had only partly understood before. Recovery was a battle, and she was going to win it. At one stage it was feared she might not walk again, but she overcame that, submitting patiently to repeated sessions of physiotherapy, at last succeeding in walking across the room, a nurse on one side, and me on the other, joking, giggling at her own ineptness, while the sweat of effort stood out on her forehead. The nurse said with satisfaction: "Mr. Bonner will be pleased."

Mr. Bonner was the surgeon. He was a type I don't care for, sharp-eyed, brusque to the point of rudeness, arrogant with the power his skill gave him. Nevertheless he had wrought the miracle, a man to be regarded with awe and gratitude. When I tried to thank him he brushed it aside. "Don't thank me. I just did the engineering. Your wife did the rest. She has a lot of guts, that young woman of yours. By the way, I've been able to reassure her about one thing. Babies."

I was taken aback. It had never occurred to me, not once, to wonder if Cass would be able to have children.

I said, "That's not important. So long as she's well, I don't care—"

He snorted. "*You* don't care, what's that got to do with it? Anyway, it shouldn't be a problem. Have to be a Cesarian section, but never mind that. Give it two or three years, though."

"Yes, of course." I had to know. "Did she ask you about it?"

235

"No. I daresay she was afraid of the answer. Anyway, she knows now."

I waited for Cass to mention it to me, but she didn't. We didn't talk about anything serious, I always careful because she was still an invalid. There could be no dramas, no reconciliation scene. The accident had wiped that slate clean.

Something about her close brush with death following her brief and meteoric career had caught the imagination of the public; her room was always full of flowers sent in by admirers and well-wishers, cards and telegrams and fan mail poured in. One afternoon she said to me, "You know, this accident has made me, hasn't it? I hope I'll be well enough to take advantage of all this goodwill." She spoke dryly, as if laughing the whole thing off.

I said warmly, "Of course you're going to be well enough. You've just got to take a lot of care of yourself for a bit. Or rather I'm going to do that for you."

"Yes . . ." She smiled, and said gently, "You are good to me, Greg."

"I love you," I said, "so why wouldn't I be?"

"Well, I'm not sure I deserve it. From what I've gathered, the whole thing was my own fault, I just walked into that car."

"You were upset," I said. "You misunderstood what was going on."

"Did I? I don't really remember."

We left it like that. She was not quite the Cass I knew; but I suppose this patience and dry good humor was her way of coping. Another time, not long before she came out of hospital, she said to me quite suddenly, "Do you remember my daydream about my father? That everything would come right, and he'd come and say he loved me after all?"

"Yes, I remember."

"Well, he did just that. This morning. Came up on the early train and he's gone back this afternoon. He was sort of bumbling and embarrassed and went round and round it, but he did say it in the end."

"What did he say?"

"Oh, something about, when you all thought I wasn't go-

236

ing to make it . . . he sort of realized that I meant a lot to him after all."

I said warmly, "Darling, I'm so glad, that's wonderful."

"Yes." With a shock, I realized that her eyes were quite empty of feeling. "Wonderful. And it didn't mean anything to me at all, you know. Not a thing. Sad, isn't it?"

I said uneasily, "You've been through a lot, darling. I daresay your responses are a bit blunted for the time being."

"Yes." She sighed. "Perhaps that's it."

While she was still in hospital, I put the flat on the market and found a house for us. It was not unlike the Smiths' house that she had liked so much, built at about the same period, but more spacious. There was a large sunny room downstairs which would do, for the present, for Cass's room; for a while, she'd have trouble with stairs.

Getting the place prepared for her homecoming took up more time than I had, and I enlisted my mother's help with things like curtains and carpets and redecoration; anyway, it needed a woman's touch. She was a bit doubtful at first about this enterprise. "Greg, don't jump down my throat—"

I grinned at her. "Do I ever?"

"At one time, frequently," she said dryly. "Anyway, it's just that I wonder if it wouldn't be better to wait until Cass is well and can do all this for herself."

"It would be a long time before she can do it all herself. Anyway, you can keep her in the picture, can't you?"

"I have, already. But she really isn't strong enough to take a lot of interest—"

"There you are then. So we have to do it for her. Or I do. With your help, if you don't mind giving it."

"Of course I don't mind. I'm glad to do anything for you, you must know that." She said this with a smile, throwing the line away. But I was not deceived. I saw on her face, behind the smile, the sad and seeking look I had observed the day of Cass's accident; and understood it for the first time.

I moved in a few days before Cass was due to be discharged from the hospital. I had engaged a housekeeper, but she could not start until the following week; Maddy came up from Stallington to help, and Mother arrived too for the weekend, driven by Russell, who tactfully didn't stay. A lot of problems seemed to have dissolved under the impact of our personal crisis, including the internal politics of Hunter's. Russell organized defeat and retired gracefully from the scene, and Hugo and I had managed to get on a new footing. The trade recession had taken hold and times weren't easy, but, working together, we would save Hunter's if we could.

There was a festive sort of atmosphere the day I moved house. Maddy arrived about the same time as the removal men; she leaped out of the car and came in with a rush, darting gleefully from room to room, going into extravagant ecstasies: "Mummy, those curtains are heaven, where did you get them? Oh, look, you can see the river from here, and there's a little terrace. You'll be able to sit out there on warm nights with long chairs and long drinks . . . Greg, this is a glorious place."

I had to smile: Maddy was herself again. We had a rather nice weekend really, working against time to get the house in order. Without stepfathers or wives or husbands or children, the three of us were temporarily a family again, the two women ganging up to tease me. Mother enjoyed herself hugely and did wonders, although, as Maddy muttered to me, she could not have so much as washed up a cup for years. In the evening we sat long over our meal in the kitchen, I opened a bottle of wine, and we were all filled with the sleepy self-satisfaction one gets from doing some untoward physical work usually left to others. Eventually, Mother announced she was dying on her feet and retired to bed.

"It's funny," said Maddy when we were left alone, "isn't it? I mean, after all the awful things that have happened, the way everything seems to be coming up roses? I suppose it can't last, but it's nice while it does last, I must say. I've never seen you and Mother seem so close. Of course she's always adored you—"

"Adored me? Mother?"

"Of course she has. First child, a son, all that. I didn't really get a look in," she said without rancor. "Of course she adored

238

you. But you've always choked her off. She asked me once what she'd done and I said I thought it must be because of Neville, and she shut up like a clam, I don't know why."

"Yes. I suppose she would." I told Maddy about Neville, and my visit to Polney. Maddy looked thoughtful.

"Yes . . . well, I must say I did wonder. Not at first, of course, I was only a kid . . . but later, I looked back, and it did seem to me there was something *odd* about Neville. Not to say," she added with a giggle, "queer."

"Don't make fun of him," I said quickly.

"I'm not. Neville was sweet; I loved him too. But it figures, doesn't it? I mean, the old Freudian thing," Maddy said vaguely, "didn't really raise its ugly head until Russell appeared on the scene. You weren't jealous of Neville; you could afford to love him because he didn't represent a threat. But Russell . . . whatever else we may think about him, he is a *man*. Poor Mother. We've always blamed her for everything, haven't we? It's the fashionable thing to do. Well, time we went to bed, I suppose. Not much left to do really. Just the finishing touches in the morning. I must get back tomorrow afternoon. Paul's very good with the kids, but his patience will be wearing a bit thin by then."

"Things are all right with you?" I asked.

"Fine. I won't say it's just as if nothing had ever happened. It's better, I think, *because* it happened. We don't take each other for granted anymore. Only I hate to think about getting in such a tiz-waz, and making things difficult for you—"

"Forget it, love. It's over. Do you think Cass will like the house?"

"Of course she will. It's delicious. Thank God it's all turned out all right . . . Poor old Greg, you haven't had much luck—"

"You could say the women who married me didn't have much luck."

Maddy said quickly, "You mustn't think like that. Oh, I know you must have blamed yourself about Tessa, but this time it was just chance—"

"You know what happened, then? Did Sarah tell you?"

239

"Yes. She was very upset, she felt it was her fault . . ."

"She had no reason to. I should have rung her. Never gave it a thought, I'm afraid."

"Don't worry. She didn't expect that, and I kept her posted." Maddy glanced at me and began again, determinedly steering me away from a touchy subject: "Anyway, I meant to tell you, she's married now. Paul and I went to the wedding. It was all madly posh. Dishy bridegroom in uniform, Sarah in white looking heavenly, bridesmaids, 'O Perfect Love,' a horde of naval ushers, and an arch of swords."

"You don't say," I said blankly. Maddy, giving me a look of relief and affection, burst out laughing; and so, after a moment, did I.

"It's perfect," Cass said. "I'm overwhelmed."

Taking it slowly, we had been all around the house in a tour of inspection. I carried her upstairs to look at the bedrooms, and she stood now at the window of the room which would eventually be ours, looking out on the garden, the lawn sloping to the river, the mirror-gleam of the water beyond a clump of willow trees. Seeing her there, I had a sense of reprieve, of absolution. We had come through; we were together again.

"I hope you don't think it's too perfect," I said. "There's a school of thought which says I ought to have left it until you were well enough to choose the furnishings yourself."

"I'm glad you didn't. I'm not much good at that kind of thing. But, Greg. . . . it must all have cost a fortune . . ."

"Let me worry about that. I did it for you. And you're worth it."

"Well, I hope so," she said. "I hope I am."

It was a time of peace, the time of Cass's convalescence, a kind of resting place between the past and the future. Our marriage, you could say, was convalescing too. We lived a quiet life in our new home, entertaining a little when she was strong enough, not going out anywhere much. Mrs. Wilson, the housekeeper, turned out to be kind, competent and a wonderful cook. I had peace of mind because, I felt, I was in control of things; when I came home at night, Cass was always there. In warm weather, we spent our evenings in the way Maddy had foreseen, sitting on that charming little terrace while the shadows lengthened on the lawn and the sun went down and we were enclosed in the warm glimmering night. There we were, in ease and comfort, the most privileged of mortals.

We couldn't make love, of course, that wasn't on, not yet, but for a while it didn't matter too much. I loved her and watched over her, untroubled by desire.

But as Cass's health returned, she began to get restless. And so did I.

She was irritable, too, especially when summer was left behind and the weather turned damp and gloomy. I'd got into the habit of waiting on her, anticipating her wishes; one evening, when she got up from her chair, I said, "What do you want?"

"I'm going to get an apple."

"I'll get it," I said, and her temper flew out like lightning.

"*I'll get it myself!* For God's sake, can't you let me do anything for myself?" And another time she turned on me fiercely. "Don't watch me. I can't stand you watching me all the time."

I didn't answer. I walked away and left her, for my own temper was sorely tried, and in a moment she came after me, remorseful and apologetic: she didn't know why she behaved like that, she didn't know how I put up with her. "You're too patient with me, Greg."

I grinned and said mildly, "I'm flattered. I've not often been accused of that before. It's all right, love. You're feeling your oats, as they say about horses, you haven't anything to do and you're bored—"

"Yes." She brightened. "I'm beginning to feel I want to get back to work again—"

"And, of course, we're not living a normal life."

"I know. I've thought a lot about that. It's such a long time. It can't have been easy for you—"

"For either of us," I said. "Never mind. You're going to see Bonner again next week, aren't you? Let's see what he says."

241

When I came home, the evening of the day she had been for her checkup with the surgeon, I heard her improvising on the piano. There was just a fragment of a theme there, one of those haunting cadences in the minor key that were Cass's hallmark. She had explained to me once that what she called real composers didn't do this, they wrote it all down straight out of their heads, without going near an instrument. To me it seemed miraculous to be able to do it at all. When I came in she looked up, smiling, her hands lingering on the keys. "It's all right." She nodded. "Clean bill of health."

But later that night, in my arms, she kept repeating, "I'm sorry. I'm so sorry."

I thought, I have been here before. Only not with Cass. It had never happened to us before. I said it didn't matter; I said it was because it had been such a long time, it was because she'd been ill, we must be patient, everything would come right in time.

"Yes," she said. "Yes. I suppose so."

With the go-ahead from Mr. Bonner, Cass began to work in earnest, writing the new song I had heard her toying with, working with her voice coach. Plans for the production of her first album, just clinched at the time of the accident, were renewed. There was a revival of press interest and she gave an interview to a woman's magazine and another for a Sunday color supplement, in which the interior of our house, looking improbably brilliant, was spread over two pages. Cass: back from the jaws of death—that seemed to be the line. I thought she looked rather tired when the interviewer and the cameramen had left. I still worried a lot about her being under strain. But she shook her head at me. "I'm fine. I'm loving it. It's so wonderful to be back in life again."

She was not, however, back in mine, not in the way I wanted her to be. We must be patient, I'd said that myself. Patience, patience . . . my middle name now for a long, long time. Hers, too, it seemed. There were no more irritable explosions, she was always gentle and sweet to me, as if I, too, had become some sort of invalid.

Time passed, Christmas came and went. In the New Year, Cass did a guest appearance on television and survived it well. One evening in February, I came home to find Jay Fisher's car outside, heard his laugh as I entered the house. I don't say I was exactly delighted to find him there, but the days of being hostile to Jay were over. I went in and greeted him. He was genial, pleased with himself, Cass pink-cheeked and excited. She went at once to pour me a drink, perhaps she thought I was going to need it. I looked from one to the other of them and grinned reluctantly.

"All right," I said. "What's up?"

They told me. Cass was going to America. Oh, not yet, they both assured me hastily, not for another couple of months, and of course she would not go without my agreement, but there was absolutely nothing to worry about, nothing. "We're keeping a tight grip on the schedule—" That was Jay. "No dashing from one city to the next with an engagement the night she arrives. And there'll be someone to look after her. I can't spare Emma, but there's a nice young woman in New York who'll meet her off the plane, go with her everywhere, iron out the problems . . . it will be all right, Greg. Honest."

I didn't want her to go. In spite of all the protestations I was afraid for her. And I simply didn't want her to be away from me. But she'd been through so much. And now she was so happy.

I couldn't say no.

243

Seventeen

"Say it again," I said. "Slowly."

It was nine o'clock in the evening. We had had dinner, I eating heartily in my ignorance. Cass had hardly eaten anything. Now I knew why.

She was standing in the middle of the room, holding herself very straight, and she was very pale, and all her features seemed to have sharpened: with distress? With fear?

Then she said it again, as I had ordered.

"When I go to America, I'm not coming back. I'm leaving you."

I hadn't really taken it in, even now, feeling nothing but a cold disbelief.

"Is that so?" I said. "Running away again, eh? Would you mind telling me why?"

"I don't know how to say it—"

"Then you'd better try, hadn't you?"

"I don't love you anymore."

When I didn't speak, she added, "I'm sorry, Greg. I'm very, very sorry."

"I see. You're sorry. That makes you feel better, does it? To say you're sorry?"

"Oh, go on!" she cried. "Why don't you say it all, how ungrateful, how unscrupulous I am? How I let you buy this house for me, and furnish it, and look after me devotedly all this time? Why don't you say how contemptible that is?"

"You've said it for me," I said. With the furious sense of injustice, of treachery, burning in my mind, I remained outwardly calm. Other times, with another woman, perhaps, I might have done her an injury. But this was Cass, who had been so ill. With her I had got out of the habit of anything but gentleness, and was thus disarmed.

"Is there somebody else?" I asked.

"No. No one. It isn't that. It's simply the way I feel. Or rather the way I don't feel. Anything. Anything at all. Greg, you've got to accept it, *there's nothing there.* Except gratitude. Would you want me to stay with you, lying, pretending, because of gratitude?"

"No," I said, "I wouldn't want you to stay because of gratitude." I made a last try: not pleading with her, I wouldn't do that. I said coldly, "Don't you think you're being a bit hysterical about this? You've been a very sick girl for a long time. It could be some sort of temporary aberration—"

"No. And I'm not ill now. It's just—look, people fall in love and they fall out of love. I've fallen out of love and I wish I hadn't but I have—"

"I suppose," I said, "it could be revenge."

It was her look of pure astonishment that convinced me.

"Revenge? What for?"

"I gave you a bad time, before the accident—"

"Oh," she said. "That." It didn't matter to her. Nothing I had done mattered to her. Yes, I was convinced.

"Well," I said, "what now?"

"My things are all packed. I thought I'd go to a hotel—"

"At this time of night? Don't be ridiculous."

"All right. I'll sleep in my old room and leave first thing in the morning. And . . . Greg . . ."

"What?"

"Thank you for . . . for taking it like this. Being so understanding . . ."

I said harshly, "I'm not in the least understanding, don't think it. But if you don't want to stay with me, it's better you get out."

Then she looked at me with her sad large eyes and nodded her head. "That's right. Hate me. That will be best for you. If you hate me."

The night Cass left England I knew exactly the time she would go: a night flight, nine o'clock. I don't know why, but that moment, the moment when she would actually leave the country, fly away, seemed the definitive, the final one, although she had already left my house and I hadn't seen her for a fortnight. And as is generally the way with these things, if you know something bad has got to happen, somehow you long for it to happen, because then the worst will be over.

I hadn't told anyone except Mrs. Wilson. She was considerably shocked and, I think, inclined to be indignant and critical of Cass, but I wasn't having that. So she showed her partisanship by fussing over me a lot, an attention I could well have done without.

I left the office that evening and made my way home as mindlessly as a carrier pigeon. It was an evening in early April, damp, with a raw cold. As I drove out through the London suburbs, the long rows of houses all the same, the wet ribbon of road before me, the lights, the road signs, the flyovers, the factories, the transport cafés, the cars and lorries and people scurrying from here to there, all made up a dark picture of desolation, of the City of Dreadful Night; with the full realization, still to come, of emptiness and pain and loss. Cass had left me before; but she had never said she didn't love me. She had never gone so far away.

I remember walking into the house that night, into that glowing, beautiful room, empty of her presence. It was so tidy these days, since she left; exquisitely tidy, with Mrs. Wilson's efficient ministrations; the piano closed, the scores put away, no records lying about, every cushion squarely in place.

I had my meal, and shooed Mrs. Wilson off to the cinema or wherever it was she was going, and sat with my coffee by the fire. The place was as silent as the grave. I thought, at nine o'clock I shall switch on the television news, and there will be voices and something to look at, and when the news is over the plane will have left, and that will be it and I shall start living again, a different life. I thought about going back to London to live, this house was too big for one; I wondered idly what it would fetch.

A taxi drew up outside, the engine throbbing while the driver was paid off. Then it moved away, the sound of its going dying away down the street. The front doorbell rang.

There was nobody I wanted to see, and I thought I might as well let whoever it was go away again. But the lights were on everywhere; the caller wouldn't be so easily put off. The bell rang again. Cursing, I went to the door and opened it.

Cass was standing outside, her small overnight bag in her hand. The light from the hall fell full on her face; she looked pale, exhausted and frightened.

We looked at each other in silence. Then I said dryly: "Forgotten something?"

She put her head down and muttered, "Let me come in for a minute, Greg."

"As you've sent the taxi away, I suppose you'd better."

She came in; I threw open the door of the sitting room, and she walked in front of me into it. There was something hopeless and shuffling about her gait, like a prisoner. She put her bag down on a chair and stood there, her face turned away.

"What about your plane?" I asked.

"It's gone."

"What happened?" I didn't feel anything. I could not begin to think of why she had come back.

"Jay saw me off. Well, I mean, he came to the airport and I checked in and everything. Jay bought me a drink and I didn't know what to talk about to him, so I said don't stay and I'll go through into the passenger lounge. So I did that, and then the flight was called, and I started down the boarding channel. I'd just got to the place where they check you out for bombs . . . and there was a queue and I had to wait and all the time I was getting more and more confused and frightened, and I just couldn't go. I turned round and ran. I suppose my luggage is halfway to New York by now."

I didn't speak. She waited a bit, and added in a small voice, "Please say something."

"Like what?" I asked. "Are you saying you want to come back to me?"

"I haven't thought it out that far. I just knew I couldn't go—"

"I see. Well, we've had rather a lot of this, haven't we?

248

Running out when the going gets rough. Running back again. There's a limit to that sort of thing. You can do it once too often."

But even as I spoke harshly to her, I could feel the hard shell I had built round myself cracking a little, and far back within me, a small core of warmth. She was there, in the same room. She was still in my world.

She turned around and looked at me, her eyes searching my face. Then she nodded. "Yes. And I have, haven't I? Done it once too often. All right, Greg."

She picked up her bag and turned to the door. She looked finished, exhausted and forlorn. Before she got to the door I called her back: "Cass."

"What?" she whispered.

"I don't want pity. If that's why you came back—"

"It isn't pity," she said.

"Then what is it? You can't call it love either, can you?"

"I don't know what to call it. I just knew I couldn't go, that's all. I don't know what I feel . . . well, no, perhaps I do a little. I don't have that awful dead feeling anymore," she offered.

There was something childish and absurd about this and it made me want to smile, but I wasn't going to let her off the hook, not just yet.

"No? Well, that's something. But not an awful lot to go on really."

She stared at me and burst out suddenly: "Greg, I know you're bitter and you've every right to be but don't play cat and mouse with me, if you want me to go away I'll go but if you don't—"

"Then what?"

"Help me!" she cried. "Help me, please!"

Without knowing it, she had said exactly the right thing, unleashing in me a burst of energy, authority, the knowledge that I had control after all, of my destiny and hers. I said shortly, "All right. Then put that bag down somewhere, take your coat off, and make a drink for yourself and one for me, while I do some telephoning."

"T-telephoning?"

"That's what I said. We have to send a cable saying you're sorry you've missed the plane and you'll be on the next available one. And we have to try for tickets for tomorrow."

She caught her breath. "Then you are sending me away, you want me to go—"

"Two tickets," I said.

She was very still. "I don't understand."

"I'm coming with you. I've a valid visa and a trip to the States lined up anyway. It's just a matter of putting it forward a bit. I'm not letting you go off on this trip by yourself, but go, my child, you must. You're under contract, remember?"

"I didn't think about that—"

"I daresay not, but you'll have to. Otherwise they'll sue, and it will cost a bomb. And if we're going to try and make a go of things again, it's no good your making a lot of noble sacrifices. Next time we have a fight—and I expect we shall—you'll be saying I gave up my career for my marriage and now look at it. We're not having any of that. We're grown-up people, Cass, and it's time we started behaving as if we were. What's the address of these people?"

"I've got it here . . ."

"Good." I started dialing. "Where's that drink?"

"I'll get it . . ."

She got the drinks and sat down quietly opposite me, cradling her own between her hands, watching me while I sent the cable, made the reservations, and had a conversation with an astonished Hugo, to whom I gave a garbled version of events.

I said at last: "Well, that's it. We're on the ten o'clock flight tomorrow morning. That means I'll have to go down to the office now and pick up some stuff."

"Oh. Can I . . . can I come with you?"

"Why not?" I grinned. "Don't look so bewildered. Drink up and come on."

In the car, driving through the darkness into London, she said quietly, "It's not like I thought it would be."

"How did you think it would be?"

"Well . . . either that you'd throw me out, or . . ."

250

"Or what?"

She said almost inaudibly, "Well, I suppose . . . that you'd take me in your arms."

"I've been busy," I said. "I didn't say I wasn't going to. Plenty of time for that now, isn't there?"

"Yes. Yes, of course."

We drove along for a bit, and she spoke again. "Greg . . ."

"What?"

"I expect this sounds funny, but I *want* to love you."

"Yes," I said. "I know."

Neither of us said anything for a long time.

Then she said, "Do you think it will be all right?"

I said soberly, "Who knows? We didn't make much of a go of it together. But it's worse when we're apart. We'll just have to do the best we can, won't we?"

The next traffic light was red, and we sat there waiting in the throbbing darkness. The car in front of us flashed its left-hand winker and in this brief illumination I saw there were tears on Cass's cheeks. I thought I knew why she was crying—not just for past unhappiness, for what we had done to each other, but for the lost paradise: the past illusions, the precious alchemy of romantic love, which turns everything to gold, and lasts for such a little time. I reached out for her hand and she clung to mine with both of hers.

Then the lights changed, I let the clutch in, and we moved forward slowly, in the crush of the traffic; forward, side by side, hand in hand, into our uncertain and probably stormy future.